TOXIC CITY

WALKERS IN THE MIST - VOLUME 1

DANGEL ANGELLO

Britain's Next
BESTSELLER

First published in 2017 by:
Britain's Next Bestseller
An imprint of Live It Ventures LTD
126 Kirkleatham Lane,
Redcar.
Cleveland.
United Kingdom.
TS10 5DD
www.bnbsbooks.co.uk

All enquiries should be addressed to; info@bnbsbooks.co.uk
Cover art by vikncharlie
Printed and Bound in Poland

ISBN - 9781999788278

In memory of Uncle Alan
KTBFFH!

ACKNOWLEDGMENTS

Firstly, a huge thanks to Kelly and David at BNBS books for all they've done, as publishers and as friends. Their support has been immense and the chance they provide to first-time authors is out of this world. They're a publisher with a heart, which I can imagine is in short supply in the industry.

Thank you!

And to my mum and Peter who provided me a safe place and the laptop in which this novel was written. Love you guys.

To my Dad who told me *never stop writing*, and I haven't.

To my Nana, because she's always believed in me!

And to everyone else who had a part to play in getting this book into print. You know who you are and I love you!

PART ONE

1

For over a month Val had been bed-bound. Each time she woke up, her first objective was to move. It was the best cure for the stiffening of her young yet haggard muscles. It negated the effects of blanket radiation which, after months to years, would sink through clothes, skin, fatty tissue, and rest on the outer lining of muscles. If this was allowed to continue then her body would slowly calcify, locking her inside. But moving hurt. Turning her head caused lightning sensations down her back, and the creaking of her bones was scarily audible. Any medical examiner worth their salt would presume she owned the organs of a middle-aged woman. In fact, she was barely six months from fifteen.

After minutes that felt like hours, she rolled from the

mattress to the floor – as it had no bed-frame – and forced every sinew to stand. She stumbled across clothes, empty bottles, and spent ration packets, using furniture for support until reaching the small closet that housed the toilet. She collapsed on the narrow pot and hissed against the burning sensation as she peed. Not much came out; a bad sign since she'd spent most of her waking moments downing litres of warm, sterilised water. Her kidneys were obviously in a terrible state and this was no surprise since she'd consumed a month's worth of radiation medication in as little as a few weeks.

"Jim?" she called, her voice hoarse. She repeated her shout to no avail.

She'd not looked for him during her struggle to the loo, but it was obvious he wasn't there.

She hauled herself to a stand, but bumped her head on a plastic sheet covering a hole in the ceiling. Pulling it away showered plaster dust, but the space up through the loft bathed her in light; not pure sunlight as the clouds hadn't broken in her lifetime, but light all the same. That meant one thing.

She had made it to day thirty-six.

Val stumbled from the table where she'd been tuning her radio and collapsed on the mattress. She remained slumped against the cold wall of peeling plaster, and listened to the fizzing static as the radio channel had yet to produce its broadcast. It'd come soon and she wanted to remain awake until then.

Rather than risk closing her eyes, she glanced about her apartment instead, of which it consisted of one long room. It had two windows covered in lead-lined, blast-proof cladding that acted as protection against the Mists. These were powerful storms that dragged radiation across the Earth and would hit any time between five to fifteen days. Sometimes, they'd experience a spate of storms and Val would find herself locked in her apartment for days.

With the help of Jim – who was the closest thing she had to family – she'd managed to erect a slight partition to the back of the room. Here, she'd built up a water purification unit, or WPU, that dripped sterilised water into a gallon jug. Behind this, on the back wall, was a hatch that she'd constructed using a pressure-door sourced from an old warship that Jim still lived in. Getting it from Barking Creek to library in Beckton where she called home had been a mammoth task. Jim had helped all he could, but she'd done much of the installation herself. Now it acted as a barrier between her less-than-sterile apartment and the makeshift-greenhouse growing veg, and brewing beer. As Jim had said at the time, *it wasn't bad going for a twelve-year-old*.

The radio's static popped suddenly. She glanced at the clock that told her it was nearly seven, but whether that meant morning or evening, it didn't matter. *ERD* would always come upon this hour. She listened ever closer to the static, waiting.

Not long now, she told herself. *Stay awake for a few minutes more.*

To her right was a stout dresser missing its draws. She'd filled the cavities with boxes of medications and bottles of water, though most of them were empty now. There was also a broken mirror that she now used to check the colour of her tongue and eyes.

She'd been called a lot of things in her time, but pale wasn't one. Muddy. Dusky. Black, even. But she was light brown in her opinion. Or she should've been. Her last mission into the Wastes far south of London had brought about such high levels of exposure that it'd actually drained her of some pigment. Now she looked relatively grey with yellowing eyes.

Her hair had fared no better. When she'd been young and living in the Sacred Hearts Orphanage, all the Sisters would run their fingers through her hair and say it was her most precious feature. Now it was limp about her face and several clumps came free when she pulled at knots; it wouldn't be long before the spots of alopecia combined, making her look ten years older.

She slapped her dry lips together, prompting her mouth to salivate, as she rummaged in the mess about her mattress, searching for a penknife. She found one in her jeans and took the blade to her straggly locks. By the time her arms were shaking from fatigue, she'd cut her hair down to a few inches; short enough to push under her beanie hat, at least.

Suddenly, she rushed with cold and held herself. Her guts churned despite having nothing in them, and now she could taste bile. Episodes like this were side effects of abusing her meds, though it'd been a necessary action if she'd had any chance of surviving exposure. Still, she'd be caught in a full-blown fit if she didn't manage to calm down.

She watched the radio as if her life depended on it. The ringing in her ears had drowned out the static, but soon he'd come.

ERD, they called him. His name meant 'Energy-Rich Drink' if the jingle at the start of his broadcast was anything to go by. He, like many others who'd hi-jacked radio channels from the Peace Enforcement Agency, reused intro themes that'd played before the End. This one seemed to have stuck and most had come to know him by it.

As if her ears had popped, the static reduced and the song broke through.

> *"It's what you do,*
> *Not what you think,*
> *So break from the chains*
> *With an Energy-rich Drink!"*

The women seemed so euphoric, as if all life's problems could be solved with a simple soda.

Val leaned back with a relieved smile. "Hello ERD," she whispered. Now all she had to do was stay awake.

'*Good morning. And yes it's morning, despite how dull it may seem,*' said the aged but well-spoken man from her slightly less static-hungry radio. ERD was a constant reassurance as she listened to his mature voice; educated in his words and gentle in his tone.

'*...and any of you up early enough would've seen the rains below Old South Quad,*' he went on. '*The clouds had thinned to such a degree that I was told the sky had been almost visible. I hope none of you did see it, actually. Not in person. Anomalies fall with the rain and we all remember what happened to Peace Ranger Rotsland.*'

She snorted a laugh – as morbid as it was – because she could still picture the silhouette from his body on the concrete column of the train-bridge heading to Sevenoaks, forming a perfect shadow of a man squatting. The explosion had decimating everything save his trousers and ID cards, as well as a pile of shit, incidentally.

'*Today falls directly in the middle of April, a spring month, or so it'd been before the End. Anyone outside of the buffered areas of Central will feel the balmy early morning reaching peaks of twenty-four Celsius, though I've heard rumour that the afternoon may tip somewhat uncomfortably over thirty degrees. So keep light and make sure you have your rations.*'

Val smiled. He appeared so caring. Not the type of *caring* where people had a job to do, like the Casuals who worked in hospitals or those peddling merchandise aimed at *relieving* day-to-day hardships. He seemed genuine, as if he had nothing to gain and everything to give.

'*You know, I was reading a book last night. It was a sorry state of a novel with its cover missing and the pages browned, but I did read that it was printed over two hundred and fifty years ago, so I can forgive as much.*'

'It was a fictitious affair, deemed a comedy in its day. The title, for what was left of the interior, was The Hitchhiker's Guide to the Galaxy. *I'll not eat too greatly into your morning routine, but I found myself more enchanted as I went and I wanted to share it with you.*

'The hero of this tale was a man with no true difference to you or I. Caught up in his life, dealing with his own troubles, thinking largely about sustaining an existence he was never much happy with in the first place. Yet, like most, he was content to sustain it all the same.

'Then, incidentally, the world blew up. Completely and utterly obliterated. Amazingly, moments before the blast that claimed the other billions of his race – as there were in the days before the End – he and an alien companion were sucked into a spaceship. Improbable, but I suppose not impossible considering the realm of things. And there began his new adventure as, well, a hitchhiker of the galaxy.'

A silence followed before he said, *'You're screwing up your face now, aren't you?'*

She softened her expression to mild surprise. If she hadn't been responsible for the making of that radio, she would've sworn he could see her through it.

'I suppose you'd have to read it in order to feel how I feel. I wish I could print a copy for everyone. Books are a blessing, an escape from the norm. Not all of us can find ourselves in the midst of a novel that keeps us turning page after page. But then, we're all living our own story, much like the hero in my book.'

His voice grew somewhat solemn.

'A while ago our world ended. Before your time and before mine. Remnants of it persist to this day but never how it was before. Children are born, grow, and die never to know sunshine, fearing the rain, and growing old before their time. Many will be fighting to preserve a life that has more ill in it than good, and yet they carry on in order to fend off what worse may come along.

'I suppose this has become quite a sermon. But to top off the few

stringent minutes I'm given, before my air runs out, I can only insist that you grab the next ride on that ship, on that train, on that bus, and find your own adventure.

'Life's too short not to be explored.'

She thought she could hear him smiling. Then the jingle played, running a little longer than the intro tune, and Val allowed herself to phase out as she could no longer fight the convulsions.

4

The evening brought sweltering heat and she snapped awake when her modified PDA began bleeping. It meant a Mist was coming and even her mattress was shaking from the mounting winds outside. She was weak and delirious, but she needed to secure the windows, bolt down doors, and activate systemic-ionisation routers to deter heavy particle penetration. Yet she couldn't even free herself from her bed sheet. Panic threatened until a shaded figure lowered over her, pushing her down by the shoulders and cooing gently. She calmed.

Jim was home.

He watered her, wiped her brow, and slurred, "Well done on surviving, chick."

She celebrated with a faint lifting of her eyebrows. Then she vomited the water back up, collapsed into her thin pillow, and shook until she passed out.

"Shit!" Val cursed as she sat upright. She rubbed at her thigh thinking she'd pissed herself again. A quick sniff proved it to be sweat so she relaxed.

The room was bright. Some of the tarp and lead sheeting had been removed from the windows. Jim must've done it, though he wasn't here now. It was a sign that a Mist had recently passed. She could even see the orange glow of the plasma layer below the thick clouds which always gleamed after a storm.

The surrounding grounds around her abandoned building were empty save for a fox hurrying for the over-grown grounds to the south, and she could hear tinny announcements from speakers coming from a PEA base two miles south-west of her position. Apart from that, all was silent.

She held out her hands, looking for a tremor. There wasn't any. She even managed to stand with rather good balance. At first, she thought she'd beaten the effects of the exposure until she found a freshly opened medi-pack by her bed. All the tablets, powders, and needles had been spent. That was a week's worth gone and no doubt used on her.

The box was red, signifying it to be a PEA ration packet distributed by the Casuals at the People's Hospital at Whitehall. The label read WALKER 32FF/VL10K. That's Jim's legal name, the type given to Walkers when they register with the Agency. It entitled him to one large ration packet a week due to his fragility; at barely forty-two, he was considered old for a Walker and he didn't half look it.

"Jim?"

She already knew he wasn't in the room, but she approved of the sound of her voice all the same; steady and with no croak.

She made for the back of the apartment for the loo, but slowed when she saw the hatch to the greenhouse had been left open. Fear energised her and she threw herself inside, finding the lights off as the generator had shorted-out. Turning it back on revealed rows of wilting pepper plants, mouldy cucumbers, and flies infesting the beds of onions and potatoes. Jim had been in here, no doubt thinking he was helping in turning the soil and bagging under-ripe veg. But she knew what the real reason for his intrusion was when she saw the brewing table had been left dishevelled. The kegs were open and cider reserves had been polished off. That was over two months of work wasted.

"Jim, you nob!"

The greenhouse wasn't the only thing that had been *violated*. Under her distillery was a small safety-deposit box, and the door was wide open. Had she told him the password? Possibly, during one of her delusional states. She found that over two hundred red stamps – known locally as Reds – were missing. Most Walkers never saw fifty Reds in a year and yet she'd earned that many in as little as six months. That was six months of bloody hard work, though.

Her anger was beyond controllable as she cried, "Jim, you *nob*!"

After half an hour, she'd donned a pair of commando trousers, a leather jacket, and a black beanie to cover her alopecia. She pushed out into the dark corridor, using her modified PDA – known as an RDAC – strapped to her wrist to light the way, and hurried down the crumbling stairs.

She didn't know what she was going to do once she found him, but he'd not like it.

The houses either side of Tollgate Road were still in good nick. In fact much of Quad: East was rather well preserved, which was why many law-abiding Walkers chose to live there. It comprised of most of East London, though it stopped short of Essex since that'd been walled off as an Exclusion Zone. The PEA said it wasn't safe, blaming flooding, anomalous activity, and Bandits for why they'd put watchtowers manned with snipers along the border. Still, as dangerous as they said it was, they'd set up a few of their own military bases all the same.

None of this really concerned Val as Beckton boasted enough estates for her to get lost in during trouble. However, much of it had been reclaimed by nature, with trees growing up through derelict flats, and sidewalks broken open by bushes and weeds. Even the road was crumbling from the grass growing up through it despite how much the PEA keep repaving.

A shuttle stop had been position just a few hundred yards from the library she called home. It consisted of a single totem with a countdown for when the shuttle was to arrive. It was the only place in the entire quad where Walkers would ever imagine congregating, but no one ever spoke to each other. In fact, most just lost themselves in their PDA's which they'd use to access AbysMA, a PEA funded information channel broadcasted from the shuttle stop's information point.

Walkers were the norm there. No Casuals would punish themselves by living in Quad: East. You could tell what job they had by the shade of their boiler suits as well, with dark blue being the most common for unskilled labourers, black being those who could lead or had a skill, and brown being those who did the most dirty jobs.

Val was as much a Walker as they were, but she'd not need to don a boiler suit until she was fifteen. However, she'd do her best to avoid it, though there weren't many legal options in order to achieve this. One way was to seek private employment, like becoming a Peace Ranger or a bodyguard which she wasn't fully against, but she'd never become a Casual. Those posh snobs live mostly to the north and whilst they have a life filled with healthcare, education, and safe housing, they do so at the cost of their freedom. A Casual is completely owned by the PEA, even down to who you can marry.

With a few minutes left to spare, Val was tapping about on her RDAC. She wasn't accessing AbysMA, however. That was run by the PEA and the information on it was limited. Rather she was trying to connect with ATOM, a clandestine server run by her less-than-legal employers known as the Palacers. It used similar relays as the PEA points, but there were more of them so the signals were weaker, thus harder to detect. And even if you did manage to detect them, accessing the server was much harder due to encryptions. Normally that was fine for Val, but after a month of being out of work, she'd not been given the new key and couldn't access it.

She'd almost lost her life on a mission that the Palacers had set up. She'd been sent to find the location of an important piece of Lecky – electronic devices made before the End. She'd not even gotten close before her *team* that the Palacers had put together had turned on each other. She'd survived and escaped, only to be forced to hide from a Mist that'd exposed her to so much radiation that for two weeks she'd been a walking zombie. It made her shudder to think what lengths Jim had had to go to in order to keep her alive. And after all she'd done, they couldn't even be nice enough to forward her the new key.

"Pack of fucks," she muttered but realised herself and glanced about those waiting. None had noticed her cursing as they were looking nervously across the road.

There were flats over there with small yards and trees dangling sap-dripping vines. Areas like that were best avoided due to clinging irradiated materials, but it didn't mean everyone stayed away. Behind a collapsed section of a garden wall was a Mallowhead and he was unnerving her fellow Walkers.

Such people were easily recognisable. They tended to be male (though it was sometimes hard to tell), with zero body fat, stick-thin limbs, necrosis of the pit areas, and horrifically swollen heads. That was the same for the figure walking back and forth behind the wall, jabbering nonsensically whilst rubbing his scaly distended belly and scanning the ground for something that didn't seem to be there.

She'd grown up seeing such people as they'd been regularly brought into the Bandit camp where she'd been enslaved between the ages of six to eleven. Bandits enjoyed many blood sports and one involved throwing a Mallowhead into a pit of dogs to watch it freak out. Sometimes they'd try to make two Mallowheads fight each other, but they were typically non-aggressive. More often than not, they'd just burn out and die or a Bandit would shoot them.

They existed almost freely in the quads as more people sympathised with them, or at least they killed them less. Despite old stories of Mallowheads being cannibalistic monsters, most saw them as harmless, though sometimes they could be a slight nuisance. In fact, the worst they'd tend do in order to move someone along was storm around jabbering and shitting themselves; it often achieved the desired effect.

It was only last year that she'd learnt of how they'd come to be in such a state. It was Jim who'd clued her in. It'd been a quiet night a few months ago, and he'd come in a little pissed and sat in the corner rolling smokes. It was often times like these that he'd decide to share his *wisdom*.

'Blanket radiation is just the same as every other radiation,' he'd begun, watching the ceiling as some do when being thoughtful. *'People say* oh that's blanket rad, *or* that's high rad, *and* that's rad rain that is. *Fact is, it's all the same rad, just delivered in a different way.*

'See, blanket rad weren't ever recorded before the nukes fell. Literally, only us Enders experience it. Hell, even my dad never believed in the stuff and he was an eighth-generation Ender.

'From what I know, blanket rad is made by the usual radiation that comes with the Mists, 'cept it's been stretched and pulled, whipped up and squashed down, making it a sort'a cream…'

He'd stopped to think it through. In fact, he'd troubled over that for so long, Val had taken herself to the greenhouse to turn soil

'Like cheese!' he'd shouted, poking his head through the hatch. *'When our normal radiation is like cream, well the radiation that settles after a Mist is more like cottage cheese.'*

She'd been nodding, but stopped to ask, *'And what's chayz?'*

He hadn't answered and she hadn't pried.

'Blanket radiation hurts you from inside,' he'd gone on to say, *'but each part of you reacts differently. With your skin, it dries out and kills all sensation; first comes months of burning as signals misfire in your nerve endings, and then nothing; just sweet numbness.'*

He'd slapped his legs which, unfortunately, had long since lost their sense of feeling and had grown gnarled.

'Your muscles can go one o' two ways. They can carbonise-'

'Calcify,' she'd corrected.

'-calcify, where they turn as hard as bone and you lose all move-

ment. Or they can age. Aging isn't so bad. Humans weren't supposed to live beyond forty, anyway. And even though they'll eventually break and leave yah crippled, for a time they're actually tougher than usual, so you can do a lot more without cramping. Mix that with the numbness and, for a while, yah kind'a pretty well off.'

She left her thoughts to watch the Mallowhead pace back and forth. He'd amassed a rather impressive pile of twigs from what she could see. Not branches. Not sticks. Just thin, six to eight-inch-long, twigs fallen from the wealth of trees that'd long since reclaimed much of Quad: East.

It was typical Mallowhead behaviour as she'd often find piles of bags, odd shoes, or even pens, hidden about alleys and quiet streets; the result of days spent searching as if it were their only reason for living.

'Your heart?' Jim had surmised. *'Well, I think that calcifies, too. Enlarges. Not sure. Your bowels? Oh wow. Well, you've smelt my guffs. Nah, to be honest it's your brain that suffers most from blanket rad. It spreads on thin and washes off easy, sure. But, bit by bit, it hardens the outer layer of your brain, like the crust atop a stagnant pond of shit. But underneath, it's hot.* Real *hot. Your brain starts to liquefy. Not a whole lot, but enough to make you go mad.'*

He'd drilled a finger into the side of his head, holding an expression of such insight that she'd been sure he'd had a personal understanding of that madness. Then he'd sighed, saying, *'Mallowhead, because it's like roasting marshmallows on a fire; outside's all crispy, inside's all soft, see?'*

She'd nodded, but a thought had struck her and she'd asked, *'What's a marshmallow?'*

She recalled how he'd scoffed as he'd slipped from the hatch. *'Like fuck if I know.'*

Even to this day Val wasn't sure what such a thing was. However, she could tell quite soundly that they were undoubtedly horrible things.

The sound of vehicles was rare in Quad: East, so the rumbling engine was easily recognised. The shuttle barrelled from the left, storming over half a dozen crumbled roundabouts where its tracks were tearing up tarmac, exposing soil for more tufts of brittle grass to grow.

It was a rather top-grade vehicle; blast-proof, radiation-proof, covering all terrains except water, and air-conditioned to boot. It had no windows (not even for the drivers at either end, if there actually were any) and black panels with glowing purple edges that acted as buffers against radiation. The triangle emblem with three stripes of blue, white, and red showed it was PEA owned, though she never saw Agents riding it.

It's donation to the Quads had been a great boon to everyone this far outside of Central. After years of warring between the PEA and Walker populations, this addition had helped cement a respect between the two peoples. Now, however, its arrival brought gasps and curses, with some Walkers going as far as to run away.

"Black Eye," muttered one of the remaining Walkers as the shuttle came to a stop. He was referring to the piece of technology fixed above the door, a lens resembling an eyeball held within a black metal socket. It spun and twisted as it focused on faces, taking their images and referencing them with data stored in AbysMA. If their likeness or chips came back with strikes against their file, then they'd no doubt have Agents coming after them.

The first bloke in the queue tried to put his ID card on the reader, but the terminal had been removed. The Black Eye was sensitive enough to pick up the chip and allowed the door to open with a clatter-*crash*. It closed after him and the next fellow held his ID up for the eye to see, and again the door rattled open.

Clatter-*crash* as another Walker entered.

Val hated Black Eyes. Hated them! Nothing annoyed her more than such intrusive pieces of technology. It wasn't fair on honest citizens who gave their all to remain registered. Sometimes it'd only take the slightest misdemeanour to deny a Walker access to transport, which would prevent them from visiting work or the hospital.

Clatter-*crash*!

Clatter-*crash*!

The man in front kept rubbing his ID card, cleaning it of oil and straightening out the creases. He wasn't young, either. A man his age couldn't walk to Charing Cross. He'd lose a day's wage and that'd mean mouths would go unfed and meds wouldn't be claimed.

His hand was shaking as he flashed the ID. The lens focused on his face, his reflection a distorted pale orb as the motorised filaments retracted, honing in on his features. Sweat dripped from his chin…

Clatter-*crash!*

Muttering to God, he rushed within, finding a spare seat in the narrow compartment where he regained his composure. The Black Eye scanned the area and found no one else waiting, so the shuttle's engine revved and off it tore back up Tollgate Road.

The Mallowhead looked from the garden where he'd been collecting twigs. He'd made a nice pile, too. As he paced back and forth, he occasionally peaked out with what little remained of his vision. But as the shuttle departed, his bulging eyes caught sight of a girl clinging to the back, ducking to avoid the camera and gripping external armour-plating as it slowly picked up speed.

Then she was gone and he found another twig.

Val was still clinging to the back of the shuttle as it strad-dled the Thames River. She watched as Tower Bridge came into view. The *bridge* part had long since fallen away, but two buffer towers sat either side of the embankment. They were older models, maybe by a hundred years. Such technology hadn't existed before the End, so it must've been hard for the younger generation of Enders to construct such a thing, but they'd done so twice and both had remained partly operational for over a century.

Much had changed since those first towers had been established. All the newer towers tended to be sword-like in shape, with smaller bases since much of it was anchored beneath the ground. The actual buffering took place in huge panels that emitted a sort of magnetic field, directing damaging material back into the sky. On the older models, the panels were kept in place by springs to make them durable during Mists and easier to replace, and this meant they vibrated. When exposure was highest, the hum was mind-numbing and it was directly to blame for the loss of birds in the area. The only place she ever saw them was south of the quads, and they tended to be stewing in a Bandit's cook pot.

Finally, they were entering Central which comprised of Whitehall, Trafalgar Square, Downing Street, and the Palace of Westminster. Most of the buildings in the area were in fairly good condition, whilst others had been left to the elements, crumbling under Mist bombardment and the invasion of nature.

Things rarely changed, but Val was surprised when the shuttle passed a construction site. Several buildings had been demolished and a huge wedge of earth had been removed, with Walkers in breathing apparatus filling hazmat trucks full of dirt. It was obvious that they weren't constructing another building as men were welding together what looked like a one hundred foot-long fan blade.

This was unlike anything she'd seen the PEA conducting before, but then she doubted it was actually their doing. She'd spotted a banner on the mesh fencing saying *site organised and monitored by* P.R.I.M.E *Industries*. She'd not heard of such a thing and wondered if it was a new government scheme.

The government was a fairly new aspect of Walker life, established fifty years ago to provide a voice for law abiding citizens everywhere, apparently. Occasionally, votes were held where anyone fifteen years and older, as well as sporting a registration number, could elect a Prime Minister. She didn't know anyone who'd ever voted, and there was rarely much advertisement before an event, but either way they had a PM somewhere, doing something.

They finally joined a line of shuttles waiting to access Central, which officially began at Charing Cross round-about. It wasn't normally such a chore to get to, and yet they'd come to a complete stop.

Worried that another shuttle might turn up and see her clinging to the back, Val jumped off and ran for the concrete barriers blocking the sidewalk. She hauled herself over and hid, hoping no one had seen her, and then she peeked over to see what the hold-up was.

She'd expected to see the large roundabout offering access to several shacks where Walkers often waited for transport. Instead, a large outpost had been constructed over the road leading in, with Agents patrolling the top and several security booths along the lanes. To top it off, there were several Black Eyes watching the turnstiles for pedestrian.

An Agent stepped out of the security booth with his PDA in hand. She didn't know what he was checking for, but the shuttle had to wait while he did. His dark blue overalls showed he was a senior Agent, as lighter blue overalls were mostly worn by standard Agents. Green was reserved for newbies, of which she rarely saw since joining the PEA ranks wasn't considered a *popular* thing to do.

Over this they'd wear black and white segmented torso armour reinforced with impact pads for blast-deflection. Their helmets were unique to each head-size as they were formed to fit perfectly around the neck and jaw, with a full-face reflective visor to mask their identity and protect from shrapnel.

Val knew nothing about guns. If there was one thing she was thankful of, it was that firearms were rare and reserved mainly for the PEA. It was due to this that she'd only ever been shot once, though that'd torn a chunk out of her calf and had left her limping for a few years.

Despite this, she knew quite a bit about the PEA weapon of choice; a lightweight, white firearm known as a small-arms, gas-operated, tri-sighted assault rifle, nick-named a Smaz Gazzar that could chuck out thirty rounds in three seconds. She'd once salvaged an older model and had sold it to her legal employer down in Sevenoaks for twelve Reds, but an unmodified model could earn a competent scavenger upwards of fifty stamps, if they had the right buyer that is. Val normally did because she was a Lancer, a *freelance* Walker who'd brave unfavourable conditions and break the law generally to retrieve Lecky or stolen goods. She'd made a career of it with the Palacers, though it wasn't exactly an easy job to do.

The shuttle was eventually given the all clear and it was

moved through. The same treatment would be given to the next, however, and she didn't fancy trying her chances with the Black Eyes. Even though she had other means in which to access Central, she decided to give it a miss.

Checking that the coast was clear, she went back the way she'd come, hoping Cannon Street station hadn't suffered the same level of refurbishment.

The entrance of Cannon Street station was a tall building made of concrete slabs and patched with tin sheets. The inside walls supported scaffolding that allowed stalls to be stacked nearly four storeys high. Goods and stamps were exchanged using baskets on ropes, with most merchants risking their lives just to make a trade.

Nearly all the ground-level stalls offered somewhere to eat. Meals on sale included items such as starch-strings in soup, roasted reformed-vegetable-matter, and highly nutri-tious but questionably-tasting balls of vitafibre - whatever that was. After waiting a moment in line, Val bought a pot of broth that tasted *okay*, even though the 'meat chunks' were more like balls of wool.

As she finished her soup, she listened to the seller's radio. A DJ was in the middle of a rant, and it'd caught her interest.

'Who the hell is Andrews? Did you hear of this Andrews fellow before today? I bloody didn't, and I got ears all over. And where was this election held? I'll tell you where, in the West and the North, that's where! Agents with finger scanners took ballet boxes to the Casuals and gave them their candidates, not caring who wins because they're all PEA lapdogs.

'The vote is a farce. It came in right after the army decimated Waterloo, killing over eight thousand lowly Walkers. That'd been a quarter of us. A whole fecking quarter of us! Not even the hoity-toity fecking Casuals could ignore it. So the PEA shit themselves, thinking their educated-goons would drop their cups and saucers in outrage, and so what did they do? Put the best of their lot in suits, sat them at desks in Parliament, and called it a government.'

"We have a new PM?" Val asked, looking about those eating quietly. "Who shot the last one?"

The vendor stirring a pot of stew said, "He dropped dead two weeks ago. Heart attack."

"Apparently," another muttered.

"Apparently," someone echoed mockingly.

The awkward conversation ended when an automated voice broke through the speakers.

Warning. Warning. Bullet train arriving. Stand back. Stand back.

Blast doors opened, giving access to the mile-long concrete tunnel lined with white lights. She hurriedly joined over four hundred Walkers as they continued along the platform where the air pressure increased from a train shooting up the tracks. It came whirring to a halt with its nineteen carriages looking slightly dusty from its exposure to the Wastes. Doors on the opposite side opened first to allow those returning from nightshift to disembark on the other side. Once empty, their doors opened and she pushed inside one of the many 'standing-room only' carriages.

She loved the train; it looked amazing with its white, shiny exterior and jaw-dropping speeds. The PEA had designed it for the same reason as the shuttles; to transport Walkers to work. This time it was to Sevenoaks in order to toil away in unsafe environments, churning out the PEA's weapons, buffer towers, and materials, and all for the purpose of improving their hold over the Known World.

Still, it was a twenty-minute ride that gave most Quad-locked Walkers the chance to see other parts of their world that were often too dangerous to traverse. Huge windows provided these views as it shot from the tunnel, going up high to look over Old South Quad.

It wasn't called Quad: South any more, not since the demolition of the factory district that had wrenched the

Quads into modernisation over a century ago. Now the levelled land was almost characterless save for a handful of landmarks. One such place was the Religious District comprising of several Houses dedicated to different religions. They surrounded a crescent of paving stones with flower-beds and buffer towers, and whilst the mosque was the largest to the west side, Christ's Church Chapel was the most eye-catching since it was an Old World church from back before the End.

Along the Embankment south of Westminster Bridge were the Estates; a mammoth shanty town built atop the ruins of older establishments once dedicated to the workers of the long-gone factory district. Now it was home to Undesirables; mainly Walkers who'd failed the registration process and weren't permitted access to anywhere north of the Thames.

The rest of the land was largely barren until the train headed further south to where the most intriguing off all post-End structures sat. It was a shanty town much like the Estates, except it went upwards rather than spreading out. It looked like a hive and was impossibly dark inside, which was down to the thick roof it purported to protect from rain, falling anomalies, and blanket radiation. It was built atop the old Waterloo station where a market similar to it had once stood, though it'd been destroyed by the Agency fifty-years-ago when they'd deemed it a threat to Central. And yet now they had Black Waterloo, as busy as ever, and just as big of a threat.

South of all this was the Quad Wall, erected a decade back to keep the Bandits out. They'd once been rife, but that'd changed around four years ago when the PEA had taken their toll of attacks, finally mounting an assault to do away with them once and for all. She'd been eleven during the raids and could recall how her camp had been blown open. Bandits had been torn apart by Agency gunfire and tanks had trampled vehicles. Even now she could see Garboa, the Bandit leader, taking a grenade to the chest that'd sent him flying out of the other end of his shack. Back then she'd been too young and broken to savour it, but now his death brought her great comfort.

After the Bandits were dispersed or imprisoned, there'd been no need for the wall. The PEA had ceased repairing it and every year it'd sustain more wear and tear from Mist activity. Its slow disintegration had been a sign of prolonged peace, and yet now it was covered in scaffolding, and worker vehicles were parked about as labourers attempted repairs. Even the lights in the watchtowers were back on.

As the train thundered on, she lost sight of the quad, but she was left pondering why the wall was being repaired. It would've been a big endeavour since it stretched three miles from Vauxhall to the ruined London Bridge, and surely wasn't necessary if the Bandits were all but eradicated like she'd believed them to be.

The answer came in the form of cold realisation when the train towered over the sorry remains of Bromley. Many of the houses were ruined and parklands were overgrown, and even the streets were impassable. But in the distance where the earth had been tilled from centuries of anomalous activity sat a new structure, towering with junk-walls reinforced by steel, with watchtowers and metres of barbed wire.

It was a Bandit camp.

The view lasted a few minutes before the soaring tracks bent for a more direct route to Sevenoaks, and yet it was still in her memory. This, like the unusual fan being built along the Strand, was another thing she'd not seen a month back when going to work, but it filled her with anger more than confusion.

The Agency could focus on building the biggest wall imaginable and all they'd be doing is giving Bandits time to thrive. And wherever a camp was, there'd be slaves just like her…

A computerised bell sounded throughout the carriages, warning of their approach to the station. It brought her to the view of the Sevenoaks factory district that was as magnificent as the Quads. It was like a second city and some even called it Eternal Night Rise because dozens of chimneys made the sky black with smoke. There were over sixty plants within its walls, making it a rather cramped, hot, and unpleasant place even at the best of times. It produced everything from vehicles and flat-packed homes, to spare parts and clothes. The chances were that if it wasn't made in Sevenoaks, then it wasn't legal.

She joined the crowds spilling onto the open-air platform lined with narrow buffer towers and wind turbines. Heavily armed Agents guarded screens with speakers projecting the *ideals of the Agency*. She wasn't used to see the PEA except during their patrols about the districts walls, and she was worried they were going to perform pat-downs and find her various illegal I.D cards as well as her RDAC. Then she realised these weren't normal Agents. Their overalls were green, showing they were new recruits and they were trying to get more to join up.

She ducked by, showing clear disinterest in being quizzed, and made for the score of turnstiles at the end. One of her I.Ds let her through where she stopped atop thirty or so steps leading down into the truck yard filled with refuse collectors auctioning off their rubbish. The auctions were often busy and fights weren't rare as factory reps shouted bids for the most lucrative looking piles of trash. That's because refurbishment was big business in a world where creating new technology was harshly regulated under the PEA. Even the factory she worked in made most of its income churning out recycled tat.

It was hard to believe this place had once been a nature reserve. Even rats found it difficult to exist here. Factories churned out smoke and the puddles were often acidic. Cars were frequent since Walkers could legally own vehicles, though few could afford the luxury. Kids busied the streets either running errands or stealing, but she kept her eye on them as she pushed on.

Eventually, she made it to the lower district where factories were older. Most worked with sewage or treated the water being supplied to Central, but this section also held the Dump. It was filled with Lecky and Lancers risked all to get inside. Its walls were over a hundred feet high and watchtowers housing snipers were always at the ready. Occasionally, she'd hear an echoed *pop* from a powerful rifle taking a shot and wonder if that was another rival Lancer done away with.

Before she could even think about getting back into the Dump, she first had to check in at work. Her factory was a six-storey sorry-state of a building with a garage door sat closed and two chimneys churning out smoke. She went through a workers entrance for the Machines Floor where several engineers were upgrading an old dump-truck. Every other floor was overlooking this one, with her boss's office being at the top. However, she needed to get to the basement, preferably unseen. It wasn't to be.

A large figure dropped from an observation platform, knocking her backwards. She wasn't surprised to see it'd been Bornis as he was now towering over her.

"Where the fuck have you been?" he asked, his mouth of brown teeth exposed in a snarl. He was a white fellow but you'd not think it due to the muck filling his pores, and he was built like a brick out-house, or so Jim would say.

"I've been ill."

"Bet you fucking have. You look like shit, too. Don't think you've got a job here. Four weeks' worth of shit's down in that workshop because of you."

"Why? Did you move in?"

He struck her, knocking free her hat and revealing a balding head of straggled hair. He recoiled as if she was wearing a dead rat on her head. "What the fuck's wrong with you?"

She slid her hat back on, saying, "I told you I got the Sickness." Then she forced a chesty cough.

"Get the fuck away from me," he squirmed, rubbing his arms as if she'd infected him. "And don't bother Pranav. He agrees with me, you're out of here."

She smirked, not believing that for a second. Pranav was an awful man at times, caring more for profit than for his workers, but he'd always taken a liking to her. *They're both paki's,* she'd hear people say. She didn't care what the reason was, as long as the Reds kept coming.

When her steely resolve remained, he huffed angrily and hissed, "Fucking muddies," before walking off.

She made it to the elevator to see it filled with trolleys. Each was packed with rubbish waiting to be sorted and she dreaded what else might be down in her department. Sure enough, when she'd reached the bottom step she found there were trolleys everywhere. Worst of all, no one had maintained the furnaces save for one, and that was likely only used to heat water to Pranav's office. It'd take hours to get them back to optimal heat. Still, she got to it, cleaning out the grates and igniting the pilot lights in each. She slammed the doors shut and sealed off the valves. With nothing else to do whilst they reached optimal capacity, she gathered what few items she'd stashed in the basement and snuck back out.

Now it was time to get some real work done.

10

The largest factory within the lower district was the sewage treatment farm. It'd actually been her first job; netting solids that'd slip the mesh-filters before the boiling process started. She'd been a little over twelve and had hated the pay, hence why she'd turned to pinching. Being small and skinny, she'd had an advantage, but she'd messed up after picking the pocket of one of the most revered men in Sevenoaks. He'd grabbed her, tied her to the back of his car, and paraded her through the streets. That man had turned out to be Pranav and she must've impressed him because he'd hired her the next day.

Still, she wasn't there to reminisce as she followed a medley of old pipes going along the walls around the Dump. Most channelled water to other areas of the district, but one had been obsolete for years now and someone long ago had broken into it behind a humming power house.

When the coast was clear, she snuck in behind it, clambering inside the rusted pipe where she put her RDAC down so that she could change whilst using its torchlight. She slid on a hazmat suit and breathing mask before bagging her coat and gloves. Then she hurried off through the darkness, rushing passed areas of intense radiation that'd make her detector bleep whilst breaking through nests of rats.

The tunnel would've gone on further, but the original users of this route had broken through the ceiling to form a shaft going up nearly twenty feet, but it wasn't dirt that lined the walls. Climbing up, she passed old fridge-freezers, washing machines, car doors, and metal sheets, all piled atop each other in mounds of priceless Lecky. That was all the Dump consisted of, and most of it had come from Essex, gathered by Sweeper Agents who'd work to find anything even remotely electronic in order to stash it here.

She was careful as she poked her head out. All it'd take was one keen sniper and *BAM* she'd be missing her head. Or worse, they'd take off a limb and she'd be forced to bleed out. Still, she scrambled up with her body intact and took a moment to look about.

The Lecky was almost sixty feet deep in some places, with some mounds concealed under tarpaulin, or locked inside containers stacked three high. Mostly it was left loose as the dump was littered with buffer towers, and from each one spanned a glass ceiling that protected the tech-nology from the elements and Mists. Still, the glass was old and dirty. In the last few years, they'd bothered less about maintaining it and she wondered if that was because the Lecky was finally becoming obsolete.

Val kept low as she hurried over the older piles of tech. It wasn't as viable as the mounds made more recently, so it was these she had to travel to. Before reaching it, however, she wanted to check on the old tunnels; routes dug through older Lecky by Lancers who'd come before her. She knew where the entrance was because it was in an area where the PEA hadn't demolished the buildings before dumping the tech, and a church's spire was sticking out of it.

She found the entrance quickly enough, but she didn't rush to get inside. Other Lancers could've come across the tunnels in the time she'd been away and set traps. It made her nervous as she slid down into them. She used the light on her RDAC to see by, ignoring offshoots that'd lead to dead-ends and cave-ins.

As the tunnel began to grow steeper, she knew she was reaching a part of the burrow that'd been her doing. Years back, she'd found the wall of an office building and broken through, gaining access to the second floor which boasted skylights and a place to camp. But even before passing through she knew something was wrong. For one, all the furniture she'd worked hard to amass had been pushed to one side of the room, and a dirty sleeping bag had been left littered with rations and drug paraphernalia. Worst of all, the dirty bastard had left countless buckets of human waste that'd formed a horrific stink.

"Fucks!" she hissed as she upturned a table in order to reach the slightly open skylight. It looked out onto the slightly messy roof, and an eroded air conditioning unit acted as cover from the nearest watchtowers. Whoever had hijacked her camp had also set up a deckchair here and left empty beer bottles and cigarette papers lying about. Hell, there was even a half-eaten roll of processed meat sitting on a car battery which gave her the impression that whoever had done this might not be far away.

That notion was soon confirmed when a four inch knife was plunged into her hip.

Val screamed as she scurried onto the roof. She kicked out more in an attempt to escape than in defence, but managed to knock her attacker's gasmask. She heard his muffled curses as he hurried to rectify it, but she was already shuffling back by then.

Almost out of instinct, she tore the knife from her flesh and nearly vomited from the pain. Her attacker managed to climb up after her and she tossed the knife far away so he'd not be able to use it again, though he had no intention of leaving it behind. As he searched madly, she scrambled to her feet and ran with a limp.

She was forever mindful to keep low, knowing the Lecky dunes only went so far before she'd be a moving target. But when she snatched a glance over her shoulder, she saw he was on her tail.

"Are you fucking *hunting* me?" she screamed.

It went against every rule of the Dump. Sure, it wasn't unusual for Lancers to fight for territory, but one Lancer moving through the Dump was bad enough; *two* would most definitely earn a sniper's attention. However, she knew this was no seasoned Lancer. His massive boots and combat jacket were typical Walker clothes, big and clumpy, and definitely not practical for the Dump. He was some stupid opportunist who'd get them both killed.

She was thankful for her upper body strength as she manoeuvred the mounds, keeping her head down and body low. He was less wary as he clambered over large objects like generators and car bonnets, causing doors to creak open and things to tumble. She spotted the knife he held and felt sick at the idea of being stabbed again, but she couldn't run fast enough. She had to do something drastic, so she fell.

The mound they'd been climbing wasn't as tall as the rest, but she grabbed the door of a washing machine as she went, dragging it with her. The displacement caused other items to fall and she was cut up and bruised by the time she reached the bottom. The Walker scurried down and pinned her with a boot pressed to her neck. Then he raised the knife. She could just about see his eyes through the mucky mask; he was looking for the best place to stab her.

An explosion of red came raining down before his body fell. It landed on top of her like a dead weight, twitching like he was caught in a nightmare before he finally died. She spluttered from shock and horror, listening to the echo that bounced about the mounds from the single rifle shot. She couldn't be sure where the bullet had come from as there was literally nothing left of the top of his head, but he was dead whilst she wasn't and that's all that mattered.

40

"This is why you don't chase people, fuck-head!" she barked, punching his side.

There she remained as scopes would be trained on that area for a while. That was fine; he was warm and she could do with the rest. She even chuckled when she found six Reds in his pocket.

Never a boring day in the Dump.

It was hard to believe Old South Quad had once been a thriving part of the City. Now it was full of men wanting whores, addicts wanting drugs, and sorry souls wanting their churches. That's why Black Waterloo was such a blessing.

She rested against a dishevelled statue. No one knew what it had once been, but the base was large and she couldn't bring herself to push away from it. She'd lost a lot of blood returning from Sevenoaks and now she was finding it almost impossible to walk the last half-mile to Black Waterloo.

The area around the Estates where she was standing was relatively busy. People had set up stalls, rickety lean-tos offered pit-fires for warmth, and horses dragged old carriages filled with unusual looking things. She'd event spent the last ten minutes watching three men carrying raggedy looking sheep off to a shack for slaughter. But no matter how long she rested for, she felt no stronger for it.

"Hey!" someone shouted from behind her. Glancing back revealed people milling about a ruined building. "Come here, my girl. Come here."

She ignored it as it was likely someone wanting to take advantage of her ailing state. But there was movement by her leg and her body stiffened when something touched her trousers where the blood had congealed. Crying, she slapped out at it, hitting a dog's snout that whimpered and leapt back. The black and white Collie was low and submissive, her large eyes wanting of affection but showing fear. Val was aghast as she said, "Cuckoo?"

"What the fuck?" barked a tall skinny woman that marched around the statue. She was decorated in tattoos, old scars, and dermatitis, but she rocked a killer pair of heels and still had all her teeth. "Val, seriously, why'd you hit my Cuckoo?"

It was Canny, an old friend of Jim's and probably one of the only women Val actually trusted in this god-awful world. That and she had a cute dog.

"Sorry, I…"

Canny said, "I was shouting at you and I - oh my god, you look like crap."

"I've been ill, and I've been stabbed." She pointed at her bloodied trouser leg.

Canny scoffed, clearly not impressed, but Val was ready for falling so she took her arm for support.

"Where are we going?" Val asked, limping alongside her.

"To the pub. Where else?"

They were sitting in Vaga's Pub on the outskirts of Black Waterloo, but they were deep enough so that the few windows made it look like midnight outside. Vaga's at least had copious lighting with running water, clinical white walls, and plenty of seating. And the beers were cheap so Canny ordered two.

There were others drinking here, but they minded their business. Vaga himself had a television playing old cartoons whilst he chewed a brown stick of liquorice. He didn't seem to care that Canny was practically undressing Val on a bench in order to get to her wound. After all, pubs weren't unusual for people to administer first aid since the beer was cleaner than the water and tipping well always turned heads.

A woman dropped off their drinks.

"Who stabbed you?" Canny asked, pulling Val's trousers down a few inches to see the stab wound better. It was an inch long and red, as well as gaping from further trauma and dehydration. When Canny tried pressing the laceration together, it instead started to bleed.

Val hissed against the pain. "Some fool. He's dead now, though. What? I didn't do it and I have no stamps for the beer."

"You'll find them. What you doing here, anyway?" Canny had managed to get a few bandages and ripped pieces of cloth off the barmaid when they'd entered, and she was using these to clean the area around the injury.

Val bit back a curse before saying, "I plan on collecting old debts."

"You think you're in any good state for that?"

"Gonna try. *Fuck* Canny!"

"That shit's infected."

"You think, doctor?"

"Exhale for this."

"Wha- Ah FUCK!"

Canny had poured the beer right into the wound and then pressed hard onto it using the makeshift-gauze. It hurt like a bitch, but she wasted no time in wrapping it in bandages.

By the time Val was allowed to pull her trousers back up, she was exhausted and her hip was on fire. Still, she asked, "You seen Jim?"

"Yeah, sometime after that last Mist. He gave Cuckoo some food. He come into some money or something?"

She scoffed as she wiped sweat trickling into her eyes. "Yeah, mine."

"What for?"

She shook her head, but Canny reached over to look

under her hat, asking "Damn, you got the Sickness? You're looking pretty bald under there."

"It's growing back."

"Sure? Coz I know a few who can help. People who can give you all this." Canny pulled her own blonde hair; it was only on closer inspection that one could see the implants.

Val scoffed as she said, "Yeah and they'll help themselves to my organs as payment."

"Only the ones you don't need." She wasn't even joking, but she was sincere as she said, "I'm worried for you, hun. Every time we meet, there's something wrong and it's been ages since I've seen you last." She wiped Val's brow as she said, "You know you can make plenty working for me, right? And I'll keep you safe. You'll be marked for good if you enlist and I've been hearing they got under-cover Agents, like *black* ones or something, real bad types. If you work for me, they'll have no right to you. You'll be mine."

"And I'll be every other sodding fellow's as well. No thanks. If I'm going to get screwed, I'll do it myself."

It'd been said in jest, but Canny read deeper and looked worried.

Val shooed it away, saying, "If I can't get a proper contract before I'm fifteen, I'll drop by. I don't want to be an Agent, but if I can get out of working for anyone but myself…"

Canny nodded. To her, the life of a working girl was perfect. She knew everyone by name, face, and smell. Her ratio of love and hate kept her crew in line and the society in which she lived could be graceful if only one was willing to bend. Canny had bent young. It had broken her a few times, too. It wouldn't be long before she became an empty sack unable to please and preying full-time on girls and boys to take her place on the clients' laps. It was good whilst the getting was high, but there was no retirement plan.

"Thanks," Val said, indicating her leg.

Canny held out the other beer. "It'll give you a boost, at least."

Val accepted. She wasn't one for turning down free things.

Val was too weak to do much else except rest. She should've been used to the fatigue, but now it simply annoyed her more.

'*You know you're becoming an adult when you're tired all the time, even if all you do is sleep,*' Jim had said once, the memory floating back as if she was there in her apartment, tending to him as he lay collapsed on her floor, too weak to even get himself a beer. He enjoyed weeks of numbness, but sometimes the burning hit his limbs and he'd be too tired to move and too pained to stay still.

'*Too old to be of any use,*' he'd mumble, disgusted with himself and dizzy from the pain medication. She'd dab his forehead and bring him cider. '*And I don't need some kid keeping me like a pet.*'

'*When will I not be a kid?*' she'd asked, tired of his moaning. '*Just watch. Soon you'll see I'm more of an adult then you give me credit for.*'

He'd laughed at this, softening even. She remembered so vividly how he'd drawn his hand down her hair which he'd never done before. There'd been no want in him, no desire; he'd simply gazed as if admiring her for the soul she'd become.

Yet his words had been sorrowful as he'd said, '*I've come to know that it ain't time that ages us. Events do; mistakes made and lessons learnt…*' His hand had dropped as if it'd been a dead weight. '*There ain't no kids today. We're born adults.*'

Her eyes opened and she realised she'd nodded off, her dream now too distant to recall. She was in a cluttered dark shop with shelves offering spare machine parts and tools, and she'd hidden herself behind a rickety counter piled with schematics and manuals. To her left was a heavy key-coded door with mechanical hinges and a protruding number pad, and she grabbed the pipe-wrench by her side as the door began to beep.

The hydraulics hissed as it opened and she was blocked from sight as a hefty woman waddled through. Her pink skirt was like a tent and her back-fat bulged beneath a green cardigan. The flesh on her ankles overflowed her yellow high-heeled shoes that were far too small, and her tights were no match for steely leg hairs protruding like worms leaving the soil. In one hand she was holding a rat-dog that yapped whilst the other was sporting a steaming cup of coffee.

Tildi they called her and, despite the blonde curls and layers of makeup, Val always wondered if someone had dressed a waste-wandering cow and taught it to walk upright.

She snatched the pipe-wrench and swung at the woman's fat knees, sending Tildi crashing to the ground. The dog went one way whilst the coffee went over the beautified manatee. Too surprised to realise what was going on, Tildi began to scream.

"Shut up!" Val snapped, slightly breathless as she towered over the beached-whale. "Where's my money?"

Her dog yapped relentlessly as it hid beneath shelves, but Tildi soon realised what was going on and, more importantly, who was responsible.

"Bitch! Little whore! You're going to pay for this you horrible, poisonous, little -"

Tildi would've continued, but her frantic rocking to rectify her position had made her breathless. It made Val remember the poster in her apartment of what Jim called a *terdle* that'd rolled onto its back and couldn't get upright again. She'd have laughed at the similarities if it wasn't so pathetic. But the bloated spud had more to come.

"*Wretch! Bitch! Broken goods*! Two tubs! Two tubs! That's what the Bandits had called you, you little whore. *Dry Val needs two tubs*, they'd say when they'd come to me with you on a leash. I'd sell them petroleum jelly by the vat full."

Val scoffed. "If that's the best you can do-"

Tildi took a deep breath to scream, but Val slapped a jelly-filled cheek. "Cry all you want, fat-fuck, I've got Canny doing a free strip-tease down the road, so there's no one here to listen."

Her rat-dog was making a racket, so Val threw a book across the room.

Tildi cried, "Be careful. Don't hurt my Poopsie."

"No, now listen! Forty days ago you sold me a compromised Initial ProtoSource Receiving unit. It was the only one that worked with my RDAC, look."

Tildi stared hungrily at her souped-up PDA and rightly so, that technology was priceless.

Val went on, "You told me the cells were fresh from the mills, yet they'd broken the moment they were used. You'd known the Adamant-Glass fuses were nearly all bust. You knew it'd pop. If I hadn't had backup, me and my men would've walked right into anomalies."

It wasn't all true. She'd purchased them before the mission that'd almost killed her. Despite the team being hand-picked by the Palacers, she'd had a feeling they'd be poorly equipped and it turned out to be true as their PDA's hadn't even sported anomaly counting technology. So she'd made them one each, except when she'd sent a bloke off to scout for signs of plasma-manifestations, the IPSR had popped and he'd walked right into a pressure-spot. It'd blown him limb from limb, sending his head through their windshield which had been their only shelter from a Mist, and seeding the betrayal that'd soon follow.

Val wasn't saying that the faulty ISPR units were to

blame for her exposure, but she was going to take it out on Tildi one way or another.

"You should've checked their condition," Tildi sneered. "It's not my fault. You should always-"

Val went for the wrench.

"Wait! Fine, it was broken *a little*, but glass fuses are seven a stamp so take as many as you want." She was pointing to the shelf where the long cylinders were located.

"I don't want more."

"Then what?"

Val indicated a hidden safe beneath the counter. "The number."

"No!"

"No? Ugh, hearing negativity makes me ill," she said, heaving. "I might vomit on you and I think I got the Sickness."

She removed her hat, horrifying Tildi with her alopecia before continuing to heave. She even forced her fingers to the back of her mouth to exaggerate the gags.

"Thirty, thirty-five, ninety!" Tildi squealed.

Val wiped her fingers on her hat as she replaced it and made for the safe.

"Don't you rob me," Tildi screamed, struggling even more to roll over.

"Well lookie here," Val sang as it opened, pushing aside useless log books and Old World coins for a shimmering book of Red stamps. They were fresh off the press as they still sat in their perforated pages within a PEA issued book, complete with foil tape and black light stickers "One, two, three… Four hundred and fifty stamps. Bet they're fake."

She squealed, "They're mine."

"I guess," Val said, not all that interested as she'd hoped for medication packets or blank ID cards; anything she could've traded for antibiotics. "Where did you get these, anyway?" she asked as she checked for hidden compartments.

"I bought them off a reliable source."

"Really? Who? Tell me and I'll bring over the hoist before I leave."

There was no other reason the shop owned a hoist other than to lift the fat cow off her arse, and the offer loosened Tildi's chubby lips, saying, "Chief Degdon."

"Degdon! He's as reliable as a wax coffee pot."

"Stamps are being phased out! There's a big rush to get them all into circulation before they become worthless, and it means they're cheaper to get hold of seeing as us merchants at Black Waterloo ain't going to give them up."

Val was laughing. "He's probably sold you marked goods in hopes you'll use them and get caught."

"Not likely," Tildi said pointedly and ran a hand down her skirt, "Me and the Chief have a… understanding."

Val shuddered. However, she'd found a hidden compartment at the bottom of the safe and Tildi swore as she liberated documents pertaining to the lease of the shop, as well as a familiar looking dented tin. In fact, she knew that tin very well. She activated the black light on her RDAC and bathed the lid to find it reflected her signature; a V overlaying an A propped up by a lopsided L. This was her tin from her safe!

She pried it open, spilling two hundred crumpled Reds. *Her Reds*.

"Jim was here!" Val cried.

Tildi looked nasty, as if depriving her of that information would be wonderful.

Val forced her anger aside and actually shrugged, pretending not to care as she made to leave.

Tildi cried, "Wait! The hoist…"

"Tell me when he was here and what he got in return for these Reds?"

"He came this morning. He wanted me to change a load of stamps for clean ones."

"But you gave him fakes!"

"He didn't mind. He'd left with double the Reds he'd come in with. I even tore them from the books myself." She was smiling nastily, knowing if he was caught with fakes he'd be carted off to the Dwells, and he'd never survive that in his condition.

Val asked, "Where'd he go?"

"I don't know and I don't care."

Enraged, Val rolled the hoist across the room where it hit the counter. Tildi was laughing as she shuffled over and hooked herself to the brace. But Val refused to leave her gloating and snatched the dog from beneath the shelf. She thought it'd bite her, but its tail wagged while it licked her hand.

Tildi stopped the hoist. "What are you doing with Poopsie?"

"I'm going to put it out its misery. This thing is inbred and suffering."

"No! Not my lil Poopsie!" she wailed, but Val had already gone.

It was late, but there was still some luminosity to the sky. She planned on heading into Central before Westminster Bridge shut, but first she stopped off at the Religious District. All the Houses were lit up and the crescent they sat before was empty and clean-looking. She hadn't visited her House in a long time and she felt bad going there with an agenda, but at least she could show her face and reassure her friends.

Christ Church Chapel was heavily fortified with bars over its stained-glass windows that spilled colourful light. As she climbed the steps, she set Poopsie down and, like before, he followed obediently. She wished he'd run off and be free, and maybe find other rat-dogs to start a family with…

He wasn't even fat enough to cook.

She pushed through the large doors and found the nave empty, except for the figure in black kneeling before the altar. She went to approach but an Agent appeared from around the entrance and used his gun to bar her entry. She glowered and he actually squared up to her, though all she could do was glare at her reflection in his visor.

Before he could get physical, she called, "Father Rodling, can you give me a hand, here?"

He turned with a face of confusion, but it formed into astonishment as he hurried to a stand where he was waving his arms. "Stand down, it's all right. Come here, girl. Here!"

He grabbed her up into a hug and then held her out at arm's length as if to get a better look. "My child! I thought you were… I lit candles and prayed and… Oh, I'm blessed. This day hasn't been the best, but this has truly picked me up. Where have you been?"

He was younger than any priest who'd held the position in decades, and wasn't far off bad-looking with short brown hair that was free of greys. His pink skin was blemish free, his teeth were white, and he sported deep brown eyes. He was a Casual, but he'd always been so down to Earth.

She said, "I've been ill, but I'm better now."

"You look tired and…" he paused at the sight of Poopsie. "Is that thing following you?"

"It's a dog. A pet. Do you want it?"

"Oh, well, we're all God's creatures, but no. Come, sit a while and talk to me."

She glanced at the Agent still keeping guard and Rodling got the hint. They walked further down the aisle to speak quietly where she said, "I wish I could, but I'm here looking for Jim."

"I've not seen him. Maybe Sister Josephine has? Let's go to her. She's been praying for you and - wait, are you bleeding?" He gestured at her leg.

"Just a sprain."

"Quite. You really should consider moving to the church. I couldn't bear to go that long again without knowing your condition. And you're almost fifteen, so you'll-"

Her eyes dropped.

Not wanting to depress her, he said, "I'm sorry, I worry, that's all."

"The church has helped me in ways no one ever has. I couldn't repay you enough, but-"

He held up a hand to silence her. "By living an honest life and keeping God in our hearts, we do for mankind what Jesus did all those years ago. Not even the End could defeat our faith, so don't let your ailing confidence mar your heart. Come, visit Sister Josephine with me, she'll rest easier knowing you're well."

With Poopsie following, they headed back outside, rounding the chapel where grounds were being cleared for a greenhouse donated by the PEA, and Rodling spoke excitedly about the produce that they'd gain tax-free once completed. He even hinted that they'd need to employ a contracted gardener in due time. With her experience, this actually sparked her interest.

The cemetery to the back was one of the oldest as it'd formed after the demolition of the factories. The fenced-in grounds were treated daily and spotted with headstones. Plants grew here, hardy ones with thick branches, dark leaves, and tiny flowers. The constant tending by the nuns kept them nice.

Of the few nuns raking the topsoil, one turned when called and her aged but pretty face lit up when she saw Val. Sister Josephine hurried over to hug her, kissing her cheeks and thanking God for her safety. She was a black woman with dark eyes and full lips, but incredibly slender with nimble hands made for turning the pages of a book. She'd aged since their time together in the Sacred Hearts Orphanage when Val was toddler, but her loving nature had gone unchanged.

"I prayed to God you'd come back to us. It's been weeks, and look at you," she said, her voice almost hoarse with tears. "You're sick? You're almost white."

"I'm getting better. I only popped over to-"

"You're not staying?"

"I can't…"

Josephine held up her hands. "Stay while I get you some food tokens before you rush off." She wouldn't allow refusals and hurried inside.

Whilst they waited for her return, Val said, "I noticed the PEA are building a wall around the Estates at the South Embankment. Has it got to do with the repairs they're doing to the Southern Wall?"

"I can't be sure, but the PEA have big plans," Rodling said. "In a year's time, they're going to do away with all these buffer towers and replace them with air purification fans. Unfortunately, I did hear that some of the Estates would need extensive renovations before that could take place. I do believe a Registration Movement is coming and it may upset many of those living unregistered along the embankment."

"That explains why the walls are so big. Walker's aren't going to be happy about that."

"Indeed. There was a riot a week ago. Several died."

"Between the Walkers and the PEA? Sounds about right."

"No, between the churches. Many see the walls as a sign of protection and due to them being so close to our church, it's fuelling the belief that the PEA are only there for the benefit of Christ's Church. I can understand why they feel this way. We have the largest congregation and so our donations are naturally bigger, though you'd not think it considering how empty our sermons are every day. Still, it's upsetting a few of the Houses."

She scoffed. "You mean the muzzies?"

"Val, please," he scowled. "It was various people who contributed to the riots. And now the foundations have started for our greenhouse, it's causing further unrest. I had asked Commander Devron to hold off building ours until all the Houses had their materials, but he'd not wait."

"Devron's a prick."

"He is a man of God and he does his best for all of us. His forces are thin, however. To have the Agency respond to every riot is a drain on their resources, and with things being the way they are…"

"Yeah, I saw the camp."

He exhaled as he looked off into the darkening sky. "It's a bad sign."

"And I saw PEA career officers looking for new recruits."

"It's working. I've seen green Agents all over the place. You've heard we have a new Prime Minister? He doesn't attend here since he's from Quad: West and they have their own church, but I met him and he seems eager to support our Houses. He's young, but willing."

Josephine returned and pushed several food tokens into her hand. "Plenty for you and Jim."

"You haven't seen him by any chance?"

"I did this morning. Early. He didn't stop, but I think he was heading to Black Waterloo."

"I'd better go."

"Not for long, I hope," Father Rodling said. "I mean, we really should talk. Tell Jim he's welcome."

"He's scared he'll turn to dust if he enters here," she scoffed.

"There's no man who's sinned enough to do such a thing."

"He's sixty per cent alcohol, Father. He's one cigarette away from combustion."

Father Rodling didn't seem to find that too funny, but then things had always been strained between Jim and the church. Either way, Val departed with the rat-dog close behind.

14

Val still needed proper medical attention and if she was going to get the right type of care, then she'd need to set aside her pride. The Palacers may've been why she'd almost died, but they'd also be the best cure as well.

She'd carried Poopsie across Westminster Bridge where many crowded to get through the gates before Central was closed off from the south. But her head was starting to spin and there was a shrill whistling in her ears. Poopsie must've noticed because he seemed adamant on licking her face.

She'd managed through the huge gates that looked as if they themselves could've stopped a Mist. To her left was the Palace of Westminster, and in its grounds was the most impressive of all buffer towers. In fact, this one was so advanced that they called it an *obelisk*, and it was nearly two hundred feet high and produced a beam of purple light that went as high as the clouds. On each mirror-like surface there was a digital clock showing it was a few minutes off ten o'clock. She'd made it across in time.

"Oh god," she said as she dry-heaved and stumbled blindly to a side road, walking on autopilot and hoping no one had noticed her weakening state. She finally dropped the dog that yipped and wagged its tail, eager to keep close as she finally made it to an alley where she fell. Her limbs were quivering and she'd come over cold, but she knew it was from a sudden drop in blood-pressure. She'd not eaten besides a few meds she'd chewed walking back from Black Waterloo, and that beer had been nothing more than cloudy water.

Eventually, some of her energy and hearing returned. She sat a moment listening to the speakers along Whitehall, often warning Walkers of incoming weather events or the radiation count. She'd not managed to visit the market along that way yet, but it sounded so much livelier than usual, and the clouds glowed from the light pollution.

Val only realised Poopsie had wandered off when the rat-dog trotted back. His tail was wagging madly as he was holding something in his jaws. Val relieved him of it, discovering a PEA ration; a vacuum-sealed foil package of soft bread.

"Where'd you find this?" she asked after eating it since it'd still been in date. To her surprise, Poopsie seemed eager to show her. They came to a break in the wall leading into a derelict room. Water damage and squatters had left a mess, but an area was cleared away and several boxes were set up, with a couple of tea-towels placed over them for decoration. Even before she saw the sloppily painted R in a circle atop the wall, she knew this was a shrine to Redemption.

She'd seen a few in her time, mostly in the run-down areas of the Quads. As usual, rations had been left there, as well other items such as bandages, creams, and scissors. She was sure such shrines existed as a salvation for those trapped in hostile environments as she herself had found them helpful during some of her adventures, especially when they'd come equipped with bags of sterilised water.

Curiously enough, there were other items that were less practical, such as toys and colouring pens, and even makeshift objects like a length of string knotted with buttons. Flowers were sometimes added, hence why they were referred to as shrines, but frankly she wasn't sure what the purpose of these was.

Whilst most of the items were random, there was one thing she'd come to expect; a leaflet. She found one nearby weighted down with a rock and kept it close as she hurried off in case someone had been using the shrine as bait.

The story of Redemption started over a century ago after the PEA had cast out many inferior members. Apparently, these people had banded together to form their own militia and had fought to save the world. Unfortunately, they seemed to believe that the people were the main reason the world was dying, and Val couldn't actually disagree with that.

It's said that they believe the world is alive, *sentient* even, and that the Mists are its way of cleansing evil. Val didn't know how much of it was true, but she believed that these people did indeed exist and for one simple reason.

She'd seen them.

It'd been a child no older than six, she was sure, and it'd been impossible to tell their gender. The kid had been blonde with pale flesh, wide eyes, and bare feet, and had been giving water to a Mallowhead when she'd stumbled across them. Val had accidentally scared them away, but she'd never forgotten that moment. And on the shrine the kid had left a leaflet, just like the one she held now.

When she was along a back road alongside barriers keeping people from entering the dishevelled grounds around the old Charing Cross station, she slid out the leaflet to have a look. It'd been hand drawn on recycled paper, bleached white and sewn with string. This one had a drawing of an Old World train pumping out steam whilst people waited at a platform to climb aboard. The pictures rarely held any meaning. The last leaflet had depicted what Jim had called penguins; fat birds that couldn't fly and lived in something known as snow, yet the leaflet had been a long ramble about the sound footsteps make in a world left silent after a Mist.

This leaflet, like the last, also held a poem.

In Mist we trust an End
    Of death without payment or pain,
    And the land blistered by men
    Will grow again.

Having wrought that which ails us now,
    We've tightened the screws and bolts.
    We'll cry when we fight the end now,
    Of which is our own fault.

Release the need to fight Her
    She barrels on regardless,
    And walk the scars we've rendered
    As this world no longer requires us.

It sounded miserable, but not unlike Redemption's style. They often spoke of the Mist's cleansing of the Earth's crust, blaming humans for the nuclear onslaught and the current state of despair. Still, there was an element of joy in their misery and it was this delusional contentment that had captivated so many. It was hard to believe that Walkers had feared them a century ago, but now they were almost fashionable.

She pushed the leaflet into her jacket and carried on with Poopsie at her heels. The roads along here had long since fallen victim to time. Buildings were rendered several storeys shorter and rubble littered the streets, but it was here she'd find the entrance to the Palacer base.

She cut through the rubble and found an oddly well-maintained corridor cast in darkness. At the end was a blast-door weighing several hundred pounds. After a short wait, there were clicks and hisses as locks were released, and with a heave it slid open a few feet. There she was greeted by a smiling lean fellow with spiked but greasy blonde hair wearing a white vest and black baggy trousers. Still, his blue eyes were sharp behind his round spectacles, and his grin went from ear to ear.

"*Bonjour*! Come quickly though, we're on lockdown," Pierre sang.

"Why?" she asked, ducking down the metal steps as the door closed behind her.

"Why? *Why*? How could you not know?" he shrilled. "The Agency are everywhere. I-" He stopped when he spotted Poopsie. "What is that?"

"Exactly," she sighed and headed down the concrete corridor with Pierre on her tail. At the end was the Command Room that boasted an entire wall of computers, monitors, and processing towers. It was ATOM, though it wasn't whirring or bleeping as much as usual. It all seemed rather dormant.

A door to the left led to a residential wing, and beside that was a glass wall that allowed her to see a well-stocked operating theatre. A frosted door ahead of her led to the hospital wing modified with a lab and technical department where the two-man team made most of their inventions. It was a large base and most of it went unused, but Pierre always hinted that there was more to it than what she'd seen.

"I was worried about you," he said, his jolly demeanour now one of anxiety. "I knew you were alive because I found Jim some time back and he'd said you were improving, but he'd not talk to me and wouldn't accept any medication. I… you're injured?" He pointed to the blood on her trousers.

"Yeah. I've been stabbed and it's in a bad way," she said, distracted as she'd been eyeing the frosted glass door to the Ward. "Is Vord back there?"

Vord was the chief scientist and owner of the Palacer group, a direct descendent to the previous head scientist.

"He's busy," Pierre said, "so we have time to mend your leg. Come, before he realises I'm not with him."

Pierre was a surgeon, but he'd been born in France, living for eleven years inside a tribe that'd existed almost completely underground. There weren't many people outside of England. Hell, there weren't many people *inside* England, but to think there still may be survivors was intriguing. But Pierre had been brought to the Known World and educated by the PEA, or so she'd assumed since he'd been an Agent when she'd first crossed paths with him. Shortly after that meeting, he'd deserted and joined as a Palacer and that was how she'd come to know of the CTGs, or Clandestine Technological Groups. There'd been dozens of them in the past, all warring against the PEA. Now, she doubted there were more than three or four still operational.

He brought her into the theatre, propping her on the bed and switching on the lamp. She slid down her trousers and watched as he cut away the bandages, recoiling at the smell.

"Is that beer?"

She shrugged and he went about the room collecting a tray of items. As he cleaned her leg, he blithered on. "I wish Jim had brought you in. I never got to see you after the mission failed. Apparently you'd asked the rescue team to drop you off in Beckton? I'd found Jim but he'd been hostile towards me and refused to tell me your condition.

All I could do was wish for the best, but I think you must've been quite ill since it's been weeks. I'm really sorry."

"Why?" she asked. He paused, unsure how to answer that. "Why should you be sorry? It wasn't you who fucked up the coordinates and sent me into the arsehole of nowhere, leaving me with a bunch of trigger-happy goons that'd tried to cut me down the moment my back was turned."

"Ah, about that-"

"And it wasn't you who sent me out fourteen hours before a fucking Mist hit."

"Val-"

"Then again, you do everything you're told by that bushy-browed prick, so yeah, feel sorry. I almost died because of you fucking idiots. And what happened to my fucking backup?"

"I was caught up! Me and the boys were right behind you with the rover, tracking you, but Bandits landed on us and then the Agency turned up by the time the Mist hit. I was knee deep in bodies by the end."

She squinted at him. Pierre was no liar, but she was surprised she'd not known about that. "I'll let you off. Fucked me up good, though. Look at this shit," she said, taking off her hat.

"We can fix that."

"Like you fix everything, with operations and horrible medicines? I'd rather be bald," she grumbled and pulled her trousers back up after he'd cut the last suture. "Just give me some antibiotics and be done with it."

She slid off the table and hobbled back to the Command Room. He was close behind, ready to say something when the frosted door opened and in strolled Vord. He had his face in a PDA and was only wearing a pair of thin trousers, exposing his ripped torso and broad shoulders. He never left the base, so working out and doing tests was all he ever did. Then he looked up and his expression turned to disgust.

"I thought she'd died!"

Val grinned and folded her arms. "Yeah, nice to see you too, you big, daft prick."

"Shut the fuck up. Do you know how much money you cost me?" Vord sneered, slamming his PDA down on the table.

Pierre said, "That wasn't her fault. Let's not blow up over this, yes?" His accent always got worse when he was nervous.

"Well, it wasn't my fault, either!"

She looked amazed at that, saying, "Excuse me, but your route led me through anomalies, your men tried to kill me, and a Mist landed on my fucking head barely twelve hours after we set off. I've been unconscious for nearly a month because of that mission, but hey, not *your* fault." She tired quickly and grumbled, "Just stop being a whiny cunt and give me the money I'm owed."

He almost flew across the room at her. Vord's ego was immense and he protected it fiercely, so Pierre was forced to get between them.

"Let's just give her what we owe her," Pierre whispered.

"What I owe her? I lost a vehicle, five men, four PDA's, two hazmat suits that I spent three weeks preparing, and it'd been her who'd lured the PEA in with her distress call."

When it was clear Pierre had very little sympathy for this, Vord threw his hands down and said, "You know what? Fine." He marched to a filing cabinet and dragged out a small bag that he unzipped. "We agreed on fifty Reds for reaching the end destination? Well fuck it, here." He threw the bag at her feet, spilling stamps. "Have yours and have the ones owed to the men that died, too."

She looked disgusted. "And that's my fucking fault, is it?"

"No, of course not," Pierre began.

"Well, who told them to leave the designated route?" Vord asked. "Who was it that stopped relaying data when you went a mile off course?"

"We were avoiding anomalies and Bandits that *you'd* sent us into."

"But you didn't scan them or radio it in, did you? No, you just left me sitting here like a wanker wondering what the hell my men, my car, and my technology was doing heading off into fucking nowhere."

"Your *men* were planning on doing away with me and driving off with your car the moment we crossed the border, so shut the fuck up with that nonsense. It was either them or me, so sorry for choosing self-preservation."

Vord didn't want to believe her, but he processed it all the same.

She slumped in a chair before ATOM and said, "I did what you needed me to do. I scanned the end destination. It's not my fault you found fuck-all."

Pierre once again stepped up to Vord, whispering for him to leave it for now. To her surprise, Vord actually left, though not before slamming the door on them both.

Pierre looked listless as he sat before her. "I don't know how you do it. I never see anyone upset him quite like you do."

"It's not hard," she mumbled. "He's more uppity than usual, though."

"Believe it or not, he honestly thought you'd died and he felt bad." He waited for her to stop laughing before saying, "He felt bad because after you made it back with the rescue unit, we found out that we'd sent you to the wrong place."

She threw her hands in the air. "Fucking figures!"

He nodded sadly as he took her RDAC and hooked it

up to ATOM, saying, "I suppose you haven't heard about Craydo whilst you've been ill?"

"They're a merc-based CTG? They're like your competition or something."

She'd done some work for them in the past, just scoping out places and finding Lecky mainly. Their endeavours were the same as Vords, to find new tech and take out the PEA, but she'd cut off contact when she'd discovered they hired ex-Bandits as mercs.

Pierre was typing as he said, "Pretty much. They've been operating to the west of the Quads for the past thirty years. The biggest employer of mercs I know. They were the reason we haven't sent teams out to find this Lecky sooner. It would've caused fights to break out and that would've brought too much attention to our doorstep. But they started talking to us out of the blue, saying they were closing down and moving on, and the word on the street confirmed it. They'd not hired a merc in weeks."

"What's all this about?" she asked, knowing Pierre could talk her head off if given the chance.

"They weren't closing down, they were being *shut* down. The PEA had infiltrated them and were using them to find us."

"Oh shit, no wonder you're on shut down."

He laughed. "Not entirely, but Craydo were forced by the PEA to trick us into finding this Lecky that Vord's been after for years, except they'd fed us false coordinates. When I look at it now, it's so obvious. They'd told us to go to Horsham and that seemed reasonable, well until the mission failed. Then we looked over the coordinates and realised just how insanely treacherous the route had been.

"Vord looked into the code, searching for any encryptions and codes. I don't know how he did it, but he figured out the actual end destination by linking inconsistencies in the logs." He spoke as if this was the kicker. "It was never supposed to be Horsham, but Hailsham!"

She didn't react.

He threw his hands down. "*Oh la vache.* Well I thought it was clever, and it was also brave of whoever fed us these coords because they'd know the PEA would be waiting for us to land, and had tried diverting us. It's just a shame we'd never realised it sooner."

"Epic, did you update it?"

He mumbled in French as he handed the RDAC back.

As she strapped it on, she said, "So it must be pretty important stuff, this Lecky, if the PEA want it, too? Worth dying for?"

"The PEA don't care about Lecky. They just want us gone like the rest of the CTGs. But let me tell you, this Lecky? It's big, and if we're right, then it'll change the course of our future."

"But it's Old World…"

"Like amber holding a mosquito, it holds answers."

"So who's manning this new mission?"

He pretended not to understand the question.

"Come off it. You've located the actual destination and have no desire to go there now?"

He pursed his lips before saying, "I'm going."

"Alone?"

"It's not your concern. Do not fret. Just focus on getting yourself well again."

"I need money, not health. Give me a list of Lecky you need from the Dump and I'll stop pestering you."

"I've not had a chance to compile one, but I've updated your RDAC so I'll send you a list when I have a need for items. But you won't get the same prices as before. I don't suppose you've heard the news?"

She gave him a sideways look.

"The PEA are looking to remove Reds from circulation. By the end of the week, you'll only be able to make lawful transactions with Cred-editors. Credits are harder to forge so we'll be working from laundered stocks. You have an E-tag?"

She took out the dog tag necklace that was chip-activated and loaded with a few dozen digital currency tokens. It was Agency money so she rarely used it.

As they walked to the door, Val said, "I'll feel better in a few days, then I'll get back to the Dump."

"I wish there was a safer place for you to find this Lecky."

"I know the Dump like the back of my hand. Honestly, I'm safer in there than I am out here"

She climbed the stairs, but he cried, "Ah *mon cher*, this dog. You almost forgot it." He bent down to pick it up and Poopsie grew excited, licking his hands and wagging its tail. But when he turned back for the door, Val had already gone.

"*Merde…*"

16

Val woke to rain. She'd been warned the evening before that it was due and had left barrels about the rooftop to collect it. Still, it'd been a short shower and the water was largely acidic, so it needed a lot of treatment before it was safe to drink.

After filling her water purification unit with what little she'd managed to neutralise, she'd tried to pass the early morning hours by cleaning up her greenhouse. She'd hoped Jim would've been back by now, but still there was no word.

The radio was playing a song from the Beatles before she realised it was nearly seven in the morning. ERD's broadcast was due, so she took herself to the living room to tune into his channel, though it played only static for the meantime.

Whilst she waited, she brewed herself a pot of tea from a few musty filter-bags she'd had left over from her last ration. Pushing aside some of the window cladding, she sat on the windowsill bathing her face in the steam as she watched the wet morning.

Just as the minute ticked by, the static died to a series of drawn-out beeps before an automated voice said, '*What follows is a paid broadcast by the PEA.*'

She slammed her cup down. "Paid fucking what?"

'*Hello residents of the Known World,*' came a deep voice, "*this is First Commander Bernard Devron of the PEA. This will be one of a number of announcements held throughout the day in which Walkers may garner information of how to better their lives, serve their world, and live in harmony with one another.*'

Val was smiling and looking around the room as if this was a joke. But the punch line never came.

'The Peace Enforcement Agency is here for your protection, and for the protection of the K.W. In the past eight weeks, we have been working tirelessly to drag the Quadrants into a more modern setting, reviewing all practices and procedures obsolete with today's needs, and building a better relationship with the men, women, and children who work hard to keep this world afloat.'

"You mean when you're not gunning us down or carting us off to the Dwells?" she asked, now pacing the room and shaking her head.

'Besides from updating Market Street on Whitehall as well as providing better resources to our hospitals, we've been cracking down on Undesirables. Terrorist organisations such as the Bravers, the RadRangers, the Red Heralds, Cradyo, and the Palacers, which have all been arrested and held within the newly refurbished Dwell Peniten-tiary, and their cohorts are now scattered and losing power.'

She doubted half of those groups even existed, but to hear him mention the Palacers made her worry. Had they been taken out during the evening? She tapped her RDAC to see everything was in order according ATOM, but still it'd birthed anxiety.

'The most noteworthy of operations to have been undertaken so far was by our covert task-force named Operation Blackstone. They'd been painstakingly trained to quell the rising Bandit influx that many had reported on the horizon of the Old South Quadrant, visible from the PEA train heading to Sevenoaks. As of last night, we have completely obliterated their settlement. Thanks to these Agents, the Wastes are now a safer place.

'To find out the latest news, listen to our segmented radio clips or subscribe to the PEA Newsprint that will, as of today, be available for free to all Registered Walkers. Thank you for listening and remember this world is only what you make it. Work Hard and Be Lawful.'

"Well that was fucking convenient!" she snapped. "You take out a Bandit base the morning before you insult our airwaves with your drivel? Great fucking headline!" She punched the radio she was that angry. "Wanna ruin my morning any more, you smug fucking cu-" She'd punched it again, but the battery had dislodged and it'd shocked her. "*Bastard*!"

She threw it against the wall, shattering it completely before she slid down and sighed. She dropped her head in her hands and whined, knowing it was going to be a bad day.

Walkers descended on the bus stop. Val kept her distance as she waited, confident that the wallet she'd made to house her ID cards wouldn't allow the Black Eyes to detect them when the shuttle finally arrived. But she'd been uncharacteristically nervous since Devron's hijacking of ERD's channel, not only because he'd claimed to have taken down the Palacers, but because she had no idea what'd become of the old man that'd brightened many of her mornings. In fact, it unnerved her more than losing contact with Jim because as annoying as it was, he was prone to it, but never had ERD missed a broadcast.

Finally, her RDAC vibrated silently on her wrist and that alone would've been confirmation enough that the Palacers were still up and running. Still, she stretched back her jacket sleeve to view the screen.

All's well here, mon ami.

She released the last of her stress with a slow exhalation. Then she heard shuffling and sniffling, turning upon realising that someone was standing a few feet behind her. Other Walkers had noticed this man and walked a little further off, but Val was standing her ground.

"They're not gone, you know?" he muttered, his eyes flickering all over the place as if aware of some unseen danger. He was a skinny man, emaciated even, with short black hair, scars down his face, and tattoos about his arms where the sleeves had been rolled up. His boiler suit was typical for a Walker, but he wasn't such a person and she knew that just from his markings.

He was a Bandit and no mistake.

He was muttering; touched by some mental issue or another. She assumed at first it was drug abuse but reconsidered it to be something much deeper. He was far from where Bandits would typical hang around, and he was dressed in a suit far too big for him, so she couldn't help but feel like he'd been left to wander like some kind of Mallowhead.

"The Badlanders," he whispered, finally catching her eye. This made Val nervous because she thought he'd directed that at her personally, as if he'd known she'd had a previous dealings with Bandits. "They're not gone. I seen them. I survived them…"

She looked along his tattoos. Most were just random symbols or tribal markings, but one was a line down his forearm that was thirty centimetres long, resembling a ruler, except eight centimetres of it had been blocked out. That was how Bandits kept a check of how many people they've killed. With each man or woman they gun down, they block out another centimetre, with the biggest and the worst of the Bandits being literally covered in black bars.

"I got sent there, didn't I?" he went on. By now there was only Val to speak to as most had wandered right off, avoiding the loon. "They got me like they got the talky man. Gots us all… Sent us there… I had to join them to survive!" He rubbed his forearm. "I had to. Had to…"

She didn't like talking to strangers, but she'd been enticed and asked, "Where were you sent?"

"The Big House."

She guessed he meant the Dwells, a savage prison north of the Quads where many went and few returned. That would explain how he'd become mixed up with Bandits.

"And how long were you there?"

He shook his head. She figured he'd lost all sense of time. He wiped his face; he was perspiring a hell of a lot. "I got there, got in with them, then they all got released. I went with them… was there with them in the Wastes, down from here. Down down down…"

"The base south of the wall?"

"Long walk…"

"Bet it was. And now all the Bandits are dead? The PEA came and blew them up?"

He was shaking his head. "Off on their tod. Off they trot…"

"They just left? No fighting?"

He made a sound like laughter, but it resulted in a cough that made his chest rattle. She was no doctor, but she could tell whatever was afflicting his mind and body wouldn't take long before it ended his life. So Val did something she'd never done before and showed the Bandit some compassion, not by drawing him down an empty alley and dropping a paving stone on his head, but by offering him a red stamp. But he seemed to have no concept of this and just smiled awkwardly.

A rumbling from down the road had him perking up. Realising the shuttle was coming, he scarpered, leaving her hand and the stamp to fall to her side as she watched him vanishing into the estates.

"Fucked up," she whispered before the shuttle rumbled to their stop.

Val had previously avoided Market Street down Whitehall in fear of more Black Eyes. Now as she walked from Charing Cross roundabout, she couldn't believe what she was seeing.

The old, mucky street was a thing of the past. Rickety stalls and merchants plying their wares from sheets on the tarmac were gone as the PEA had issued stalls of white plastic and shiny metal, with merchant's names purported on LED boards. There were goods from fresh veg to meat; it came in BioBags to show they'd been lab grown, but still it was advertised at a great price.

Buildings once left crumbling had been reinforced with scaffolding, and now each supported a colour screen. Propaganda played nonstop with speakers broadcasting the ideals of the Agency to anyone going slow enough to listen. The Walkers who were willing to brave the increased PEA presence and numerous Black Eyes about the stalls seemed enamoured.

She passed the People's Hospital where queues waited to receive their rations. Further on was Downing Street that held their new Prime Minister. There were screens here, too, broadcasting a Casual news reporter sat at a desk reading from a PDA. The screen changed to a chubby young man with reddish hair and freckles – a Royal if ever she saw one. It had to be Prime Minister Andrews.

It then swapped to another figure, and this one there was no mistaking. Commander Devron was a short man, but well-built and smart-looking in his dark blue uniform beneath Agency armour. He was talking intently to whoever was holding the mic, but there was a figure behind him looking sullen and this face always brought about a rush of tingles.

It was Second in Command Erga Roman. Tall, broad, and bald. He held a face of constant contempt and had been a high ranking Agent for over a decade. He'd also been the man who'd led the Agency attack on the Bandits that'd led to her freedom four years ago. She could see him towering over her and the other slaves, his grenade launcher smoking and his hand held out for her, ready to whisk her away to freedom.

She should've ended up in an Agency complex, or inside some type of training program, but fortunately Jim had been present that day when they were getting chipped and registered. They had all been so scared and untrusting of the PEA, so she'd leapt at the chance to get out of there. He'd taken her to his boat to live with him. She couldn't imagine what she might've turned into if he'd not found her that day.

By the time the screen changed, she was already gone. Reaching the end of Whitehall, she stopped before she reached the grounds ahead of Westminster Bridge and turned for a dugout leading beneath a dishevelled building. As the stairs went underground, she passed the neon sign of a glowing green lion, which made sense since this was the Glowing Lion Pub, and continued down a dreary corridor of sloppily plastered walls for a door at the end.

"Marco," she greeted the massive bouncer at the end and pushed her way into the pub. It was a small room with booths around two of the walls and rickety tables in the middle. It looked relatively empty, though she didn't draw attention to herself by looking around. Rather, she turned to the bar covered in wire fencing decorated with old road signs, spotting Loris standing behind them.

"Has Jim been in?" she asked the skinny man in a shirt

and dinner jacket that looked miles too big, and some rumoured he didn't even wear trousers back there. But he was a wretched human being with a lopsided face and nicotine-stained fingers, and he hated her as much as she hated him. So whilst she'd expected an onslaught of insults, he'd in fact given her a smile and said, "Well no, I ain't. You off to work, pet?"

She almost threw a load of abuse, more out of instinct than anything, but the question had caught her off guard. Then she noticed his shifting eyes and knew he was trying to tell her something. For whatever reason, he was being covert, so she played along and approached the bar.

"Yeah, soon. A bottle of Bruch, please."

Pronounced *Broosh* if you wanted to be posh, it was commoners wine and she drank it because it was low intoxicating and thankfully quite tasteless. He slid one over and she pushed a Red through the cavity in the barrier, but rather than take the stamp he grabbed her wrist instead.

"I only work in creds now, lass," he growled. "It's the law."

"You need to get the fuck off me before I liberate your testicles from your diseased husk."

It was a ploy. Both were playing along in order to get close enough for a quiet exchange, only made possible when he grabbed her face with his greasy hand and dragged her through the barrier.

Yeah, he didn't wear pants…

"I'll smack yah about until your mamma hurts!" he spat before whispering, "*I kicked Jim out the night before after he paid me with a fake fucking stamp. He was waving 'em about like he was rich.*" Then he shouted, "And I'll cut you three ways from Sunday if yah get rude, you little cow!"

"Did you tell on him?" she whispered.

Loris threw back his head and laughed; he was sick and

horrible, but he was no grass. He let her go where she bumped something hard. Turning revealed an Agent. He was wearing a dark blue overall with partial armour about his chest and arms, but he must've been off duty because he didn't have his gun or helmet.

"Problems here, Loris?" the senior Agent asked.

"I got this," he said, pushing a bottle of vodka across the bar. The Agent eyed her before taking it to a dark corner where two other Agents were sitting, but their uniforms were green and they looked tired.

"Come on lass, a credit for the drink," Loris said, accepting her e-tag before scanning it at a small terminal.

"What happened to Jim?" she asked.

He didn't seem comfortable as he replied, "I had to kick him out. He was getting rude to them lot."

"Did they follow him when he left?"

For the first time in as long as she'd known the greasy freak, he looked concerned.

"Where'd he go?" she asked.

He didn't answer, but he did put a walking stick on the bench. It was Jim's. When drunk, he miraculously found his balance and leaving it wasn't unusual, but this time it felt ominous.

She took it and the Bruch. As she left, she glanced to the Agents where the largest fellow who'd bought the vodka ignored her. The others were more interested however, and the way their eyes were glued to the stick spoke volumes.

She had to find Jim.

"Val, you really need to take this thing with you," was the first thing Pierre said when he let her into the base. He was referring to Poopsie dancing on tiny paws around his legs.

"Nope."

"Vord's going to see it and blow a nut."

She dropped her backpack beside the mass of computers and said, "Do a nut, Pierre. Blow a nut means something else. Anyway, I hear you're famous now. Devron's been boasting that he'd taken you lot out."

"Well, we're still here," he said, as if it wasn't much to celebrate.

She glanced to the frosted door. "Where is he?"

"Vord? Why?"

"I need someone finding. I've lost a friend."

"You have friends?"

"Pierre…"

"All right, I will help, you know I will, but there is something I want you to see first. Come."

He walked her through the frosted glass door for a corridor that went along a ward. Observation windows revealed several medical beds and one recovery chamber. She'd seen it before and Pierre had said that Vord slept in it after operations or when he needed restoration from exposure. She wasn't sure how he ever got exposed considering he never left the base, but she guessed it was more for his vanity than his health. When his own face was one of the only things he ever sees, she guessed he liked to keep it well preserved.

"Is he in there?" she asked, pointing at the chamber.

"Not today. He's been rather well restrained when it comes to some of the old *nips and tucks*, but he's due a tooth out in the coming days so he'll be unconscious for a few hours, then I can use the lab without him moaning at me. Talking of labs…"

He stopped before a door at the end that she'd never paid much attention to, mainly because she rarely came down this far. It had a glass panel that exposed the darkness beyond, but it was slightly relieved by a lamp. When he pushed through, she found a workshop cluttered with Old World tech, large mechanical devices, and Vord at a table soldering a laptop's motherboard. He turned out of curiosity, but threw his chair back in surprise to see her standing there.

"The fuck, Rocky?"

Pierre was resolute as he said, "I think she has a right to see this, considering what she went through."

The lab was pitch-black, but she could make out much of the technology about the walls and worktables. There were generators being modified, weapons laid out in all their parts, and the back of the lab held an extensive chemistry set-up, but when Vord stood before a tall unit as if to block it from view, she smiled.

"What you got?" she asked.

Vord sighed heavily before saying, "It's the *thing*."

Realisation hit her. "The Lecky from Hailsham?"

Vord stood aside and she hurried to the containment unit, or that's what she believed it to be. It had a hefty base supporting a glass compartment with fans built into the top and bottom. It was dark inside, however. She couldn't make out much of the Lecky, other than the fact that it was as long as her arm and looked somewhat charred and deformed.

"Can't you turn a light on?" she asked.

"No," Vord said, handing her some night-vision goggles. "Its components are power- absorbent; light, movement, and heat-exchange all charge this device and I need to keep it powered down."

The night-vision displayed it in better detail. It was a jointed device of some kind, like an arm, except she wasn't sure how it'd move since it had no hydraulics. Its metal frame had warped from extreme heat and the white chassis had cracked and peeled back. There was a fair bit of damage inside, but mostly the circuit-boards looked in good nick. However, leaning in closer revealed these weren't the workings she was familiar with when it came to computers and machines.

She took off the goggles and looked at Pierre. "So, you went to Hailsham and got it?"

Pierre said, "I retrieved it the moment we cracked the correct coordinates. With the PEA distracted at Horsham, it'd been the perfect cover. I'd found it within its case in someone's back yard, half sticking out of the mud. Whoever had found it originally hadn't even realised what it was."

"And what is it?" she asked, but they seemed uncertain, so she said, "Well, power it up for me to see it in action."

Pierre said, "We can't. This is the reason we're on lock-down. It sucks in light and heat like a sponge and it fires itself up into action. As soon as we got it into the base things started happening to our computers, and then the next thing we knew ATOM was being invaded. This Lecky gets in using remote wireless connections and tries to overrun the mainframe."

Vord added, "And it's smart, too. It knows we have a firewall and bombards it with generated keys to pick apart our encryptions. It'd take days of constant attacks to get in, but ATOM used so much power keeping the encryptions modified that it pushed our energy levels over the cap, risking us becoming visible to the PEA.

"ATOM has been forced to shut itself down several times since then to keep the fucking thing out." He sighed as he said, "So far it's shown great interest in intercepting all devices connected to the mainframe and burns out anything I use to reverse the signals." He nodded back at the busted laptop. "That thing just blew up in my hands the moment I tried to intercept it."

"So if you've never known what it does or what it is, why'd you risk everything trying to get it?" she asked.

"Because it's a smart-ass fucking computer," Vord said, pushing her aside to shine a laser into the circuitry.

It wasn't your standard motherboard of fibreglass and wires. Chips and tracks were still visible, but the rest of the boards were made of green looking glass barely a few millimetres thick. Parts of it had crumbled away like shiny sand, but much of it seemed intact and rather clean.

When the laser's light hit it, the beam bounced and refracted through tiny cubes that looked like crystals, amplifying the ray whilst splitting it up and diverting the light all about the board. When he turned the laser off, the circuits were left glowing ever so slightly, showing a minute amount of charge.

"What did I just see?" she asked.

"It's Holometric tech. If I'm not mistaken it's the technology boasted about by the Regen Program started by the MindZyi organisation over in America before the End."

Val was amazed as he'd said something she recognised. Most of it was just babble, but she'd heard of MindZyi before since much of the Lecky found in the Dump had been manufactured by companies using MindZyi technology. It was the only Lecky she received plenty of stamps for, even if she had been pulling it out of kettles, ovens, and washing machines.

"So other than making a fancy-talking microwave, they

made stuff like this?" She pointed inside. "And is that a glass circuit board?"

Vord said, "What you're referring to is a brand name. Good stuff if you want a smart kettle, but that's it. This tech here was made in very limited amounts. Most of it was confined to radically-designed laboratories for scientific endeavours, and the majority of those labs are lost in Europe and America. I've got multiple documents referencing the tech, but this is the first piece of actual Lecky I've found with it inside.

"But the *big deal* about it is the vast amount of data it can store. My most powerful RDAC can store data in terabytes whilst this thing stores in exabytes. That's one million-million bytes of data. It bypasses petabytes altogether. It could even store in zetabytes if I had more of the circuitry intact."

He urged her to wait as he fetched a box from a safe. He withdrew a vial and unscrewed the top, gesturing her to hold out her hand. He poured a tiny green crystal onto her palm that was no larger than a grain of sand.

"Squeeze it," he said. With the crystal in her fingertip, she did. It flattened and when she let it go, it bounced right back into shape, even glowing from the build-up of kinetic energy. He said, "It's called Holometric because the design is holographic; the sum of its parts contain the whole of its information-technology. As long as you have just one tiny bit of the original motherboard, you'll hold the entirety of the data stored on it. Unfortunately, I still need a certain amount of the stuff to actually gain access and even this may not be enough." He gestured the Lecky.

He must've seen her waning interest because he said, "Let me put it into perspective. Before the End, there was over two and a half exabytes of data generated *daily*. That's around two and a half billion gigabytes. A monumental amount of machinery and power was needed to process it all. We don't have those levels today, but regardless as this Lecky alone could've processed the world's virtual data with the right cooling and power supply."

Pierre jumped in. "It's made of a type of crystal silicone, but not as we've come to know it. It's all about pressure and cooling rates. If glass cools quickly, it makes it brittle and weak. The slower you cool it, the tougher it is. Same goes for silicon, but even then it's never been strong enough to survive the power needed to make this tech work.

"But this silicon-crystal formation is called Hyperpure Silicon and is solidified so slowly and under such amazing pressure that it makes these tiny crystals hugely dense and yet still maintains the fluidity of the molecules inside. The more pressure applied means the denser the crystal can be, but also smaller. You might think you're holding one entire bit, but that grain is made of dozens of even tinier crystals that are linked together using carbon-silk fibres put in place by lasers larger than this base, and with accuracy so great that it could write the full first act of Shakespeare's Macbeth on a strand of your hair."

"It's really a lot more complicated than that, Val," Vord said, taking back the bit. "I couldn't expect you to understand it."

She scoffed as she said, "Well that's great and everything, but if you've never been able to access it, and all it does is sit there, well then how do you know all this?"

Vord's face dropped whilst Pierre was holding his head as if she couldn't have said anything worse.

But she was standing her ground, saying, "Don't get me wrong, I'm tingling hearing all this, but I bet most of what you're basing this on is what's written in documents made before the End. Pierre told me this could answer every question relating to the end of our world." She shrugged, looking indifferent. "All I see is a glass-mechanical-arm-thingy."

Vord's explosion wasn't out of character, but it still made them jump. "And that's all you'll ever fucking see, you Waste Monkey!"

"Marcus!" Pierre gasped.

It was water off a hog's back for her as she said, "No offence, but I'm not the one standing here pretending a piece of glass is going to save the world."

Vord grabbed her. Pierre tried to intervene, but Vord already had her pressed against the containment unit.

"This-" Vord indicated the crystal in his hand, "- will not save the world. *I* won't save this world. I don't have a clue what will, but do you know what got us into this mess in the first place?" He came closer, seething. "Ignorant, pig-headed little pricks who only care about themselves is what got us here. People like you."

He shoved her away and stormed off, cursing beneath his breath as the lab door closed behind him.

"Bit harsh," she said, straightening her jacket.

"He's just-"

"Nervous? Yeah, like a rabid dog."

"I'm sorry-"

"Don't be. I kinda did it on purpose. He's easily triggered. Nah, I think this shit is cool. I just think he needs a reality check once in a while. Stuck in here, trying to live forever… He's repeating the mistakes of his old man."

He guided her out, saying, "I suppose you don't think it's worth risking your life for now?"

She scoffed. "I didn't do it for the future. I did it for the Reds. Now you got time to help me, or not?"

Back in the Command Room, they sat at ATOM and Pierre said, "What can I do to help?"

"It's Jim. Been a while since I've seen him and I think he's been turning the wrong sort of heads."

"We're on shut down, it won't be easy. It gets in everywhere, that tech."

"Honestly?"

"I'm not sure how serious it is, but that technology outweighs anything we got going on in here."

"Can we not risk Jim's life due to suspicion?"

He paused. "Is it that serious?"

"It might be…"

Pierre got to it, opening programs and putting in information all of which was lost to her; she could build computers rather well, but programming was a different game entirely. What she did know was that these things took time; she just hoped Jim could keep out of trouble until then.

PART TWO

A shot immune system, hair loss, irregular temperature control, and a slowly-healing stab wound had fixed Val up for a bad day. Still, she'd completed a full shift at Pranav's and had even caught six or so hours roaming the Dump.

Now, the evening was drawing in. She was walking slowly towards the train station with her headphones in, hoping to hear any news of ERD. She'd had the radio on all day, listening to DJ's also showing concern over the loss of his channel. Now as she shielded her face with her jacket to keep out the smog, she tuned in to his station only to hear Devron broadcasting his propaganda.

It seemed ERD wasn't alone as several other stations had been taken off the air as well. As she arrived in time for her train, she wondered how long it'd be before all Walker voices were removed, and where would it end?

Val woke up swearing, but her rasping breaths were loud in the quiet of her apartment. She rubbed the sweat from her brow and laid back, hating the dizziness and cursing her over-active memory.

The nightmare hadn't been scary, but it annoyed her to remember such horrible events. Why couldn't the past stay in the past? She was worrying about Jim and it was often stress like this that'd bring the Lady in Black to her dreams. She wasn't some imagined spectre, either.

It'd not been long after her liberation four years ago that Jim had realised she was ill. Val had refused all medical help, distrusting of everyone, especially men since they'd been her main abusers in the camp. But her stomach had blown up and she'd been in such agony that walking had been impossible. That's when *she* arrived.

The Lady in Black.

Val had never brought it up after, and Jim hadn't either, so she didn't know where the woman had come from. But she'd been gentle and caring, despite being hidden from head to toe in what looked like a burqa.

Maybe even Jim had thought Val was Islamic and had sort that church's help as if it'd be the best thing. Still, the woman had kind, though she'd fed Val awful-tasting medicine and yet her condition had kept getting worse.

Val hadn't known what was wrong, but Jim must've had a good idea. This was because the moment her pains had grown more extreme than ever before, he'd known she'd been suffering contractions and had rushed about gathering blankets and water. All she could remember was an intense burning sensation between her legs, a tearing in her guts, and then…

Val sat up and looked at her jeans. Her apartment was dark because the windows had been blocked up again, and it made her jeans look black. And in her memory, her legs had been covered in watery blood and between her knees had been a baby.

Jim had held her as if he'd expected her to start crying. However, she'd only felt relief and immense intrigue at the underdeveloped baby no larger than a spud, with spindly arms and legs laid on the sheets, its heart taking one last beat before going completely still.

She should've been devastated, but she guessed a still-birth was something an eleven-year-old just couldn't comprehend.

Huffing loudly helped return some reality, and she eyed the clock to see the early-morning hour. There was also the slightest sound of static coming from her radio as she'd left it playing all night. She'd hoped ERD would come through, but only Devron had busied the channel. She left it on as she abandoned her bed, making for the greenhouse that still needed stripping. She tore plastic cladding from the walls and wrenched up the rotten veg-beds. She knew she could have it operational again within a month, but it'd be a costly endeavour. Still, if Rodling really was looking for a gardener then-

'Hello?'

She staggered. "Jim?" She shot from the hatch, but the main room was empty. She ran for the door, only pausing when a voice sounded from within her apartment. It was the radio and she could hear breathing.

She turned the dial so the volume went up.

'I hope you can hear me. I don't know how long my transmissions

have been lost to you, but please don't think I've left you. I haven't. I'm here.'

ERD had come through without a jingle and the static was still present behind his meek words.

'I know some of you will do your best to spread my messages, to let my listeners know that I haven't left you.' He scoffed as he said, *'I might as well be a world away with how easily my station has been overtaken. And here I sit in my little room with only this radio, and I think to myself 'can anyone hear me?''*

She lowered to her knees; she'd never heard him sounding so hopeless.

'I don't know what's happening. I hear things, terrible things, and it makes me wish I was able to help. I do so hope the whispers are wrong, but if life has taught me one thing, it's to hope for the best and expect the worst. So I'll make what may be my last transmission one of caution.

'Nearly fifty years ago a structure was completed in an area above Quad: North, in a patch of land surprisingly stable in such a hostile place. It should've become an extension of our world, for Walkers to live in, to build up, and to expand our tiny existence. Instead, it was hijacked and from it came the Dwells.

'Many stories circulate, but I tell you now the truth. It was a man, a Royal no less, called David Dwells, the youngest son of a prestigious family in the West. He'd had dreams that were beyond his station, dreams that were not proper.

'He went against everyone who fought his wish to fulfil these delusional dreams. He put men and women at risk as he broke his boundaries and made it north, finding this Promised Land like some delusional Moses. And where he fell and died they did so find a land of great worth, and on it they built the prison in his honour.

'I've seen videos, images, and I've been told stories from people who have seen cattle trucks taking citizens to the Dwells, people whose only crime is failing Registration, and there they are imprisoned. Men,

women, and their children have been torn from their homes and may never be seen again.

'It is not a prison. It is not a correctional unit. It is an abomination! It should never have been built and it sickens me that, of all the horror in this world, of the cancer, and the sickness, and the constant Mists, that the most terrifying thing to befall mankind was made by us.

'Will we never learn?'

ERD regained some composure, but now he was wheezing.

'I do not know how long this will last, how long I will last. You were my only beacon of hope for so many years and if this is taken away then there will be none of me left. But the world will continue whether I take up your time or not. This is why I implore each and every one of you to fight against the Dwells. To fight against your oppressors! But most of all to protect each other. We are already in an awful place. We are already in our own prison. Let us not make the only viable places of our world places of such horror.'

Silence followed his last shaky breath. She waited, watching, listening… She even shuffled nearer to turn up the volume.

'Hello? I hope you can hear me. I don't know how long-'

She sat back, deflated. His transmission had started again, but ERD was gone. As she searched other channels, she found his same message there, too, repeated by those sympathetic to him.

She slumped. This – mixed with the fatigue and nerves – was almost enough to make her cry, and she'd not felt that way since Jim had misplaced her RDAC during a *spring clean*. Yet when her RDAC vibrated from an incoming message, Val almost cheered for the distraction and raced back inside her greenhouse where she'd left it. She allowed the program to finish downloading before it decrypted, and the message came through in full.

Jim's turned up on our screen. Less than an hour ago he used his card to get rations from Central. Will message you when we have an idea of where he is now. Take it easy, mon chou.

She slumped against the peeling walls and pushed tears from her cheeks.

"Jim, you nob…"

"The fuck is that?" she whispered as a black, reinforced vehicle stormed Tollgate Road. She'd been waiting with a dozen other Walkers for nearly ten minutes and had looked up at the roaring sound coming from the far end. Whatever was approaching now was not their usual shuttle.

Some Walkers ran off and Val was one of them because the front and back of this new shuttle was manned by Agents. Black Eyes she could fool with her various IDs, but if one of the soldiers decided to check for themselves…

She watched from behind a garden wall as the beast of a vehicle came to a stop. It was three times the size and churned out smoke, and there were black eyes and buffer panels all over it, as well as a white, tri-sectional triangle on the side to show it was Agency owned. The Agents never stepped down as they remained amidst the roll-cages with their guns across their chests. After picking up the few brave enough to enter, it drove off and she was left stranded.

"Fucking great," she hissed and stormed off in the other direction.

It was a forty-five minute walk to Barking Creek. The areas around it had been flattened by floods a century ago. Once cleared, it'd left mounds of debris for people to trawl through, but some of it had been put there on purpose. Why? Because it hid a lopsided battleship left over from the Old World that previous survivors had turned into a secret base. In time, it'd been forgotten about, but Jim had found it and made it his home.

She crossed the rubble to reach the top, finding the hatch amidst the rubbish. Stairs led into darkness so she used her RDAC's torch to navigate, passing a stairwell leading to her old bedroom. Rather than head there, she went further along to a room Jim normally spent most of his time in. She stopped by the slightly open door, looking in at the slanted room made level again by secondary flooring. Furniture was strewn about and the horded mess harboured an awful smell. This was all normal for Jim's abode, and since the odour wasn't of decay, she was happy to leave it at that. She'd always respected his spaces and she'd not start snooping just because he'd gone AWOL again.

She backtracked for the stairs, heading down into a dusty, damp room that Jim had fixed up with furniture and a bed for her years before. Much of what was left she'd outgrown, but there were a few things she could still use, like hazmat overalls, gas masks, and a double ended paddle to her kayak. Armed with these, she made for the exit, stopping only a moment to press a note onto a nail.

Call me!!!

Once outside, she made it to the bank overlooking the shallow waters of the Thames. Slipping to a dishevelled quay maintained in secret by Jim and herself, she pulled a rope leading off into a cavity formed in the river wall. Out came two kayaks. The larger one was Jim's, the smaller red one was hers.

She felt a stabbing emotion as she pushed his kayak back and, after donning her suit, set off up the river.

It took nearly three hours to get to Central. She'd managed it in less than that before, yet she clambered from the plastic raft at an abandoned section of the embankment under the ruined bridge of Charing Cross Station, and laid there panting.

After a few minutes, she struggled from her suit and hid it with the kayak. Despite the fences and PEA patrols, she made it from the ruins unnoticed, but that's when she spotted smoke.

She stumbled when a six-wheeled PEA cruiser shot by with one armed Agent sat atop it. It may have had several more within, but it didn't slow as it turned into the street the Palacer's base was on. This cemented her fear as she rushed to it, peeking around a crumbling building to see a sight she'd always expected but never wanted.

A handful of Agents were standing in the street and four Agency buggies were being filled with burnt computers and boxes of documents. Watching it all was Devron wearing a dark green military uniform and a slanted cap, and he was making comments as charred sections of ATOM were being thrown into the back of a vehicle. Two soldiers emerged holding the arms and legs of Vord, his head lolling lifeless as they loaded him into the back of a cruiser. The door cranked up, shutting him inside before Devron slid into the front seat. Then it vanished up the street, but the soldiers remained.

She threw herself from the wall and ran. She needed to find Jim, now more than ever.

22

Val headed to the People's Hospital, but not for rations. She avoided the swamped Walk-in Centre for a side road leading to the private A&E and surgical department. It was away from the Market so even though she could still hear the racket of announcements and merchants, she at least wasn't swamped with Walkers. That's because this road was usually reserved for Casuals who – for whatever reason - couldn't access private clinics in the north and so were forced to brave the rough City Centre.

She passed through the open gates but the entrance was barred by an Agent who spoke through the speakers in his helmet. "What do you want?"

"Someone's missing. Please, I need to make sure he's not in any of the wards here. He might've been admitted in the last-"

"Go to the Walk-In centre and-"

"The line's longer than the road! It's been days and things are bad. I need to know."

He grabbed her to ensure she listened. "You need to do as you're bloody well told! This ain't for Walkers."

He pushed her away, but she didn't relent. "He's come into trouble. I know it. He's old and ill and he might've been targeted by-."

"Go to Trafalgar's Head Office to report the crime. If Walkers attacked him-"

"They were Agents…"

He was standing with arms folded and for a few seconds he was silent. Then his sigh came thorough distorted, but he stood aside.

She rushed into the waiting room. The desk was tidy with no frosted glass or bars like that of the Walk-in Centre. There was even a little box on the side requesting visitors to leave their comments and experiences, and a few casually dressed individuals were sitting on the couches. They watched her almost fearfully, but at least the nurse behind the desk seemed friendly.

Val said, "Please, can you check if a Walker's been admitted? He's been using his Benefits Card at the Walk-in Centre, but I need to know if he's reported any illnesses or injuries, or if they'd taken him up into the wards."

"I can try. Are you a relative? Okay, what's his registration?" She put in his details and looked through the files. "No. No one's been admitted under that name. It does show he'd had rations out recently, but he's made no further requests or admissions."

"When was this?"

She looked closely at the screen. "Last night and this morning, both time using his Benefits Card at the People's Walk-in Centre."

Val almost collapsed with relief. The nurse seemed

happy for her, but she said, "He has two strikes on his account, though. Apparently, his finger-print recognition failed on two attempts and the card's been locked."

"His card works even when the finger-prints don't match?"

"Only twice. The People's Hospital allows the dispensing of emergency rations when security fails, but now the card is unusable. Just make sure he re-registers at the office over at Trafalgar, yeah?"

"I will, thanks."

She left feeling dazed, and she unsure why the woman's words had numbed her so. She eyed her own palm filled with all manner of little cuts, lumps, and grazes. She'd never failed her scans even with such injuries. It also seemed odd that he was claiming rations at all. He'd helped himself to hundreds of her Reds, so why was he settling for welfare hand-outs when he could've bought the better stuff from Black Waterloo?

She hurried further along the street to where the road sloped to an underground parking facility beneath the People's Hospital. An Agent in an external cabin ignored her as she went beneath for an office jutting from the left wall, and the vans parked beside it all read 'refrigerated' and had a skull emblems and biohazard signs underneath.

Val banged the safety glass of the office. "I need assistance!"

The light was on and a computer flickered in the corner, but it was unmanned.

"Hey? Someone? *Anyone*?"

A man with a biscuit and a coffee poked his head into the office.

"Please, I need help!"

"A&E is further up, honey," he said. He looked in his early thirties, skinny but handsome, dark-haired and tall.

"No, please, just help."

"I'm not a doctor. This area is for the morgue. If you-"

"Do you keep records of everyone who comes through here?"

"You mean dead people? If they're registered, then yes."

"I need you to check your system."

He realised now she wasn't hurting; she was panicking. He set his drink down and brought an office chair to the computer. She read out Jim's legal name, but he smiled as he said, "Not on file."

She didn't share his relief. "What's your backlog?"

"Excuse me?"

"Do you have bodies that you haven't identified yet?"

"Well…" He looked to the black refrigerated vans.

"How far back?" she asked.

"A few days."

She wiped her face of sweat, bracing herself. "Can I check them?"

"I really wouldn't recommend-"

"I need to. If he's in there…" Her voice quivered. "He's all I have."

"Right," he said and took a card from his pocket before leaving the room. A moment later, the security door beeped and he joined her in the parking lot. He gestured to the Agent that things were fine and walked her passed the vans.

He said, "These were from today. How long ago did he go missing?"

"At least two days ago, I think." That was when he'd left his stick in Loris' pub, at least.

He led her to a garage door that'd been partly raised, taking her into a clean corridor lined with vinyl and tall concrete walls painted white.

He asked, "Did you check the hospital?"

"They don't have a record of him. Would it be normal for a body to be brought straight to the morgue?"

He seemed a little surprised at how she'd gone from nearly crying to sounding so detached. Yet he said, "Yes, it's not unusual. If they died at the scene or in the ambulance-"

He stopped talking as a woman in scrubs watched their approach, but didn't ask questions as they passed. Several double doors were present, but most were sealed with air-barrier plastic. The last few were accessible, but it was an entrance marked 3C that he stopped at.

"The bodies through these doors were brought in a few days ago so I suppose this would be where we should start, but it's pretty full in there."

"I can do this alone."

He was more hesitant than her. "Fine, but listen, we care about the living and the dead, but what you're about to see is what happens when we just can't handle the work-load. I'm sorry. If he's in there-"

She eyed his I.D and said, "Adro? If he's in there then he's dead and he won't give two shits about which way up you've stacked him. Just let me in."

Failing to dissuade her, he pushed open the door for a wave of cold mist.

Then there was the smell...

Adro had been starring at the computer for nearly an hour. The office was a mess of paperwork, computers, and filing cabinets. He'd completely forgotten about the girl in 3C. Still, she hadn't rattled at the sight of the corpses (a hardening caused by Walker life, he'd assumed), so he'd left her to search on her own as requested.

The wheels of a mortuary bed rattled as Elna came along with three bodies laid atop each other. She nodded a greeting through the door and he nodded back, looking at his screen before realisation set in.

"Wait!"

She was at the plastic curtains of 3C. Scowling, she asked, "Why? These guys stink."

"But why you sticking them in there?" he asked nervously.

"Because 3D and E are full. Move away."

He didn't.

"What's the big deal?" she asked.

"Someone's in there…"

"Loads of people are. It's a morgue."

He didn't find that remotely funny.

"Is that girl still in there?" she asked. "It's been an hour! She'll freeze. Shit, Adro, she might be scanning them for BioChips, you idiot. Get her out, now."

He hadn't considered that, so he hurried in. The large square room was empty in the centre since the bodies had been piled against the walls as much as four high (with other bodies slumped against them for stability). Newer arrivals were further back and in a dreary corner the girl was sitting. On the floor was a fully clothed male covered in frost, though she'd wiped his face that looked swollen and misshapen from blunt force trauma.

"What are you doing?" he asked, nervous that she might be harvesting after all.

"Mourning. Is that news to you?"

"Sorry. Is this…"

"Yes. His name's Jim."

"It's not wise you being in here so long. I'm afraid

you'll have to-"

"The tag on his leg said he was brought in by an ambulance."

He was wearing no boots, so it was easy to see where he'd been labelled. It was green, which meant the paramedics had indeed tagged him.

She added, "Another tag on his wrist says he'd also been admitted to the emergency room here in Central."

"Well, if that's what it says. Please, come along now, you're frozen."

Once in the corridor, Elna took the bodies through, leaving them to speak but not looking happy about it.

"I went to A&E and they'd had no record of him. Is it common for someone to be treated but not be put into the system?"

"No, I wouldn't say it was."

"So someone admitted him, he died, and they then removed him from the system?"

"They may have forgotten to scan him in the first place."

"Would the ambulance pick up someone who isn't registered?"

"No…"

"Then he was scanned."

"What are you implying?"

"Jim was beaten black and blue. Someone phoned him an ambulance and he was admitted only for records to be removed once he'd died. I want to know who phoned in that ambulance."

Adro was rubbing his head. "Well…"

"Can't you do that?"

"I can, I suppose."

The doors opened with Elna bringing the empty bed through. She looked ready to say something, but Adro shooed her along. Once alone, he took Val to a terminal in the corridor.

"This is going to be difficult to find without knowing the ambulance registration-"

"The tag had a reference number. 18-84-XA3."

"You remembered that? Well, all right. Like I said, none of those bod... *people* have been processed yet so there might not be... okay, here we are. Ambulance eighteen responded to five calls and he was the first that morning."

She leaned against the wall, watching the floor as she asked, "Was he alive?"

He read the screen. "Yes. Found at the bottom of a flight of stairs, barely conscious, no evident bleeds but he did have a concussion and broken bones in the face and head."

She knew his injuries were far more extensive than that.

"Then he died in A&E?" she asked.

"No records. It doesn't even state when the ambulance dropped him off. I don't know what to say."

"When can I get him cremated?"

"Err... It'll be at least a week-"

She hovered her e-tag in his face. "At least seventy creds on here. Take it all if you have to. Get it done ASAP."

"No, I don't..." He waas shaking his head. "We have to do a coroner's report, an autopsy, we-"

"All this for a Walker?"

He rubbed the back of his neck. "Give me a few hours."

"Fine. One more thing."

He looked as if she might shoot bullets with the next question. "Yes?"

"His personal belongings?"

He was relieved that that's all she'd wanted and said, "Sure," before hurrying for the office where Elna was tapping away at a computer.

She droned, "I've got eight folders here filled with thirteen forms in *each*, can you call – what are you doing?"

He'd dipped through a door at the back.

She cried, "We're not allowed in there without authorisation."

She listened as he rummaged about, cheering before re-emerging with a large brown bag.

"Adro!"

He hurried into the corridor where Val was rubbing her face of the tears. He tried to pretend he hadn't seen that and handed it over. "It has a coat in there, and boots by the looks of it. I don't know what else, but the form says illegal items were confiscated."

She assumed those to be the fake Reds.

"Thank you." She turned without looking at him, making for the end of the corridor.

"Wait, I need a name and contact information."

"I'll be back in a few hours."

"But-"

He followed her to the end, but she'd marched for the road leading out of the lot, her head down and her hands gripping the bag so tightly that her knuckles whitened. The Agent said nothing as she passed, and then she was gone.

Elna came up behind Adro, asking, "Did you just do something monumentally fucking thick?"

"Maybe."

"Idiot," she hissed, shaking her head as she went back inside.

Physically and mentally drained, she was forced to rest. As before, an alley offered cover as she sat, putting the bag of Jim's things between her knees as she regained herself. Then a noise caught her attention and she shuffled to where the wall had collapsed and looked into a room housing a mountain of bags. Not just any bags, but shopping bags, all Old World and some in good nick. They'd been scrunched up and pushed together, and walking around them was an emaciated Mallowhead with a swollen skull that weighed so heavily on his brow that he was almost blinded.

"You good?" she called. His grumbling didn't change, though he seemed to turn to her, his legs covered in faeces and his body showing welts from infections. He whispered as he was walking about the room, searching.

She tore the top off the bag and tipped out the contents. She then threw the empty packet into the room where the Mallowhead stood, but he was too busy muttering quietly to himself to notice.

She sorted through Jim's things, putting aside his heavy boots that he'd worn the life out of. His coat was long, brown, thick, and imbedded with dirt, but it was all the warmer for it. A single ID slid from his pocket, of which she could recycle for a few stamps at least. Still, his Special Benefits card for the People's Hospital was missing. She realised now that someone had been using it after he'd died, hence why Pierre had believed him alive. It made her sick.

Her mind flashed back to the Agents who'd glared at her as she'd left with Jim's stick. Had it been them? Had he walked in, daft with drink, flashing his fake Reds and mouthing off to bloated Greens? She'd seen him acting up before and knew how he could be, and sometimes even she'd been tempted to shut him up. But all it would've taken was a slap and a harsh word. He'd have calmed down. But what they'd done to him was horrendous and to know he'd been alive through it all, possibly suffering…

She wiped her face on his coat and felt something in the inside pocket. It was a long envelope folded in half, sealed with PEA tape which had already been broken. She pulled out the document and the title read, *Official Adoption Papers.*

Val forced the envelope back into his coat and threw it aside. Her hands were shaking, her breathing was erratic, and she couldn't think straight. Tears streamed without her say-so and she angrily swept them away. She cursed as the sobs came thick and fast, but she couldn't fight it now and lay trembling against the wall.

At least it wasn't painful; not anymore. Keeping in the grief and the worry had hurt a great deal, but the pain had mounted slowly, allowing her to suffer without realising. Now, all she felt was relief.

Jim was dead. He'd snuffed it in a horrible, lonely fashion and it burnt in her a level of hatred that she hadn't felt since seeing that Bandit camp, but she also knew there was nothing she could do for him now.

The Mallowhead mumbled as if suddenly waking up. He kicked about rubble in his continued search for bags. Then he coughed, defecated, and kicked that around too before wandering deeper into the ruins.

She sighed as she took the documents back out. The paper felt wonderful; slightly textured, and coloured a nice shade of brown. *Cream* if she wasn't mistaken. The left-hand margin sparkled from PEA silver foil boasting official insignias, and the top corner was pierced with a golden chip surrounded by spiralling ink. This was the real deal. *This* was why Jim had taken her Reds.

She read it.

'*This document, registered to* WALKER *32FF/VL10K has qualified for the adoption and future three-year employment/ownership of a Registered minor under the identifier* WALKER *33GR/E163D effective immediately upon official stamping, signing, and dating by Agency Registrar made lawful by the E.O.W Peoples Registry Act of 199.*'

She skipped most of it for the declaration at the bottom.

'*I [Jayms Enetti] hereby swear that the above information, and all subsequent documents provided for the acquisition of this legal paper of official adoption is true to my word, my knowledge, and my understanding. I coherently accept the* WALKER *stated above is to be my property for the next three years upon which this contract will be void and further contracts of-*'

A teardrop hit the page.

Had he been planning this for a while? Jim wasn't impulsive so she assumed he had, and with the impending abolishing of Reds, he'd have panicked to get it done all the sooner. He'd never strived to be a dad, and even until then she'd never thought of him as such, but he'd been the closest thing to a father and now she'd never get to tell him.

"Jim, you…"

She breathed against the sobs and struggled to her feet. As she trudged off, she slapped the naked Mallowhead on the back. "C'ya, buddy."

He jabbered on, barely noticing her departure as he grabbed the paper bag, screwing it into a ball before adding it to the pile. Then he was off to find more.

I'm sorry for your loss…

Adro's words played over and over. Had he been? Maybe he genuinely felt for her, but she doubted he'd been actually *sorry*. Sorry is what people say when they hold an element of blame; if Adro was even partially responsible, then everyone was. She didn't accept that since revenge would be much harder to achieve on an entire population of people.

Jim's ashes had been handed over in a bag secured with a zip-tie. She'd seen burnt bodies before and had assumed their ashes to make up more than a handful. Still, it sat easily in her pocket as she walked aimlessly, too fraught to eat, too hot to sleep…

It was dark by the time she reached the Religious District. Her legs burnt from fatigue, but the cooler air was welcomed and a drop in humidity made her itch less. Not to mention there wasn't a soul around to pester her. Not living ones, anyway.

Christ's Church was quiet as she rounded it for the cemetery. No nuns bothered the plants at this hour, but she saw that a few graves had been decorated with flowers. Nice ones, too; daffodils and tall bushy roses.

Val didn't cross the fence. Unless walking with Rodling or Josephine, she'd never go inside. She wasn't the type to end up buried there; she was neither rich nor religious enough, not to mention she still hadn't been baptised. But that didn't make this any less a special place for her.

She stopped at the eighth fence post. It was near a ridge of earth placed as a perimeter marker for the chapel's grounds, and trees had grown behind it. Few had reason to walk this way, which made it a more private place to be. But despite all the grooming by the nuns and landscapers, a single rock the size of her head remained. It was a piece of natural earth rather than a slab of concrete, and had been worn down on one side where a symbol had been etched; a solitary cross. Beneath was scratchy writing made with a knife, but it'd faded and the rock was mucky. She knelt before it, wiping dirt from the grooves and tugging weeds from the post.

She muttered as she did so. "I haven't been for a while. I've not been all that well, to be honest. I thought I'd end up coming to see you in person, but I guess that'll have to wait."

Mentally prepared, she rolled the stone aside and began to dig. She didn't have to go far before her chipped fingernails snagged cloth. It'd been white when the parcel was originally buried, but now it was brown. Dry, however, which made the process easier to bear.

The urge to open that cloth almost won. *No*, she thought to herself, closing her eyes against the images she still nurtured from years before. *Don't Val. You already have enough horror to contend with…*

Instead, she placed the bag of ash beside it and covered them both in soil before patting it down.

She hadn't buried her baby for a long time after the birth. She'd not known she was supposed to. Jim had brought her and it to the church, though he'd seemed against the idea at first. Still, he'd been as lost as her during that time.

She remembered the nuns and the priest had been so sorry for her, and yet they'd turned her away because it hadn't been baptised. Jim had thrown a fit, cursing them out and damning their God, and it'd taken several others to drag him away. She'd not understood his anguish, but they had when realising what'd been in her bundle.

As they'd trudged off, a young priest had hurried to them, secretly requesting that they return at the dead of night. They had, and not only had he introduced himself as Eric Rodling, but he'd brought with him a person that'd burnt her guts with emotions that Val hadn't felt in a long time; fear, yearning, love… It'd been Sister Josephine from the orphanage Val had been stolen from whens he was six years old.

On that night, they'd dug the grave by the fencepost, and Jim had found the stone.

Four years ago and yet it could well have been a lifetime.

She replaced the stone and took out her penknife, etching a second larger cross beside the first. Atop it she scratched *Jim*. The rain would likely wear it down as the rock was too soft to last, but in the light of her RDAC she could just about make out the words she'd etched into it on her first visit.

Here Lies A Baby,
Born With

HOPE

BUT WITHOUT A CHANCE

25

The morning was damp from humidity and it made her itch. It didn't help that she'd slept all night in an abandoned building, hugging herself to keep warm. She ached all over and the three bottles of Bruch she'd consumed wasn't helping her mentality none.

It was nearing midday by the time she arrived at the Glowing Lion where the bouncer simply said, "Don't cause trouble," before letting her through. She fell onto a stool at the bar and shouted, "Drink!" even though Loris was right there.

He looked around nervously. "What do you wan-"

"Something wet!"

He cursed beneath his breath, but he did as told, opening a bottle where she drank heavily. Then she leaned closer and whispered, "Where are they, Loris? I saw 'em coming in. Where are they?"

"Get out of here," he hissed, though he kept his

creaking voice down. He shot glances behind her, so she turned. Surely enough, the same green Agents from yesterday were present, but this time there were only two. Their senior wasn't there.

"Just go," Loris sneered, "he ain't worth getting thrashed for."

She caught his eye. "Was it your stairwell he fell down?"

He was clenching his teeth so hard that his jaw muscles were flexing.

"Did you hear him tumbling down each step? Call an ambulance for your old friend? Your most loyal customer? *Hmm?*"

"I warned him-"

She spat, "Shut your hole, you nonce."

He wanted to argue, but she'd already slid off the stool. He was so unnerved at her brazen approach to the two Agents that he didn't even demand payment for the drink.

The Greens seemed amused at the sight of her, that is until she was close enough for them to see the yellowing of her eyes.

"You got the Sickness?" the small skinny one asked, his visor up so she could see the bags under his eyes and three-day-old stubble.

She didn't hear him. "A few mornings back, were any of you here?" she asked, her voice hoarse but forceful.

"What?" scoffed the larger one. He wasn't wearing a helmet so she could see his wild ginger hair and sallow skin.

She dragged over a chair and slumped at the table so that her arms were hanging down between her legs. The men covered their pints as she spoke. "Think back to an innocent Walker who was beaten and thrown down a flight of stairs, just out that door I'm guessing. He was taken to the hospital, alive apparently. Alive enough for someone to try and save him, at least. But he died. I'm just here wondering which one of you lot called the ambulance. Which one of you lot foot the bill?"

"Kid, you need to watch yourself," the largest said darkly.

She looked annoyed. "Ah calm your tits. Just tell me why you killed my dad?"

"We didn't kill no one!" barked the skinny one. His reaction screamed of guilt.

"Shut it, Reg!" the other snapped, but rolled his eyes since there were no secrets now. "So what if he died? What you going to do? You're just some kid."

"Exactly, nothing to worry about," she said, scratching under her hat where it was so dry that they could hear her nails grating across her scalp. "So tell me why you beat him to death."

"He came in here throwing stamps around," Reg snapped. "Buying everyone drinks and making a scene. He didn't even have that much money on him, so fuck knows what he had to celebrate."

"So you killed him?"

"No! We took him outside and questioned him. He got rude. Laughing at us. We're the fucking PEA, get it? You don't make a fucking joke out of us."

The larger one grew tired. "Get the fuck out of here, kid."

"Fine. All right," she said, making to stand as if to do as told before sitting right back down. "One more thing, his ration card…"

Reg's face dropped.

"What?" the larger one asked, eyeing them both as if confused.

"See, he died a few days ago, but records show his

rations have been collected twice. I'd like it back. Being his daughter, it falls into my ownership."

"We ain't-" the Agent began, but Reg was acting shifty. "The fuck, Reg?"

"It fell out after the medics had taken him."

"So you fucking claimed on it?"

"I'd have told you, but you were off-"

"Guys?" she said, holding out her hand to indicate she still wanted the card.

Reg slapped it aside. "I threw it away. Fucking depleted it, didn't I? Shame because you look like you need some meds."

The other Agent scoffed.

"Oh yeah, I do. I need it badly," she said. "Sick, me. But at least I haven't got-" she paused, listening to something no one else could hear. "-herpes simplex type two? Ouch, is that the one that makes your bits itch? I'm scratching just thinking about it."

"The fuck…" Reg said, looking to the other guy before reddening.

"Yeah, I hope my dad's rations helped you there. Shame you didn't share it with Tony here."

Tony looked ready to explode at the sound of his own name. He clearly had no clue how she'd come to know it.

She went on, "Nasty case of the squirts, I'm sensing. Bit of IBS is it? Anxiety induced, maybe? Can't be easy being a low ranking Agent of only three months, yet you've been in the medical offices four times to get checked up. Let me guess, PEA food a bit rich in fibre?"

"How's she know all this?" Reg asked. "How the fuck-"

She snapped, "I'm no fucking idiot, that's why, Reginald Wittland, Walker 81LA/B47G. So green to the Triangle that they've not even updated your registration status. Maybe they're waiting to see if you survive the trial period."

Tony had her by the back of the neck before she could finish, throwing her across the room. She slid to the bar where Loris barked for restraint, but he was facing down Agents now. The bouncer was quick to intervene however, standing between her and them. He dwarfed Tony and Reg by a good margin, hence why they desisted.

"That's enough, fellas," he rumbled. "Been enough bloodshed now." He lifted her up, adjusting her sleeve to hide the RDAC that'd been scanning their implants and feeding the info through her earpiece.

Before he could get her out the door, Reg had his say. "Don't think about getting any of your Walker justice on us. His death was judged lawful."

Tony snapped, "Reg, leave it." The skinny bloke did as told, but he swore under his breath as he returned to the table. Still, she heard Tony mutter, "She'll be next, anyway. They all will be."

She didn't doubt it and followed the bouncer to the stairwell. He made sure to keep close until she reached street level where he said, "Try to let it go. Jim wouldn't want you getting mixed up in his business."

"His business was my business."

"*Was*."

She could've taken that wrong. It even stung. But she knew his statement was a sensible way of looking at things. It was simply a shame that Val was very good at keeping grudges.

Tony was hissing insults at Reg as they returned to their seats. Then a door opened from the W/C and an Agent in blue overalls and white armour approached, shaking his head and cursing. Senior Agent Haido said, "Good job, dickheads."

"Sir, it was just some kid," Tony muttered.

"A kid that knew both your names?"

Reg shrugged. "She probably just overheard us talking."

"You two talk about your itchy balls a lot, like?"

Reg winced. "Fuck's sake…"

Haido gestured to their drinks. "Finish. We have business."

"Seriously?" Tony asked, astounded someone of his rank would care about some Walker kid.

"She had a restricted piece of technology. I saw it when you threw her. She'd scanned you both when she was sitting here. Maybe got me in there, too. Fuck knows where she got that tech from."

Reg downed his drink and dropped Tony's helmet in his lap. "Let's reunite her with her dad."

They went to leave together, but Haido let them go first as the bouncer had been watching them since he'd returned.

"Problem, darky?" Haido asked.

"I knew that girl's Pa. He didn't deserve what he got. She don't deserve it, either. If she don't come back after you lot have gone, you'll have a good few of us to deal with."

"You lot? Like Darkies?"

"Walkers."

Haido nodded as he slid out his PDA and asked, "Care to make a statement? A complaint?"

The bouncer remained quiet.

He switched it off and put it back in his pocket. "Thought not."

He left for the Agents above, but it'd rattled him. He

needed her arrested; tech like that shouldn't be on the wrist of a teen. But now it limited him to how he was going to take her down. He drank there all the time, for fuck's sake. He'd need to be careful.

"Where'd she go?" Tony asked, looking both ways up Whitehall thick with people.

Haido said, "She's sick. She'll not get far. Reg, you go towards Westminster Bridge, Tony come with me to Charing Cross. Just keep visuals."

They set off as Haido took up his radio, but first he asked Tony, "What's the politically correct term for Walker darkies now-a-days?"

"Duskers?" Tony asked.

"Yeah, you'll go far," he scoffed and radioed for an APB of the Central area.

She roused, her head spinning and vision failing to focus. Someone was dragging her by the feet as her arms flailed around her head. The floor was smooth and she could smell sterilising agents. The white lights and gleaming walls gave the impression that she was inside a very clean building before being dropped and left to loll about, rolling onto her side and groaning as the drugs were wearing off. She could still feel the sting of the needle, administered through a gun where it had impacted her hip. She couldn't even remember passing out.

This wasn't the first time she'd come to. She'd opened her eyes whilst on the floor of a PEA wagon. The three Agents from the pub had captured her and were in the back with her as she was being transported. Tony had been holding the dark gun whilst Haido had been playing with her RDAC. He'd slapped her into consciousness where he'd demanded she turn it on. She'd pretended to be unresponsive so Haido relied on his powers of investigation to make it work.

He'd said, "It's got some kind of finger scanner on it. How fucking basic." She'd kept her eyes closed as he'd grabbed her hand, tearing off her gloves and forcing her thumb into the scanner.

Even now, laying on the cell floor with her guts doing somersaults, she couldn't help except smile as she remembered.

"There, it's registering. Silly cow-" he'd begun, but an explosion had cut him off. It hadn't been huge, nor had it damaged Haido, but it'd ruined the RDAC and had caused enough of a fright to make the cruiser swerve. Still, her PDA was completely destroyed.

She'd never imagined someone would fall for the finger-scanner trick, but they had and it'd caused her to burst out laughing. Haido had not only smacked her, but Tony had stuck her with another needle, sending her back to black.

Now she was alone inside a tiled room with a lit ceiling and a one way mirror going all around the sides. She managed to sit up, tasting bile and blood as she swallowed against her dry throat. A click foretold of an unlocking door, so she scrambled to the furthest wall as an individual entered. At first, she was surprised. Then she barked her laughter.

"Are you shi-"

Her words caught in her throat and she coughed uncontrollably as Commander Devron – armed with a chair – entered in order to sit a few feet in front.

Once free of the fit, she leaned back and sighed. "… shitting me?"

He was wearing his green uniform but no armour. His boots were the heavy sort, shiny, with high-treads caked in dirt from his time out in the Quads. His dark hair was rather greasy, slicked back, but he looked a lot less block-headed in reality. He took a device from his pocket and read from it.

"Daisy Riner?" He paused as if expecting a response. Shrugging, he said, "Leanne Trescot? What about Alison Fowler? No, I didn't think so. You don't look like an Alison."

He was reading the names on her fake IDs. She would've been a little better off if she'd discarded those before pulling her stunt.

"Agent," Devron called. A large fellow in full PEA gear entered with a second chair. He set it heavily beside her and left. Whilst she struggled to sit, Devron took a medicine box from his belt, revealing three syringes.

"You have the Sickness," he said.

"I know," she rasped, falling ungracefully into the chair.

"Not full-blown. A day or so old. Three-tier Panacea can cure it at this phase." He indicated the box.

"For a price," she mumbled.

"It's free," he chuckled. "All you need to do is register. Properly."

She closed her eyes and shook her head. "That's a price. Why are you here, Devron?"

"Because I'm going to interrogate you on the threatening of my-"

She cut him off. "No. Why are *you* here and not some officer-goon?"

He snapped the medicine box shut and rested it on his knee. "You accessed sensitive information from mainframes you shouldn't have had access to. That's a terrorist level threat worthy of my time. You were in possession of illicit tech, one linked to an infamous criminal *terrorist* syndicate that I just recently did away with. Don't bother ever trying to contact the Palacers again. I've neutralised them all."

"All of them?"

"Every single one."

In that short exchange, he'd demonstrated that he knew very little about the Palacers. Her RDAC was Palacer tech and that would've been obvious to any Agent savvy with today's CTG's. But what he'd revealed was that he thought the Palacer group was comprised of many members when, in fact, it'd ended with Pierre and Vord. She could use such ignorance in her favour.

She said, "I work for anyone with the dosh to cover my

expenses. Always someone wanting a job done in London. Is that all I'm here for?"

He pulled his chair a little closer. "We ran your DNA. You weren't on any of our Undesirable lists and didn't flag prior convictions."

"I've been a good girl."

His smile remained, but it was tainted with distaste. "Do you know what the punishment is for defrauding registration?"

She shrugged.

"Now-a-days it's a spell in the Dwells. That's the current law. If I get my way, it'd be a swift execution."

"And I bet a pro-active fellow like you is already piloting that scheme. Oh, can I be a beta-tester? Can I? Please?"

He chuckled as he sat back. "You think that low of us, huh? I'd never kill a child. Children are our future." His eyes caught hers. "But children are echoes of what has come before and when I look at you, I see them." His smile died.

"Who?" she asked when the silence lingered.

"What's your mother's name?"

"I don't have a mother."

"Your father?"

"Dead, too."

"So who was this Jim fellow?"

"He rescued me when I was younger. Your Agents killed him."

He looked away, a little annoyed as he said, "They did. They were clever enough to tell me why you'd confronted them in the first place. Walker deaths at the hands of Agents is on the decrease, but slip-ups happen."

She merely sneered.

He went on to say, "Your father died a long time ago, just after your birth."

She realised he was making a statement, not asking a question. She tried to comment on this, but acid shot up her throat as if she were to vomit, but settled on a vicious bout of coughing. She hacked up yellow bile and the smell was awful.

Devron took a needle from the medicine box and stuck it in her calf. "You'll need a few more, but you should be okay, Val."

She flinched at the sound of her name. Her reaction made him smile, but she couldn't deny him the satisfaction. She realised now he was far more in control of this situation than she'd given him credit for.

She groaned, "I hate to admit it, but I have no idea what the fuck is going on."

"You're a Big Banger."

She went to laugh, but coughed. With teary eyes and half a smile she said, "I've been called some things before, but-"

"I hope you're not playing dumb with me." He held the medicine box as if threatening *not* to give her the rest.

She rolled her eyes, but his patience only went so far as he grabbed her shoulder and squeezed. She screamed, not expecting such pain. Her confusion was evident until he tugged down her top, exposing where a BioChip had been implanted in her shoulder. She had no recollection of that taking place.

"Shit," she panted. She'd never been chipped before. "Fine, my name is Val. Just Val. That's all I know. I've never been part of any fucking Bangers, which I'm assuming are some clandestine group? And the PDA your Agents confiscated off me was just some tech I stole off a dead Lancer in the Dump-"

She'd been forced to stop after he'd thrown a hand across her face. She almost toppled off the chair, but he pushed her back upright. "Don't lie to me," he warned, sounding calmer than he acted.

She fought the pain and dizziness as she seethed, "I've spent nearly my entire life around cunts like you. If you think *this* is going to break me, then you better try harder."

He actually looked amazed. "Holy hell, that's some fire. Very well. Say I believe you. You're a Lancer and you found that tech. Why did it have programming on it found within a clandestine group-"

"I'm a *Lan-cer*," she droned, rolling her eyes. "I've sold Lecky and traded with terrorists since I was ten years old. Hell, I was making Varista Units for chump Agents making their own currency at seven years old."

"At seven? Under what organisation did you operate?"

"That one you do a lot of business with. You know, *Bandits*?"

He said darkly, "We don't do business with Bandits."

She smiled. Maybe not Devron personally, but if he thought she'd buy that piece of shit lie…

He took a moment to collect his thoughts, eventually saying, "It's safer to assume everything you're saying is a lie, but I can be lenient if you give me information that officers can verify. What I'm referring to is your dealings with clandestine groups."

"What do you want to know?"

"Names. Locations. Dates. Items traded. Information gained. I want to know everything."

She shifted, looking noticeably uneasy.

He leaned closer to make sure she was listening. "I want to know about the Palacers, what they've been up to, and about the Bangers. The more open you are with me, the more you'll benefit."

She fidgeted and he grabbed her knees to keep her from doing so.

He said through gritted teeth, "I need *you* to cooperate. Got it?"

She was shaking her head as if fighting some inner turmoil. Even a tear trickled her cheek. She leaned forward as if she might whisper; instead she vomited on his boots. As Devron flew off his chair, she sat back and sighed. "Fucking hell I needed that."

Devron looked horrified at the watery mess on his boots. An Agent hurried in, but with Val almost unconscious in the chair and Devron holding up a hand of restraint, the Agent stood down.

"It's the Panacea," Devron said, replacing his chair and sitting down. "It'll likely get worse before it gets better."

He was oddly calm as he stuck her with the second syringe. Maybe he was thankful that she'd thrown up on his boots and not his head.

"I can tell you everything I know," she said, almost intoxicated from the relief, "but there'd be no point."

"I'll be the judge of that."

"I sold mainly to the Palacers." She slowly regained herself and wiped sweat from her face. "I only knew the Whitehall base. I traded with others, but through third parties. Before you start asking, no, I wasn't a member. I just weaselled my way in and they tolerated me, to a point. I'm just some Lancer to them. That's all."

Was he convinced? She doubted it, but he was quiet as she went on.

"I access the Dump through an old pipe from the BioFirm where your lot turn my lot into glue and plant feed. As for the items I trade? I swap Lecky for rations and food. Are you surprised? Well, you shouldn't be considering I eat better and get more medication living this way than I would as some registered dog who'd be lucky to get vitamin D tablets from your pathetic hospital. You can't even offer more to the sick and needy, forcing them to work to death even as their bodies erode."

He twitched a smile. "This is about Jim, isn't it?"

Her jaw clenched.

"I get it, Mr Enetti wasn't your father, but he meant a lot to you. We've questioned a few in the area of your verbal assault on my Agents. They say despite him being very ill and drink dependent, you were quite fond of him, and he of you. Mutual, I hear. Within the law.

"We even managed to trace you back to Christ Church Chapel. I made a few calls and got through to Father Rodling. He was almost desperate to sing your praises. But he also told me how you'd spent time as a Bandit slave. If there's one thing I've come to realise is that slaves tend to be just as bad as their Bandit masters." He leaned closer. "Be thankful I have a lot of respect for Eric Rodling. He's the reason you're in here being questioned and not where we normally send your lot."

She actually shuddered, but she blamed it on the meds.

"This has been a very lucky day for me," he went on, crossing his legs before spotting the vomit and putting his feet back down. Still, he smiled. "If it hadn't have been for that illegal Lecky found on your person, my men wouldn't have handed you over to the outpost, and they wouldn't have forwarded you to me as a possible terrorist. I'd not have found the adoption papers, giving me the legal name of Jim, and would never have run your bloods. In as little as five hours, I've solved two decades worth of mysteries."

He took from the tin the third needle and stuck it deep to reach muscle.

Her head spun, but she did her best to keep with it. She'd never had the Sickness before, not like this anyway. She did regular detoxes and transfusions to prevent sepsis, and her immune system had always been hard-core. Still, there was only so much she could take.

Most Walkers would die within a few weeks with no treatment, but Panacea was the strongest combination drug going. She didn't like the fact he'd used it on her, however. Now she assumed she owed him.

"Amazing thing, blood," Devron said. "It can tell us so much about a person. We keep records of people's DNA as a way of identification."

"Yeah, I remember. You said mine didn't pull up any files."

He laughed at that, shaking his head. "No, it pulled up *loads*, just none on you." He went for his PDA, but thought against it in order to look her dead in the eyes. "You really don't know, do you?"

She didn't bite.

"I've got mixed feelings about this. What I have here could make or break you, you know?" He didn't wait for a response as he indicated his PDA. "Jim's file. I almost didn't run his Walker number when I saw the papers, but there was something niggling at me. The first file showed he'd been cremated recently. Even then I couldn't bring up much until I saw an indication marker that he had a previous file.

"See, the Agency did a scheme ten years back for Undesirables to come clean and to make them honest registered civilians. The New Start Initiative. It was a way to drum up support for the government. Jim had obviously opted for it and, in return for being chipped and processed, his records were somewhat expunged. Yet, with a push of this icon, I get his old file straight away." He was showing her the screen where a warning sign flashed in the corner. His finger lingered there as if waiting to see if she'd protest. She didn't, so he pressed it and read the screen. "Here, Jayms Enetti, one hundred and eighteen cases filed against him."

She was impressed.

"He never stood trial for a good few of these, of which

141

he'd have surely received the death penalty, but I hadn't been in power back then, so what can I do? Did he ever speak about his history? No? Let me indulge you.

"Jayms was an only child of a registered couple in Quad: North. Posh," he said as even back then it'd been reserved for Casuals. "Due to financial issues, Jayms became the property of the PEA at eight and between that age and twelve he'd been reported AWOL a record number of ninety-four times. Trespassing, theft, brutality towards other fellow child recruits, you name it he'd done it.

"He'd broken the containment unit of his apartment at the age of twelve, infesting the complex and calling for immediate evacuation. That'd been the last straw. Jayms was imprisoned in a young offenders institute until he was fourteen. His parents completely disowned him by the looks of it as his papers were sold to the Home Office.

"At fourteen he was released. Never enlisted, which is odd. Maybe he was too much of a handful? Wouldn't happen now-a-days. But this shows his first warrant for arrest as an adult was issued the day he turned of age; wanted for association with various Bandit groups."

She caught his eye. Had he expected her to react? Either way, she grew defensive. He didn't feed off this and continued.

"He spent three months inside a low security centre for being found repeatedly drunk and disorderly, for fighting, and for carrying weapons, as well as his association with Undesirables. He was arrested but never charged for drug paraphernalia. In fact, he never did any hard time until he was caught stealing from Quad: West and sentenced to three years in the Dwells."

She'd always had the impression Jim had experienced the Dwells, but hardly anything Devron said sunk in. She was still fighting with the idea that he'd associated with Bandits. She wouldn't have judged him on the things he'd done as a young adult, and the hatred he'd had towards them in his later years made up for it. Maybe Devron saw this growing defiance because he pushed on with an angry tone.

"Jayms left the Dwells at eighteen. He removed his chips, defied his probation, and went underground, later enlisting with the Big Bangers as a mercenary. I suppose they're old news to your generation, but for a very long time the K.W was victim to their ways and they were at their most brutal during their dying phase. Jim was a part of all that. He was, it shows me here the he was very much a contributor to a level of chaos unrivalled by even the Bandits.

"Individuals fitting Jayms' likeness had been captured on security feeds, showing how he'd traversed illegal sectors of the Wastes, hijacked Agent technology, and infiltrated Essex Exclusion Zones."

He showed her the PDA, flicking through grainy coloured images of a lean young man with a skinhead, broad shoulders, and sporting a bandana and goggles as well as a massive automatic strapped to his back.

"Oh, wow, what a bad man," she muttered.

He barked, "His team were responsible for countless Agent deaths." He showed her images of these groups, of whom Jim may or may not have been present in, shooting Agents in a courtyard.

Devron said, "Men and women getting up on a morning to make ends meet for their family, but instead they were faced with car bombs, booby-traps, poisoned water units, raids, *all* later claimed by the Bangers with plenty of links to Jayms' involvement. File after file after file."

He was flicking through the images and notes, stopping on a black and white pixelated shot of armed raiders in a research facility, with Casual workers on their knees and hands behind their heads. Several had already been shot and were face down in their own blood. One of the armed men looked eerily familiar.

"Your *father* was a cold-blooded killer!"

"Well, the PEA at the time obviously didn't care if they *expunged* his record," she said, listless now.

He tensed. "I'm still trying to find who'd authorised it. When I do…" Then he caught her eye. "Your parents were quite a colourful lot, too."

She frowned, thinking he'd made a mistake there. Her parents were…

"Esha was your mother," he said without delay, again reading from his PDA. "She'd been born an orphan, raised on Agent funding, and was property of the PEA. She should've completed her training at sixteen, but subsequently ran away. It says here no one had known what'd become of her between the time she went AWOL to her death, so now we can add birthing a bastard child to the list.

"Derek Glimford was your father. Yes, your blood dragged up his file, too. Youngest of three boys born to a registered Walker couple in Quad: East. He, too, went off the map around the same time Esha disappeared. His family had been quite distraught, I'm guessing, because Peace Rangers were hired to find him, but with no luck.

"He'd become a delusional member of the Bangers and I can only assume Esha joined him. They'd no doubt have known Jayms since they're confirmed in footage to have carried out these raids together.

"I can tell by the look on your face that you'd had no idea Derek and Jim had both been very close members in one of the most notorious clandestine groups in the K.W."

She wasn't buying it. Jim had suffered much in the past few years, surviving exposure and sickness, as well as operations to repair his liver that'd drained his body until he couldn't even remember her name at times. Hell, he'd even walked away from being shot in the head. If he'd ever known anything of her dad, it might've gone the same way as his last set of kidneys; down the surgeon's toilet.

"In fact," he went on, "it says here eighteen years ago that a list of Most Wanted Undesirables was released. The first and second positions were held by Bandit Lords. The third was the Banger's leader, Jonas Anderson. The fourth was Derek, your father, for the killing of countless Agents and registered civilians. And a step down for the same offence was Jim."

He showed her a spread-sheet of these *most wanted* and it struck her like a rock. She'd seen the exact same notice laid about in Jim's home years back. In fact, she even knew where it was now; stuck to the wall above his radio like some kind of souvenir.

The PEA had released only a few of their criminal files in order for freelance Peace Rangers to help bring them in, and she could almost see Jim's name on the list. She'd simply failed to make the connection.

He asked, "Do you know how they died?"

Silence.

"Well, I came in here thinking you'd be an integral member of one of the most secret conspiracies of all time. And I find you're just… well, a child caught up in life."

That was, in no way, genuine empathy.

"Do you know anything about the Big Bangers? They'd been as big as Redemption, but our Agency whittled down their numbers. They were a cult. This is no general state-

145

ment. They were fanatical about exploring the unknown world. They believed the Mists were the result of some galactic event taking place right here on our little planet. They believed this so thoroughly that they killed anyone who didn't.

"Their biggest slaughter came days before their own demise when a group of eighteen Bangers ambushed an outpost on the east coast, killing over forty people and taking ten boats, sinking two vessels, and destroying a twenty-year-old mission dedicated to the exploration of France and the surrounding countries. These *Agents* your parents helped kill were volunteers. They were unarmed. Hell, we have evidence that the researchers had even surrendered before they were executed.

"The next stage saw these eighteen members crossing the Channel to France in the stolen boats. It's said they were searching for some new promised land, or some secret base operating in the Mists. Take your pick. What they found instead was a cluster-heavy anomalous area and a megaton-Mist ready to blow them the fuck apart. I'm not kidding. I have pictures."

He threw the PDA onto her lap. Her clammy hands made grease marks on the screen, but there they were; grainy images of a dreary brown land. France? It looked bright despite the cloud cover, but not a shred of greenery. About the ground were pockmarks of black earth from anomalous explosions. What she thought was burnt wood scattered about was actually scorched limbs and bits of clothing. Even in the Wastes, she'd never seen anything like it.

He leaned closer, saying, "Your mother abandoned you so she could go and die in France. She'd opted to walk that godless terrain with cannibals and Mallowheads rather than be here with you. She left you to be enslaved, to suffer, to lose your kid…"

She shifted suddenly, as if the seat had become quite unbearable. Feeding from this, he said, "Easy for a girl exposed to all that to go bad. Do you want to end up like them, Val? Want to become a godless, fanatical, loon?"

"Can't be worse than ending up like you," she said, strained. She was perspiring now, and growing faint.

He scoffed. "What a stupid thing to say."

"Not from where I'm sitting."

His smile dropped. "What's that supposed to mean?"

"It means, with all respect, I think I'm about to purge all over your shoes again."

She suddenly tensed, as if preventing something from getting out of her body. It was followed by a very loud, and very ominous, gurgling of her digestive system.

Realising the third needle was about to get to work *detoxing* her, Devron shot from the chair, cursing and calling for an Agent.

"Sir?" the Agent said in the doorway.

Val slid from the chair, tensing in a foetal position as she hugged her somersaulting guts.

Devron growled, "Get a hazmat team down here, now."

"Sir!"

As he left with the Agent, Devron added, "and bring the power washers."

I'll need more than a high-pressure hose for this, she thought as nature took its course, but mind over matter made her block out the horrific scene. With what she'd been told, she had too much on her mind to leave her enough energy to care about explosive diarrhoea.

28

"They're making you sweat," Jim said, his voice echoing as if he was speaking through a metal drum. *"It's a tactic they use in conflicts to break a person's will. They'll hold you up for days on end. No food or water. No stimulation. Just rats, constant dripping, and blistering cold…"*

She mumbled something.

"Nope," he answered. *"They don't always do it to get information out of you. Sometimes, they do it to make a point. Just keep your chin up and your mouth shut."*

A hard nudge rolled her over.

"Get up," barked the Agent.

Val couldn't make out his face through the visor, but a female officer in a dark military jacket and skirt was kneeling over her, zipping closed the paper suit she'd put on Val. How she'd managed to wash and dress her without once waking her up was amazing, but she allowed them to help her to stand.

She was walked out of the bright room for an even brighter corridor, empty save for doors that showed prisoners behind frosted glass. She was marched to the end where a surgical room held a gowned and gloved doctor. He didn't say a word as he checked her arm where she'd been chipped.

"That's not like any chip you'll have had before," he said, cleaning the site before applying a dressing. "It's been superficially implanted into bone and rupturing it will cause a caustic compound to eat away at your arm until you either seek medical attention or die. So be careful."

She'd never heard of such a thing. In fact, she barely even believed it.

She was dressed once again and led to an office filled

149

with men and women sitting behind desks. None paid her any attention as the officer sat her before a terminal.

"Now my dear, please prepare for registration," she said, her fingers clacking on the keyboard. "This will be quick and you'll be linked into AbysMA. This new Smart-Verse technology was woken a few weeks ago so it'll watch where you go, log where you work, what centres you're active in, and update a point system that, if high enough, will reward you with free entry for transport, local leisure-centres, market areas-."

"All of this is for me? Oh god I feel so special," she shouted, pressing her hands to her eyes.

The Agent nudged her with the butt of his gun. "Stop the sass!"

The officer said, "Well, we'll send you a newsletter. Where do you live?"

"I don't."

"Very well. Your age has been estimated at fourteen years and forty-nine weeks. Yes? Not long now and you'll be of age. Want me to sign you up for an induction course into the Young Adults P.E-"

"God no!"

The officer pursed her lips as she finished inputting this information and shot a look to the Agent. "Done."

They guided Val to another room marked Lab Diag-nostics that was empty save for several machines. They had brown casings and some were supported from the ceiling, and there were a few medical trays set about with a stretcher-trolley to the end.

The first machine had a narrow opening where the Agent *helped* put her head inside. The glass walls looked ominous and dark.

The officer's voice came through muffled. "Hold still."

A bright light ran up and down as if scanning her, and

then she was hauled out and stood before a box boasting a pair of goggles. When her head was pushed against it, a mechanism clamped over her eyelids and made it hard for her to blink.

"Watch the birdie," the woman said, tapping the glass screen several inches from Val's face.

"The what-*ah!*"

Two puffs of intense air hit her eyes, making them water immediately. Temporarily blinded from the tears, she was walked to a stool before the hospital bed. The officer had a tray of unusual items, one being a large tub of petroleum jelly as well as two metal rods that were as long as her hand.

Val backed off. "Whoa now, where are they going?"

The officer said, "Please put your face gently into the pillow, and exhale on the count of three. One, two-"

"No fucking wa-"

The Agent smushed her face into the pillow.

"-three! There we go."

Her horror dissolved when several hairs were plucked from the back of her head. She'd nipped them at the base to salvage the root. Once released, Val could breathe and see the officer lining the bulbs and hair shafts with the jelly before feeding the entire strands into the cooled tubes.

"What the fuck is all this for?"

"We're giving you a free health check," she smiled. "We'll test for softening of the brain, for glaucoma and diabetes, and to test the levels of radiation you've experienced over the last year or so. We can tell all of that from your hair." She then pointed at the bald spots. "Do you come into contact with hazardous materials regularly?"

Val burst out laughing.

The woman was confused. "What?"

"I can just tell you live in Quad: North. All you idiots ask the most fucking obvious questions."

The butt of the Agent's gun hit harder this time, knocking her laughter but not her grin.

The officer's lips almost disappeared due to pursing them, and she led Val down a corridor where more cell doors sat flush with the walls. One door was open, revealing a bed, a toilet, and a tiny sink.

Val grumbled as she entered, "Cold in here…"

The woman tutted as she pushed a tray of rations and medications closer to where Val was standing. "I suppose gratitude can't be administered in capsule form."

"No, it fucking can't."

Before the officer left, she said, "For your information, I was raised in Quad: West."

She snorted. "Fucking figures. Dirty Royals…"

The woman gasped and stormed off. The Agent, however, was shaking his head as he left.

Val leapt onto the bed and sprawled out. "See, they're not trying to make me sweat," she said as fatigue forced her quivering muscles to rest.

'No. This is much worse. They're being kind.'

Her smile died as she allowed herself to sleep.

The officer woke her. She didn't know how much time had passed, but enough for her arm, head, and guts to hurt a hell of a lot. Still, she felt far better than she had before.

She'd been allowed to dress in the same clothes she'd arrived in. Fortunately, someone had gone to great lengths to get them cleaned. She was led out under the escort of the female officer and an Agent, and the corridors were growing busier the further she went. Eventually, it turned from a jailhouse to an office-like set up and she was brought to a sign-in desk within a busy reception. The officer signed Val out and then took her to the front doors where the bright morning hurt her eyes.

"Am I free to go?" Val asked, looking down the steps to the clean courtyard of paving stones and cobbled paths. It had to have been Quad: West because there were Solid-State towers all over the place and the buildings were well-maintained and sparkling. Towering poles exuding artificial light that bleached the clouds and the slight hum of cars drowned out the droning silence that she was all too used to.

At the bottom of the steps where the road bent into the yard was a PEA buggy; an open top four-wheeled vehicle with a roll cage where Agents could stand in the back. The Agent behind her nudged her with his gun and said, "Get in, Walker."

She didn't need telling twice and hurried down the steps two at a time, brushing past officers heading to work whilst turning a few heads. She didn't know where this was destined to take her, but if it got her out of the precinct then she'd be laughing.

"Wait," the officer called as she followed. Val didn't.

She leapt into the backseat where an Agent had been waiting behind the wheel. Still, he didn't drive off as the officer arrived and set a backpack beside her.

"There's a wig in there, and advice on how to dress for an interview."

"A what?"

"It'll keep you looking presentable until your real hair grows back. There's a uniform in there, too. All you'll need is a clean pair of shoes and you'll be ready for employment." She stepped back and saluted. "Work hard and be lawful."

"Yeah, right…"

She had meant to say *thank you*, but by the time she went to correct herself, the buggy had driven off, breaking into a tidy road sided with houses with triple glazing, blast shutters, and bleached brickwork. Every chimney sported a humming vent to process smoke and prevent environmental pollutants from getting inside, and she even spotted door numbers and street names. A moment spent at traffic lights revealed a corner shop where windows boasted amazing deals like *two pounds of bacon rashers for thirteen credits*, or *a whole jug of orange juice for less than a credit*.

Buy one tub of BioDeradicaliser and get another tub free!

They even passed a roundabout purporting a billboard offering discount dental work to children under thirteen.

Val sat back with a tired grin on her face. "Give me Quad: East any day."

'Ha! That's my girl.'

30

Val didn't need to go inside to know it was all gone.

She'd kayaked home after the Agent had dropped her off at Central. After stashing her stuff, she'd trudged back to Beckton Globe Library to find her apartment had been gutted and even set alight. It'd gone cold by the time she made it there, but there was no reason to investigate. It was all gone.

With little choice, she'd returned to Jim's ship. It'd always been big enough for the both of them, and yet Val had been desperate to live on her own since she'd landed in his care. He'd understood and, once she'd been well enough, he'd helped her find somewhere safe to call her own. Back then, that area of Beckton had been a quieter place, but populations had grown and she'd not moved out in time. In the end, too many people had come to know where she'd lived and she'd lost a lot of tech due to it.

She pushed down the slanted corridor running through the length of the ship, unable to see due to not having her RDAC anymore. Jim's room was dark save for solar-powered lights that still twinkled, though she imagined the Sol-Stations would be in need of a good cleaning by now. The same went for his ancient WPU in the corner and the air-purifier that was likely adding to the pollution than taking away from it.

She pushed through hoards of useless junk for the nest of pillows and blankets before a tea-table propped up by books and empty beer kegs. There she slumped down, weak and trembling, before blacking out.

She kept waking due to the pain in her arm, a result of the BioChip. The swelling was bigger and it bled when she pressed it. She shouldn't have been surprised that it was infected, but without Pierre she'd not be able to remove it.

Now they were dead and she was truly alone.

She dropped her face into her hands and sat for the longest time. The ship offered a wealth of creaks and drips, but still the silence managed to deafen her. This felt like her life now and it was terrifying.

She grabbed the backpack the officer had given her. In it was the wig of black hair that she planned on selling for a few Reds, as well as a vacuum-packed uniform that she left on the side. The bottom of her backpack held a few medications that she tore open and consumed dry. She didn't know what they were, but she doubted they'd make her much worse.

She finally traipsed to the WPU and recoiled at the smell of the water it was producing. It needed a bloody good clean. It even had a full tank of rain water, but without running generators it'd not be able to purify anything. To find the generator, she followed the wires running along the walls, making for a curtain at the back. She'd not noticed this room before and imagined it was his bedroom, except it opened to a narrow area barely big enough for her and it was cast in darkness.

After finding a torch, she returned. The generator was to the left and cranking it up made everything rattle, but at least the ship came alive. Directly before her was a cabinet of VHS tapes and old players, though she doubted any of them worked. And to the right was something that made her stop and stare; not out of astonishment, but intrigue.

Two heavy-duty military trunks had been propped up to waist height. On either side of its top were two burnt-down candles. In the middle a hand-held radio had been secured using poly-cement and the tiny red light in the top corner brightened with each low *beep* that it released. She wasn't surprised to find it was a TriStar radio, a post-End product that'd benefited hundreds of people after they'd lost most of their communications due to the clouds.

Using customised signal-boons, early Walker communi-ties could track each other using such devices, and as the technology improved, the signals were able to travel further, bouncing them off the clouds and adopting existing towers to power the signals further. They were as good as junk now with today's technology, but it didn't surprise her that Jim had one. But why was it transmitting and what purpose did it have in this room?

She looked closer at the other items. One was a framed picture that'd faded to such a degree that she could barely see the outline of two figures. Before it was a load of dried leaves that she picked up and turned for inspection, realising it was a dried-out black rose. That's when she dropped it and backed off. She'd not found some odd terminal; this was a shrine.

Jim had been the least religious person she'd ever known. He'd hated the church. It wasn't an unusual mind-set given the life he'd had, but she'd never asked him why. And yet the only thing this set-up was missing was a cross.

And what did the radio play in all this? Its line was open, so anyone on the other end could've spoken freely, but all she could hear was a gentle static. It was being powered by a Sol-Station, but there was another lead reaching into the trunk, and she opened the lid a little to spot the device inside and it made her gawp.

It was a Jettison Mark II signal booster, a large device comprised of much smaller pieces of tech working together to form a super-computer the likes rarely seen outside of the military. Its purpose was to digitally boost a signal to far off locations, altering its output by constantly reading the environment, radiation levels, and weather conditions to guarantee a strong feed. It was something she doubted Jim actually needed as it was generally used to track other devices outside of England, and yet here it was boosting some two-bit radio.

It fed her annoyance and she almost smacked the radio off the stand. Rather, she stormed from the room and slumped onto the couch, knocking Jim's weed and tobacco off the table so she could prop her legs up.

She'd always known she'd end up losing him, and she'd expected a far worse death than that which he'd sustained. And yet she'd never predicted the hurt and anger that settled in her now as hot tears trickled down her temples whilst watching the ceiling. And despite it all; her serial-killing parents, Jim's involvement with Bandits, her blatant fraudulent activities, and her connections with CTG's, Devron had still let her go, and this frightened her.

He must've had something in mind to use her for and she'd be damned if she'd allow those plans to come to fruition.

Val had no ID cards, but she did have a nifty new chip in her arm. She prayed this would be all she needed to get on the Shuttle. Sure enough, when the big black bugger rolled up to Tollgate Road, the Black Eye scanned her and the door sighed open.

After forty-minutes, the shuttle pulled into Charing Cross station, stopping at one of a dozen shelters that were busy with Walkers preparing for their morning commute to work. This had been the first time she'd visited the shuttle station since the renovations and it was actually quite stunning. Each stop had a glass shelter with televisions and speakers, as well as terminals for Walkers to access AbysMA. It was enough to mask the several Black Eyes keeping watch about the roundabout, as well as the wealth of Agents weighing heavy on the market.

Whitehall was even busier than before. The new market and bright screens were winning over the wary Walkers, and now some of the stalls were inundated with customers. The People's Hospital was unchanged, however. She climbed the steps as the queue was low and waited a few minutes before reaching a frosted glass window. It was one of many with a nurse hidden behind, except now there was a Black Eye above each terminal.

"Walker 33GR/E163D," the hidden nurse confirmed, her voice coming through a tinny speaker. There was nowhere for her to scan her cards now. Everything was chip activated and the Black Eye's lens never left her face.

"Am I registered for rations still?" she asked.

"You are. Please collect them and move along."

The drawer smacked open and inside was a tiny blister pack of medicines.

"Work hard and be lawful, Val."

She paused at that, her colour draining fast as those words bounced about her head.

"Move along," the nurse ordered and she did as told, making for the exit where Walkers crowded the steps and drank from small bags of rationed water. But her eyes were about the walls and billboards, no longer trusting of the very air itself. She was being watched and they knew who she was. They were waiting for her…

Panicked, she rushed off into the crowd. Never before had being herself felt so hostile. It needed to change.

───────

Bornis saw her coming. His legs were dangling over the side of a platform overlooking the Machines Floor where a few workers were neutralising oil spills. She had hoped to hurry beneath him unseen, but he barked a laugh and this made others look as he jumped into her path.

"Well now, how the mighty fall, eh?"

He indicated her one piece blue Walker suit and surgical mask. The only thing she'd kept of her clothes was the beanie hat. Go back a month and she'd have shot herself rather than dress like a Walker, but he was right; she'd fallen hard.

She tried to walk around him, but he kept getting in her way. "Where you going, *Registered*. We ain't got no *Registered* Walkers working here. You been marked. It's all over your fucking face."

"Well you do now," she growled and went to barge by. He grabbed her arm, latching on to where she'd recently been chipped. Screeching, she pulled away and bumped a supporting wall where she stayed to regain herself.

"Damn girl…" he said, cautious of her at first. Then

he leaned in with a scrutinising eye. "You've been broken, haven't you?"

She tensed. Those words had cut much deeper than even he had intended.

He added, "Bout time someone gave you one and wiped that smile off your dirty little face."

She snapped. Lunging at him with teeth and nails, she managed to land a few good hits before he caught his bearings and laid her out in one fell swoop. She hit the deck like a bag of shit and remained there, unashamed but definitely hurting as her head was spinning.

Bornis hissed as he touched the cut down his temple. "I'm gonna kick your dirty fucking head in, nigger!"

As his boot aimed, a shout brought them all to a still.

"Back off, Bornis," Pranav said. He was five floors up, looking down to the Machine Floor from his office door. He was eating a carrot, which made him look like even more of an asshole, but he gestured with it and said, "Bring her," before retreating to his private space.

"Fucking aye," Bornis whispered, grabbing her by the back of her boiler suit and wrenching her to her feet. "Move!"

32

She was sitting dazed in the chair, thankful for Bornis's punch since it'd taken her mind off the pain in her arm. Pranav was quiet as he was behind his heavy-duty metal desk lit up with a lamp. It also held a computer, a filing tray, and a ceramic cup with tealeaves in the bottom.

He was acting as if she wasn't there, sorting through registration cards in a tin as if counting money. She recognised a few of the cards as rather official items, ones that could get people into high up places, but she was more interested with the map on the wall; it showed the world in all its glory, long before they'd lost contact with over ninety per cent of it. She'd seen it on previous visits, but that'd been years ago.

His office had a window, frosted, lead-lined, and narrow, but the addition of natural light was soothing. It bathed all his fine things in a gentle glow, like his wall-mounted guitars, a set of golf clubs in the corner, a fine couch, oil paintings, restored vases, a drinks cabinet, and a rug. If this was his office, she could only imagine how lovely his home was.

The other thing that always caught her eye was the pictures on his desk. One was of a pretty, slender woman with long black hair and dark skin. She looked like Val's kind of race, unlike Pranav who was a little more bronze and his aging hair was dark brown rather than black, with white strands poking through showing his age at around forty-five, maybe fifty. On the woman's lap sat a little boy and both were smiling happily. His family, she assumed.

Another picture was of an elderly chap, *tanned* rather than dark skinned, but the image was faded so she couldn't tell. Yet his eyes were a shade of blue and his titanium white hair fell thick around his tufty beard. He had a jolly smile and round cheeks. In his sixties at least. She wondered if he'd been Pranav's dad.

Sighing, he dropped the tin of cards into a drawer and brought out a pear, chomping noisily and speaking without swallowing. "They got you."

"What gave it away?"

He scoffed. He was a big fellow, fat, but he carried it well. "How did they get you?"

"They killed Jim."

"I know. It's fucked up. So you on a revenge trip?"

She scoffed, thinking he was taking the piss. His accent was different to normal Walkers, making it hard for her to take him seriously. He wasn't French like Pierre had been, but she found him somewhat pleasing to the ear. Especially his swearing. His *fuck* came out like *foik* and he always spat his consonants.

"Where did they take you?" he asked.

"Quad: West."

"Oh, posh. Because they knew of Jim and the Bangers, huh?"

"What the absolute fuck do you know about that? And how do you know about Jim all of a sudden?"

"Jim was a terrorist, you know," he said, throwing the pear's core into a waste-paper bin. "He was what they called a technological fanatic. Not like he was tech minded. Couldn't wire a plug, eh?" He leaned on his desk and whispered as if the office was bugged. "He was a merc, you know."

"I know."

"Oh, he told you, huh?"

"No, Devron did."

"Devron? What's he know? Fool of a man. Anyway, ignorance kept you safe, I think. Do you know where I'm from?"

"Bornis says our lot come from Pakiland."

"Bornis can suck a dick. My family were from South Africa. See?"

She eyed the map he pointed at. Africa was south of their little island, but to travel such a distance seemed impossible. Still, Pierre had come from France and even people of her generation found it hard to believe anyone could survive even that far out.

"My father was born there, but his grandparents had come from Australia. They were aboriginals, but you don't even know what that means."

"Barbarians?" she asked.

"Bornis says this?"

She nodded.

"He's a fucking barbarian."

"How many of you were there in South Africa?"

"Fuck if I know. I wasn't born there. I was born on the boat coming here. I grew up with a few of the survivors. A dozen at the most. The PEA kept us in camps when we got here. For most of my childhood, all I ever knew was that ship and all that water. Couldn't walk straight for years once we landed.

"I grew up in PEA complexes being marvelled at like I was some prize fucking turkey. But my older brothers and uncles had some memories, God rest them. They'd said South Africa had been hot, and when the clouds broke, the sun would set fire to the land. Ah, God bless England and its miserable fucking weather."

"What's your point?"

He seemed solemn. "It took years to get here. My mother almost died. Many others had to be thrown overboard. They had to land a few times along the way and they said Father found other people hold-up in their own way, surviving the Mists and the heat and the radiation. There was no way we could've taken them with us, and I think most didn't even want to go, but some were desperate. I think leaving them had done irreversible things to my father's mentality.

"He'd promised them he'd find civilisation and mount a rescue, but the PEA wouldn't listen. He spent his early years here with us in the camp, getting healed, educated, and indoctrinated, but it drove him more over the edge. I could handle it; I took to it like a true grunt of the Agency, but the others got illnesses and turned to drink, all sorry for the families they'd never be able to return to.

"Fact is, the PEA didn't care about survivors. They only cared for resources and when they discovered South Africa was outside their capabilities, they turned us loose like unwanted pets.

"I made a life of it, but my father? No, he never settled. That's where the Bangers had come in."

This made her sit up.

"They were just some joke before he took over," Pranave went on. "A nasty joke, though. Killers. But father abandoned me and my mother for them. I went on the straight and narrow, working to keep my mother's latter-years comfortable. She never saw him again. I met with him in secret, but he wasn't the same man. He was the true meaning of fanatical.

"The Bangers could give him what the PEA couldn't; passage to the unknown world. Passage home. He thought they'd provide the means necessary to survive the trip back to Africa and rescue those we'd left behind. But something changed him along the way. Something made him lose sight of his goals."

He tapped the picture of the bronze man with white hair. "He was a charismatic man, my dad, and he could worm his way in and build you up as if everything he uttered was gospel. But turn your back on him and he'd fill you with bullets. I can't tell you how many men and women I'd seen him kill."

He took a photo from the drawer as if he'd had it ready. She accepted it, viewing the group-shot of a dozen or so people. The middle man was his dad, and Pranav said, "Jonas Anderson. My Pa."

"And that's Jim!"

There was no doubt. He was bald, tall, lean, sporting an armless shirt, thick trousers, several guns, and muscular arms crossed over his wide chest. He was dashing besides the stubble, muck, and smug grin.

Pranav took out an apple and a fruit knife, and as he peeled he said, "Aye. Jim was my brother."

She almost stood up in protest. "Like fuck he was. He was as white as hell."

He burst out laughing. "Well true, not by blood. We spent time together in the same complex. I think he was an orphan, but he was bloody good at all that commando shit. We got on very well, sneaking out to meet up, but he saw my Pa as the dad he always wanted, and Jonas saw him as an asset. It wasn't long before he joined up with the Bangers. I never stopped being his friend, but we drifted…"

He chuffed a laugh as he sliced off chunks of apple. "Remember when you tried stealing my balls from under me by having a good feel about in my pocket? Ah, you almost did away with my Reds, yah little tea-leaf. But I got yah and I was going to bake you on the roof for a day or so, really teach you and the other fleas a lesson. If it hadn't have been for Jim hobbling along to fetch yah, I'd have done it. Instead, he convinced me to hire you and I'd done right in doing so since you've made me a good deal of money. Mind you, I'd not seen him in years and it'd shocked me to see he was in such a bad way. Had his brains blown out, I'd heard."

She nodded. "We'd been in Quad: East, rummaging. A Walker got him and pulled out a gun." She trailed off as she was in no mood to relive that story. That's when she spotted another face. "I know him."

He didn't finish the apple as he set it and the knife on the desk. "Did the specs give it away? Father went out to France often. He'd even get the approval of the PEA to scout about since they were too chicken-shit to do it themselves. Jim was on that mission when they found him. Just a kid at the time. I heard he'd lost his whole family…"

It was Pierre. He had the same daft grin and thick glasses, but he was handsome with his flock of blond hair and lean frame. He seemed right at home next to Anderson who was holding his shoulder as if they were father and son.

Pierre had known Anderson, and so Pierre had known

Jim. The evidence was there, and yet she couldn't believe it.

"Are my parents in this photo?" she asked.

"Maybe. Jim knew them, but I never did. Keep it."

She pushed it inside her boiler suit and stood. "Can I get to work now?"

"No. We don't employ Registered Walkers," he said, matter-of-factly.

"I'm no fucking *Registered*!"

He tapped the desk with his finger as he spoke. "Twenty-eight hours ago I got word that you'd been picked up by the PEA, brandishing Palacer tech and a wallet of false IDs. I knew from the get-go they'd run your bloods, do a background check, and they'd know exactly what I know. You, right now, should be in the fucking Dwells. Instead, you walk through my door. That shit me up big time. Every scanner I have in this place lit up like a Christmas tree." He indicated his computer. "You're not just registered, you're fucking *owned*."

He was shaking his head, as if refusing to acknowledge even the sight of her. "I run a tight business here. I had my men destroy every last thing in that basement that could link me to what you've been up to. Your Lecky got me stamps, but that's no good when I got me an empire to run, eh? I'm expanding. I build tech for the Agency now and it's going to get me out of this shit hole. Going to get me into high-up places. No, I'm sorry, you're broken goods."

"What?" she asked through gritted teeth. She'd been called it before, but there was no tolerance in her now.

"You're almost fifteen and I'll be breaking the law if I try to hire you when the PEA already have a claim. Sorry love, but you're as much a Registered Walker as those milling about the Quads, and I can't waste resources keeping you here."

She could've thrown a tantrum. Instead, hot tears rolled down her face.

He refused to look at her. "Don't try that with me. I'll not take pity on you. It weren't me who got you chipped."

She stumbled to the desk as if she'd lost balance. It was a ploy, a distraction for her to land near the fruit knife which she grabbed before he could realise.

"No!" he cried, throwing himself from his chair as blood spilled, but he scrambled to his feet, watching in horror as she drew the blade a second time across the lump in her shoulder. It burnt, but desperation drove her as she scraped the tip of the knife against bone. She cried out as agony worse than anything she'd ever experienced pulsated through her body. She'd broken the chip and the caustic powder was eating away at her. She threw the knife down and took up his half-eaten apple. Into the wound she pressed it, squeezing to make the juice mix with the frothing, burning solution.

"What the fu…" he began, but realised what she was doing and rushed for the door. His shouts silenced the machines and, a moment later, a man entered with a medicated acid-wash used to neutralise alkaline burns. She poured it in and screamed unashamedly, but it did the trick. The acid had stopped eating away at her flesh, but the wound was gaping.

"Crazy bitch," Pranav panted as he washed it out with a ration-bag of water and wrapped her arm with a handkerchief.

"I'm no Registered," she whispered, her voice hoarse and eyes bloodshot as she marched for the door. "There's a basement full of scrap down there with my name on it, and I'm going to sort that shit out and send up what's salvageable. I'll expect credits, and I'll expect my first day's pay by the end of my shift."

"You'll get what you're given and only until you turn fifteen." He shouted louder as she left the office, "Then you can get the fuck out of my face so I can be done with you forever."

"Deal," she muttered, stumbling into the elevator going down.

33

Pranav hadn't lied when he'd said he'd had her entire department gutted. Other than the trollies of trash, there wasn't one thing left of her belongings. She'd managed to reinstate the furnaces however and had already reduced several trollies into scrap metal, but there were more to come and she was weakening fast. She hoped Pranav would keep to his end of the bargain and pay her at the end of the day.

One of the trollies looked like general waste and this was confirmed when she found tattered bags and torn coats, as well as mouldy rations and empty medication packets. It looked like personal effects taken from the dead, but it was only good for burning. However, just as she poured it through the furnace door, a piece of paper caught her eye and she yanked the coat back out, jumping away to avoid the spitting fire. She stamped out the blaze before salvaging the leaflet. Surely enough it was from Redemption and she hurried to her workstation to take a look.

It was relatively clean but badly crumpled. It, like the others, had a picture drawn at the top, but this one was of an Old World bus with a cartoon face and comically inflated wheels. She didn't bother to work it out and laid it open to read the poem.

The dust in us ebbs and flows
And quieter nights we rest best
As the Mist's song grows.

Stuck to ground when others reach heights,
They're the angels of the dust,
Whilst we walk its flesh like mites.

Men come and bring big haulers,
Their guns make echoes
And bleeding holes make babies into bawlers.

Now dusty lands hold bodies in mounds
And Big Brother's talky box has bad sounds.

She shuddered, feeling as if that last line had echoed in its solitude.

Big Brother's talky box? She thought of ERD. And the only big haulers she could think of were PEA cruisers and cattle-trucks. Maybe Redemption had seen the Undesirables of the Estates being carted off in their masse as reports had said on the radio. But what chilled her more was the tone of this poem; of all the macabre they spun, this sounded the most harrowing.

She took herself upstairs to a side room off from the Machine Floor. Half a dozen workers were sat eating their rations and drinking murky coffee, but they seemed thrilled when she entered. She didn't know why, but she did ask, "A trolley filled with clothes and bags was just sent down to me, where did it come from?"

They shook their heads, though one man suggested, "Dump trucks?"

"But these were off people. Like, dead bodies?"

A lady said, "Quite a few died yesterday after a

chimney burst in the hydrogen factory. It gassed the entire place."

"Ah, that might be it. Fine."

She went to leave, but a man said, "Sorry to hear they'd got you. Glad you're back. None of us work the furnaces like you do."

She felt uncomfortable, but one lass said, "They got you for tracking down Agents who killed your dad? No one blames yah. They're monsters."

Shit, she thought, *my life's become a source of entertainment.*

"We got your back here, Val," another man said, making her feel worse. "Just stick with us and we'll keep the fuckers back." He held out a beer. "Drink?"

She took it, forcing her best smile and thanking him. One guy turned the telly back up as the little pep-talk had seemingly ended, but as she downed the drink, she realised the television was playing the news. It was a report being made at the South Wall and she coughed against the warm alcohol when a familiar face took up the screen. She gave no explanation as she left, heading down to her department before dragging the picture Pranav had given her out of her bra.

The reporter had been interviewing the Second in Command Erga Roman, and it'd made something click. Despite how long she'd been eyeing the faces in that picture, she'd been more on the lookout for her parents. And yet it was glaring now. To the far left, almost as if standing away from the others, was a bald, muscular, hateful looking man with his arms crossed and a rifle leaning against his leg. He had to have been in his mid-thirties, but it was Erga all right.

She collapsed into a chair and watched the smoke escaping the furnace, uncaring as her mind whirred. Erga had decimated that Bandit camp and he'd found her hiding amongst the slaves. Barely a day later and she'd been released to Jim. A year on and she'd met Pranav, Jim's ex-bestie, and Pierre shortly after that. None of it had been a coincidence, and they'd all known.

They'd all been in on it.

The anger burnt as she forced the picture back into her bra, but she kept the rage in as she got back to work.

It had been Val's second day back at work when the news aired that a nasty riot had broken out at the Religious District. Several were reportedly dead and the foundations of Christ's Church's greenhouse had been destroyed. She'd dropped everything to head there.

It was midday and it was hot, and yet still Walkers came in groups to protest in the grounds of the religious houses. There was still smoke from where the foundations of the greenhouse had been razed, but now a wall of Agents were keeping people back. There were tanks, cruisers, and buggies, too. It'd take just one command for the Agents to lay waste to anything that moved.

There was no way she'd get to Christ Church chapel through the front doors, so she took the long way around the back. Men loyal to the church were keeping guard and looked unnerved as she approached. She made sure to keep her distance, but tried to remain in sight for anyone brave enough to look from the church. When a nun poked her head from a side door, she spotted Val waving before dashing back inside. She rarely prayed, but this time Val's lips twitched as the seconds passed.

The same elderly nun as before broke through the wall of men and gestured to her. Val rushed over the fence and between the gravestones, making it to them as they hurried her inside. The kitchen was the first room she entered and it was laid up with injured Walkers. The same went for the nave as every pew had been turned into a medical bed, with Agents keeping guard by the main doors. The chanting from outside was loud, but it softened as she was led down a corridor of small rooms. Each was modestly furnished with a bed, a side table, and a chair. She was put into one and urged to wait.

Moments later and footsteps sounded as a frightened Father Rodling rushed into the room. "My child! God be praised. How you manage I should never know." He knelt before her, taking a hand in his as he looked over her tired face. "You look half-dead. How did you ever escape?"

She couldn't answer as Sister Josephine arrived soon after. He moved aside so that she could see to her, rubbing Val's face with a cloth and taking off her hat to expose the dermatitis. "You've been sick, I've seen this on others."

"I was, but I got the Panacea and it's helped. This still hurts, though." She unzipped her boiler suit to expose the wound on her shoulder. Josephine almost passed out, but rather she urged Val to be still and rushed off.

"I came when I heard about the riots," Val said.

"It's chaos, but the PEA have control." He brought a chair closer and took her hand. "But never mind that, you're safe now. No one will hurt you here. Tell me, in confidence, where does it hurt?"

She looked a little confused. "My arm…"

"No," he said. "Don't put a hard face on just for me. I know what's happened to you, where they sent you, and what they do to girls in the Dwells, but your recovery starts now."

"No, Father, I didn't go to the Dwells."

Josephine returned with a medical kit and allowed it to fall open on the floor, exposing items for cleaning and suturing. Father Rodling said to her, "She didn't go to the Dwells."

"You didn't?" Josephine asked, pausing with a vial and needle in hand.

"No."

"Then where did they send you?" she asked. "The PEA caught you. They called you a terrorist!"

"They just let me go."

Josephine didn't seem convinced, but she didn't argue as she went about injecting the wound. It burnt and made tears prickle, but it numbed a moment later.

Rodling said, "He'd called here. I'd pleaded with Devron to return you to me. He told me about Jim being in a mercenary group and that he'd been bringing you up to be the same. He'd said Jim had died…"

Josephine muttered a prayer.

Val said, "I'm no terrorist. I'd like to be, but that's a lot more dedication than I'm willing to give."

Josephine muttered something else.

"They chipped me and I got it out. I made myself ill by working, but I had no choice."

Rodling almost flew at her with the 'you could've come to me' line, but he held off.

"You're here now," Josephine said. "That's all that matters." As she finished the last suture, she put aside the medical bag and took Val's hand, asking sincerely, "My girl, is there anything else you need?"

"Food would be nice, oh and if you guys could stop treating me like a retarded arsehole that'd be great, too."

Even Rodling looked astounded.

Val rolled her eyes. "Yeah yeah, act surprised. I, on the other hand, absorb shock like a fucking sponge."

"What's this about?" Rodling asked before Josephine could die of asphyxiation after hurriedly reciting whispered prayers.

Val said, "Jim was a Big Banger. Did you guys know?"

"No!" Rodling said.

Josephine agreed. "I've no idea what that even is."

"All right, how about Derek and Esha? Those names ring a bell?"

Josephine said, "No. Are they your parents?"

"Yeah… Then who dropped me off at the orphanage? Come on, one of you know something and I'm always the last one to fucking find out!"

Rodling still looked bewildered, but Josephine had fallen quiet. This told Val everything. She said, "Well? Tell me the truth now, because I've just found out that my life has been public knowledge for the past decade and the only idiot who wasn't laughing along was me!"

Josephine's words caught in her throat as she struggled to think up a response. Rodling put a hand on her shoulder and said, "I think it best you two have a talk. I need to see to the others, but I'll be back."

Josephine didn't look ready to be left on her own, but she also couldn't stop him. When the door closed, she had no excuses left and her shoulders drooped. Finally, she said, "I'd not meant to keep anything from you, but I'd assumed Jim had told you."

"Assume he'd told me nothing. Start from the beginning, please. Tell me everything."

"Do you remember Sacred Hearts?"

"Sure. It was small, falling apart, and it looked out onto miles of brown fields."

"It was top of the northern quadrant. Do you remember the Sisters?"

"Some, but I've only ever found you again."

Josephine watched the walls, possibly listening to the chanting outside. She eventually said, "Abbess Mary ran the sanctuary. She was old by the time I joined. There were eighteen girls and ten boys in our care and it'd been the only orphanage outside of PEA control at the time. You don't get them anymore; they're all raised in complexes now."

Josephine smiled as she recalled that time long ago. "You were a good listener. It unnerved the other Sisters. You'd stare. You still do." She picked at her tunic. "I first remember seeing Jim on the outskirts of the orphanage. I'd been in the kitchen steam-cleaning flannels. I'd had no idea who he was and had called for the caretaker to move him along. Glen was his name, as old as me but firm. He'd been the only man allowed in the orphanage and I'd expected him to scare him off, but instead he'd invited him in. I hadn't known why other than that he'd drop off donations now and then.

"We'd needed all the help we could get. Despite Quad: North growing in investment and Casuals, we'd been seemingly forgotten about and it was looking dire. We were forced to grow our own food, make our own clothes, and to protect ourselves. And we'd all feared the out-dated buffer tower would eventually blow up on us, but when it had, we'd not expected it to be due to Bandits."

"They're not common up north."

"They were back then. Very common. The PEA were keen to keep them back and now they're nearly unheard of, but it'd taken the deaths of four nuns and eleven children to see it happen. Do you remember the attack?"

"I'd hidden with a girl in a cupboard. Can't remember her name, but she'd been blonde and loud, and she'd only had half a hand."

"Drea, yes, she'd been lovely. She'd made it out and found a good family to adopt her. I spoke to her a time back, she told me she was doing well…"

Val shrugged. "After that, all I remember is leaving the cupboard, finding the tower had fallen though our bedrooms, and then men began snatching us up. I'd been thrown in a bag and spent ages travelling. They'd tried selling me but no one had been interested, so I'd ended up at the camp."

Josephine looked teary as she held Val's chin. "My dear. You came out a strong person when many would've fallen to the vices. You are an inspiration."

"But what about Jim?" she asked.

"I still didn't know who he was, but he'd arrived shortly after the attack to check the surviving girls, and then the bodies. He'd said you weren't there and left. I didn't see him for years, not until, well…"

"But you knew Jim wasn't my biological father?"

"I assumed he was. But this Derek and Esha…"

Val produced the picture. Josephine rightly identified Erga Roman and nodded heartily at the young, enthusiastic looking Jim. But the rest had her stumped.

"My girl, I wish I could help. I mean, this lady looks like you, I'd say, but as for your father, it could any of them."

"Esha doesn't sound exactly… I don't know, white?"

"She may not even be in the picture, my dear. Don't give in to such faith when it may well be preparing you for disappointment."

"I'm sorry I blew up at you," Val said, replacing the photo. "I've just come to assume everyone knows everything about me. It's been a rough few days."

She kissed Val's knuckles and said, "And yet you're still strong. I've seen you go through horrors no child should, and it's only done to strengthen you more. But you must rest and eat. Let me fetch you something."

"Thanks."

Josephine hurried to the door but stopped to say, "Jim hated this place. He hated us." She looked around the room as if it represented the entire church. "He couldn't forgive my failure in protecting you, but he put it aside so I could help you at your weakest. He may not have been your biological father, but he-"

Val shooed the rest of it away; she was too tired to handle such emotions.

Josephine wiped a tear and left, half closing the door. Val, however, slumped into the bed and listened to the growing anger of the rioters outside.

Val worked late into the evening. The trolleys she'd cleared the day before were back, but she went at it with all the vigour she could muster. The only break came when Bornis arrived. She was half dressed due to the heat, with only her bra and the lower half of her Walker suit covering her modesty. He didn't seem bothered at what he saw and she didn't care, either.

"Come on," he said. "Pranav wants yah."

She threw aside the trolley where it smacked the wall, making one of the various metal panels shake.

"Watch the fucking panels, *Two Tubs*! If that comes off, we'll find a way to make you pay for it."

Val was standing with her back to him. She was still, not breathing, her muscles tense…

His smile widened. "Sorry, don't go by that name no more?"

She turned. Bornis had always been an awful person, but she'd assumed it came with the territory. But the way he'd said it, the vindictiveness in his tone and the darkness in his expression, it made that nasty ball of hatred in her gut return.

"You a Bandit?" she asked.

He scoffed at the question, as if it'd come out of nowhere. Unarmed and looking like the weak little girl that she was, he didn't feel threatened when she neared him, but he grew ill-at-ease when she stopped an inch before his face.

"Are you a Bandit?" she repeated.

"The fuck you think?"

"I *know* the only people who used to call me that were Bandits. I *think* you're either one of them, or you have friends who are, and that – in my book – makes *you* a Bandit."

He cracked his knuckles as he loomed over her, but even when he pressed his sweaty, dirty forehead to hers, weighing down like the brute he was, he never broke his smile. "I ain't no Bandit, *Two Tubs*. I ain't friends with them, neither. I just know people who *know* people and they say you earned your stamps in more ways than one."

She held his stare.

He whispered, "They say you were so dry, it took two tubs o' lube just to get in."

He chuckled, but she simply stood there in all her five-foot-fourness, glaring into his face. His smile started to waver before he saw her hand edging towards her pocket. His realisation was too late. Before he could react, a foghorn blasted, making him leap out his skin as the furnaces bleeped. It was the warning signal for the crucibles to show they'd reached optimal pressure and the horn signalled the vents opening. She'd known it was coming, but he'd not.

"Fuck's sake," he hissed. "Think you're funny, bitch?"

She stopped on the lower step of the stairs, saying, "When people used to call me Two Tubs, I didn't earn stamps, or creds, or anything. I was lucky if they fed me. Not to mention I was only eight years old."

He didn't have much of a conscience, but even he knew those visuals were rather grim.

She flipped him the bird as she continued up the stairs.

"Oh, it lives," Pranav said, glancing over his glasses where he'd been reading forms. "Sit."

She did.

"Eight trolley's in twelve hours," he said, indicating his computer. "Masterson says you've churned out eight grams of gold and three grams of platinum from the scrap as well. Didn't fancy pocketing it anymore?"

"It's life or death now."

"Good, that's how it should be. No one deserves a free ride, especially not you."

He held up a digital tablet for her to take. It was scuffed but in working order. There was a video on pause and he gestured her to press play. She did and it revealed a scene that was sketchy and dark. The green hue showed it was using night-vision, but background radiation meant the image was flecked with white flashes. She still recognised the sight of a settlement in the Wastes. The cameraman was one in a team of several making for that camp of tents and partly erected walls. Watchtowers were being put up and the business-end of a buffer tower lay towards the back, waiting for implementation. The men were Bandits; thick skinned, tattooed, clad in bullet-proof gear and night goggles; they were just as she remembered.

"What's this?" she asked.

Pranav opened a drawer to extract a potato, which he began eating raw. He said through a full mouth, "I don't deal in Bandits. Never have. Never will. Agents are the lowest I'll go."

"Sure? Because I saw your parliamentary admittance card the other day when you were rooting through your things. When it comes to the lowest of the low, rubbing shoulders with the Royals is lower than my boot."

He didn't look ashamed. He even smiled.

"What's the coffee like in Westminster?" she asked. "I heard they do these things called *paninis*?"

He ignored her and said, "I'm not a politician, but I know how to milk them. Anyway, just play the rest. The man behind that camera is one of my guys on the inside. Keeps me in the know."

The footage continued as the man turned where she caught sight of a child slave stirring a pot on a fire. She couldn't have been older than five and something inside Val gave way. Pranav noted her reaction but made no response.

The cameraman turned his attention to a trailer. It meant nothing to her, at first. Then the door opened to a huge man wearing a heavy military mask, his arms exposed and thick with scales, and he was sporting two fully automatic rifles strapped to his back. His chest was on show, exposing a large scarification-mark of a sun with blazing tendrils reaching about his torso, but it wasn't a tattoo he had by choice. It was a scar from where he'd taken a grenade to the chest nearly half a decade ago.

She finally uttered, "I saw him die…"

Pranav shook his head. "Evil doesn't die. It just goes away for a while. And Garboa is as evil as they come."

"How recent is this?"

"A few hours."

"He's been free all this time?"

He shook his head. "He'd been incarcerated in the Dwells. I only found this out a few days ago. I have interests in the Wastes around here, and Bandit activity had been at an all-time low. Next thing I see Bandits everywhere. The rough kind, the kind who know how to keep control.

"I did some digging. Garboa never died. He and his ilk were up in the Dwells living it large in the high-security wings. But there's been word for a while that Devron's been crying for a high security facility to be built that can hold over ten thousand people, like a prison, but he's been too secretive to employ an outside company to make it.

"So what's Commander Devron go and do? Flushes the prison, releasing the filth down south and I'm guessing it was with the understanding that they stay away. Well, surprise surprise, they've not been listening."

"But why release them?"

"The Dwells has been done out. The cells were removed, the gates torn down, the surfaces cleaned, and even the land around it has been renovated. Now it's home to over a thousand Unregistered Walkers. I hear they've got workshops in place to give useless Walkers some skills, and they feed you propaganda to twist your mind, eventually releasing you as the Registered civilian they want you to be."

She was shaking and she couldn't hide it. She didn't need to know about Garboa, that life was behind her now, and she felt sick that Pranav had brought her into it. She just didn't need that right then.

"Can I go? I mean, I have work to do."

Pranav looked confused. "Don't you want to know the rest?"

"I know enough."

When he didn't argue, she made for the door, pulling it closed behind her. She barely saw the steps as she thundered down. She tore past workers before taking the long passage to the basement where she slammed the door shut and collapsed against the wall. There was nothing to vomit and there were no more tears left to cry, so all she had to give was blood. She punched the wall, breaking the skin on her knuckles as red smeared the metal panel.

'*You're breathing, aren't yah?*' Jim said, his voice haunting. '*Then there's always a chance. Keep breathing and you'll keep getting chances.*'

"Fuck you, Jim," she sobbed into her hands. "Just fuck you."

Several heavy bangs on the door garnered a gentle woman's response. "We're not open yet, honey. Come back when the night lights on."

A short silence, then *knock knock knock*.

"Hun, fuck off please. We're not working yet," Canny shouted, trying to sound sweet whilst slowly losing her temper. But the third set of knocks had her flinging it open in order to use her freshly painted nails for exactly what she grew them for. However, she stopped short. "Val? Get in here."

Cuckoo bounced excitedly, but Val didn't have the chance to play with her. There were several women around a table in the living room, making use of a collection of cosmetics, and a few pretty men lounged on couches or propped themselves on windowsills for passers-by to check out the wares.

"This is Val," Canny said as if she'd talked about her before. They didn't look impressed, so she whipped off Val's hat as if that helped, wiping down her freshly shaved head and rubbing the smudges from her cheeks. It might've made things worse, but it didn't dull Canny's smile. "We'll wash you up, get a wig on you, tart up them eyes because, honey, they'd melt men like butter."

"I just need somewhere to sleep…" Val put several Reds down and asked, "Will this do?"

The largest of the women snatched them up and nodded to the stairs.

Canny said, "Right this way, honey-buns."

Val sat in the bathtub with Canny. The water was almost too hot, but neither of them minded. A touch of bleach helped kill off what the heat didn't.

"Luxuries of being a girl of leisure," Canny said as she poured water over Val. Her sudden exclamation as it stung her bald head made Cuckoo bark excitedly and she tried to jump in. "No! Out. Not tonight, girl. Later."

After ten minutes, the water was brown enough to put Val to shame. Slipping out, they knelt before the fireplace to wipe down with alcohol, but Val was silent during Canny's constant chatter. As if only now realising this, she took Val's chin and asked, "Hun? What is it?"

"Do you take Bandits as clients?"

"Oh babe, I wouldn't know one from the rest."

"*You* would."

She threw Val the towel and fetched some clothes, saying, "It's not like I can pick 'n' choose. I'm like a doctor, see? I can't discriminate. Plus, after all the years I've been doing this, I'll fuck anything for a warm meal."

"If you knew the things they'd done, if you'd seen what I've seen, you'd not let them touch you."

Canny turned, looking angered as her pride had taken a punch. But she knew all too well what they were capable of and she softened. "I…"

"No," Val said, indicating the clothes Canny held for her. "I'll wear my Walker suit."

She didn't argue, but she threw her some clean frilly underwear to go with it.

Whilst Canny dried and combed her long, blonde hair, Val spread out on her bed. It wouldn't be long before the doors opened to clients, so she'd need to find a place out of the way to sleep. Until then, she relaxed.

She must've dozed because she woke to find Canny

sitting beside her. Val normally visited after her shift when her makeup had run and her hair was a mess. Now her foundation was flawless, her eyes large and outlined in black, all caught under butterfly wing eye-lashes. Her ruby lips were puckered from all the pinching and even her hair was beautifully set in flowing ringlets. She was stunning.

Canny asked gently, "If I made you a promise, would you make one, too?"

Val looked troubled.

"You'd not lie to me," Canny said surely as she lay down beside her, half naked and still glistening from moisturiser. "You're the most honourable person I know. If you made a promise, I know you'd keep it."

"What promise?"

"I'll turn away Bandits if you promise to join me here. Become one of my girls and live an easier life. You're guaranteed to get the itch either way, so at least here we can watch each other's backs."

Val had never been so tempted before. It was this that made her uncomfortable. Canny understood, making no comments as Val moved to the window, barred and lined with wire acting as low-level buffers against radiation. The Estate was dark and flat rooftops stretched for a few hundred metres until the lights of Central across the Thames sparkled. But several heads shot by the top of the yard wall. Another couple rushed into the street…

Val said, "Something's happening."

"Eh?"

Knuckles rapped the door before a young man looked in. "Come see this."

Val pulled on her boots as Canny slid on a coat, and down into the road they ran. A few others joined as they wound around rubbish in the streets, making for the south of the Estates overlooking Black Waterloo. The empty lands between it and the Estates sometimes acted as a road, though it rarely saw much traffic. Now, dozens of PEA cruisers nipped here and there, with some parked by the statue and others driving as far as the outposts south of the market. But one vehicle stood out not only due to the lights along its roof, but the sheer size; thirty feet long, nearly ten feet high, with a side that opened like a stall. Men and women were rushing to it as official-looking Casuals doled out supplies.

All trepidation vanished when it was found out they were giving away free Bruch, vacuum packed food, clothes, and minor medical packs. Canny grabbed a fellow rushing back into the Estates, his arms loaded with stuff as she asked, "The fuck is this?"

"Listen to the radio. To compensate us for all the work they've been doing over by the churches, they're giving us this." He indicated the rations and wine bottles.

"And you buy that drivel?" Val asked, annoyed.

"Listen boy, just get it while it lasts."

Canny rolled her eyes as the fellow hurried off, but more were rushing from the buildings to get in on the goods. Maybe they felt safer because the van looked amazing; sleek, glossy, and not an Agency emblem or Black Eye in sight. Still, it didn't mean the PEA weren't about, and the Walkers were walking right into it.

"What now?" Canny asked her.

Val answered by turning from the masses already drunk on the free brown wine, and returned to the brothel. They entered a room of nervous-looking people.

"We'll get plenty of work tonight, girls and guys," Canny said, "But not an Agent walks through that door, just to be on the safe side."

The lad closest rolled his eyes. "I'll man the alleys, then."

As he slipped out, the older of the women said, "Get her out the way. She'll scare off the punters."

Val knew the score and took Cuckoo to a cubby hole to sleep.

It had indeed been a busy night for Canny and the others. Val had slept through most of it, but had woken to Canny beckoning her to the very back room. It was kitted out with sofas, tables, and large chairs where they'd been celebrating the money they'd made. It hadn't lasted long and nearly a dozen men and women, including her and Canny, now slept about the room as the dull morning light woke her.

The room had an exit into a yard where bins and generators sat. It was ajar, letting in the cool wind of the morning. It'd likely grow to stifling temperatures through the day, so she enjoyed it while she could.

As Val put on her boots, Canny rolled over, exposing her messy locks and smeared makeup. "What's the time?"

Val looked to her wrist. Of course there was no RDAC. "Early."

"Go back to sleep then, sugar."

"No, I got work to do."

"At this hour? Trains won't run until nine."

Val ignored her, so Canny threw a rolled up sock to get her attention and then pointed at a table along the far wall. Mirror fragments had been fixed to a board forming a sort of vanity table, and there was a zip-bag containing makeup.

"What's this for?" Val asked.

"Practice. It's your colour, so just do it how you've seen me doing it, yeah?"

Val didn't know where to start. There were creams, oils, and powders, vibrant pigments and glittery gels, all in shiny metal tubs and plastic vials, as well as kohl-black eyeliner and mascara. She'd found makeup before and tried it, but she'd felt like a clown. Still, if she ever did become one of Canny's girls…

"Will you show me?" Val asked, but no answer came. Canny's smoky eyes were closed as she slept. In the very early light, she looked younger and more at peace. How could someone who'd lived on the end of every man in the Estates still hold any element of humanity? Canny was stronger than most gave her credit.

Val did something she'd never done before and crept close, bending to kiss her forehead. Canny didn't wake up, thankfully.

She crossed the sleeping bodies for the hall leading to the front room, hoping she'd grab a spare bottle of Bruch on her way out. It was empty save for Cuckoo by the front door. Val was about to call her, but a shadow passed a heavily curtained window. Whoever was there, they were going to great lengths to not be heard.

"Watch em!" she hissed, pointing at the door. Cuckoo's ears went back and her teeth showed as she growled. Val hurried back to where they were sleeping, heaving open the back door and accidentally waking a heavily-built woman who swore and went back to sleep. Val rushed into the yard and hoisted herself atop the wall. What she saw was staggering.

"Shit! Wake up everyone, wake up!"

As she leapt down, the wall spat chips where bullets had struck it, and the sound of rapid gunshots had thrown her senses. She went stumbling into the wall and a crash within the house told her that the front entrance had been kicked in, and Cuckoo barked once before a bang silenced her forever.

"Move!" Val cried. The fat woman was trying to get up now, but a canister landed within the mess of people and, instinctively, Val threw herself back. The blast blinded and deafened her for an instant and she was showered with glass and stone. It'd even thrown the generator off its stand where the tank spilt fuel. She could smell smoke, burning hair, and when her hearing returned there was screaming.

'*Run!*' barked Jim. '*Get fucking moving.*'

"Canny!" she cried as similar explosions rocked the Estates. The earth moved, making her stumble every time she tried to stand. Then she spotted the half-decimated body poking from the door. It was Canny, or what was left of her, but she didn't need Val's help now.

'*Fucking move!*'

Gloves appeared over the wall as a man in black armour hoisted himself up. His need for balance meant he couldn't get his gun when he saw her, but she refused him the chance and punched him in the face. His breathing mask and goggles hurt her knuckles, but it'd also hurt him as he flew back with a cry. She scuttled over the wall and into a street with black soldiers at either end. She darted for cover.

'*Just keep low. If you hear a sound, go the other way. I'll be right behind you. Don't be afraid.*'

The alleys were winding and narrow, and each time she saw movement, Jim shouted *Duck!*

"Canny…"

'*Up and over, honey. Just keep going.*'

She scurried over another wall and hid there. Men and women were peeking from a cracked window as plumes of smoke messed up the sky. She glanced over the wall as soldiers with guns at the ready blasted doors and shimmied over walls, rushing into houses where muzzles flashed and screams were silenced. Their black visors and helmets buzzed with communications as they went systematically along, releasing controlled sprays of bullets before shouting *area clear!* They weren't Agents, but they were PEA, that much she knew.

'Wait for it…'

A house along; one soldier knocked down the door and three more flooded in. When the last entered and the street was momentarily clear, Jim barked, *'Now!'*

She hurried down a side road where an army jeep shot by, eventually skidding to a stop when she was spotted. Bullets followed her feet, but she was gone before one could hit home.

'They'll chase yah, chick. They'll follow you until they can radio in Target Down. *Don't give them the satisfaction.'*

She had to think this through.

'Head for freedom, but stop before you get there. The most important part of any escape ain't running the furthest, but making them think you have.'

She jumped a ruined wall leading to a seven-foot drop as a crater had opened up from previous warfare and anomalous explosions. Buildings leaned over, ready to fall, and tarmac hung down, acting as shelter.

'They'll never expect you to stop, to hide, to be right under their noses…'

She ducked within a cavernous area with water up to her ankles. Boots thundered above, men and women shouted, there were screams as Walkers were shot, and a distant speakerphone burdened by static warned of the coming *eviction*.

Desist and await instruction. Resistance will be met with deadly force. This is a lawful action…

Her pursuers ran around the ruins in search of their target. All it would take is for one soldier to look back, to consider the crater a viable place of shelter, and then she'd be seen.

"Keep going. Keep on fucking going," she whispered.

The soldiers left her sight,

'*Keep your nerve, don't be zealous…*'

She planned to. She wasn't afraid now. She'd done this many times before as Jim had taught her well. She could even feel him smiling as he backed off, letting her do her thing. And right then a straggling soldier nipped around the crater, keeping an eye on the rear as he hurried after his comrades.

She dashed out the hole and went the other way, heading south of the Estates where the Embankment overlooked the Thames. She could see boats along the waters, their rifles pointed at the buildings where Walkers scattered like roaches. Some dropped because they were afraid, others because they were dead, and she ducked only when needing others to distract the scopes.

She was near Westminster Bridge where the Agents had built the wall. It made sense now: the refurbishment, the surveying, the feeding and watering of the Walkers! All these idiots had fallen for it, making themselves drunk and lame, and now she was one of the trapped.

The areas nearest the bridge were heavily damaged from countless Mists with many buildings consisting of nothing more than ruined structures. She dipped behind a wall to hide from soldiers scouting here, their guns up as if eager to shoot. She wasn't alone, either. Walkers had stopped here to wait for soldiers to pass, and some were mere feet away. She knew someone would bottle it, and she waited for the distraction.

As predicted, a man cracked and took off running. A bullet bit him and he hit the deck, gurgling since most of his neck was now painting the ground. The horror drove the others to flee and she was thankful that they were running *away* from the bridge, taking the scopes with them.

She set off running for the wall, but it was only when

she got so close that she saw the gated entrances were closed. Walkers amassed here, banging on the gates and screaming for help. Black soldiers were approaching from behind them, forming a wall so no one could escape, and the order to aim was given.

Finally, the gates blew open and Walkers shot aside as their regular Agents rushed through. Rather than set upon the Walkers, Agents aimed at the black soldiers, barking for them to stand down and urging Walkers through the gates. It was a stand-off between the two divisions.

Then several figures emerged. Their religious robes showed they were Islamic and Jewish priests, guiding the terrified survivors to safety and waving their arms at the soldiers, imploring them to have mercy. But when one face she knew appeared, Val started running.

The wide eyed Father Rodling looked horrified at the black soldiers and bodies littering the ground. But he caught sight of Val who was crying for him as she escaped the ruins, and he latched onto her, dragging her through with those running for the churches. Nuns and Agents were standing outside Christ Church and they hurried for the doors; it might as well have been Heaven since she'd just survived Hell.

No one had said a thing when Val had arrived at the factory, mainly due to it being so deserted. She was thankful since she looked like shit and was covered in as much since she'd rode the dump trucks to reach Sevenoaks.

Now she was standing before the bellowing furnaces, seeing nothing but flames, smelling nothing but destruction...

A hissing sound knocked her from those awful memories of earlier that morning. The furnaces were at their capacity and she momentarily opened all the vents. And yet even in this racket she could still hear Rodling's pained cries as she'd run off, but she'd been unable to stay. Agents and Walkers were bringing the injured and the dead to the Religious District, and the state of their bodies had been awful. Even in the camps she'd never seen such carnage.

She coughed against the lump in her throat and slammed the last vent shut. The noise reduced enough to allow her radio to play through, and the voice made her skin crawl.

'*...the riot sparked by the Undesirables had spread fast,*' Devron said. '*Our Agents had responded, but the weapons in the possession of these criminals were devastating, and we were forced to bring in our special units.*

'*Our efforts to control the gunfight were strained, with many known criminals fleeing the initial raid, taking refuge in homes elsewhere in the Estate where the fighting had spread. The amount of people consorting with these offenders was astounding and acted as further proof that Undesirables had been taking advantage of the Quads for too long. But not anymore.*'

His voice darkened as he said, '*I promise, we won't rest*

until every single Undesirable is ousted from our good city. Work hard, and as always, be lawful.'

She reared up, grabbing a trolley from the lift and throwing it across the floor until it smashed against the wall. The metal panel rattled and a few bolts fell out, but it remained firm. And so again she dragged it back and threw harder still, screaming as she did so as rage rose like bile and made her eyes water. The clashes were causing sparks and a wheel broke, leaving the trolley at an angle as she drew it away again, but this time she was unable to maintain its balance and it crashed to the floor, spilling rubbish and scrap. Over it she stooped, her sobs heaving out of her chest and tears stinging her bloodshot eyes.

In the commotion, she'd not see the wall break. The panel had lost every last one of its screws and now it laid flat on the floor. The crevice it exposed was black, but dust spilled out into the turbulent air kicked into a frenzy by the heat, and she could smell mould and damp. The crawl-space had finally been rendered exposed and taking up a torch, she shone it inside, revealing supports, wires, insulation, and studs.

It was only now that she took a moment to consciously consider her plan. She'd needed covert access to Pranav's office and this was the best way. She'd even used it before, years ago, but back then there'd not been metal panels about the wall. Breaking through would be her cover, hoping they'd put it down to her recklessness and not her desire to trespass. Still, she doubted she'd be around long enough for anyone to discover it.

She shimmied from her Walker suit to prevent it getting dirty. Semi naked, she climbed inside, ignoring the itching insulation and jagged edges, but she crawled up into darkness until she was above ground level and a grate exposed the empty Machines Floor.

Her fingers stung as if everything was made of acid, and the air tasted caustic. Still, she made it to the second level where a woman was rewiring generators. Another woman turned up and rubbed her leg to get her attention. "You all right?" she asked, but the woman shook her head and began crying.

"It's all gone. I've seen it," she sobbed. "I've seen the entire thing ablaze. They say eight thousand people were trapped inside. Black Waterloo's all gone."

Minutes passed as she climbed, eventually reaching the top where a panel offered a level of silence not experienced elsewhere in the factory. She thumped a grate loose and spilled into Pranav's office.

She couldn't see any movement through the distorted glass of his door, but she remained quiet as she crossed the carpet for his desk. The drawers weren't locked, so she found the tin containing his key-cards easily enough. She sorted through them until she found a blue and white striped card.

Someone moved outside. She returned the office to how she'd found it and hurried back into the cavity. Pranav might find the card missing in the morning, but by then there'd be nothing anyone could do about it. There'd be no stopping her now.

A dump truck had gotten her to Old South Quad, after that it'd been a long walk home. It was almost dark by the time she'd made it to Jim's ship. She'd slept whilst water boiled for a bath, and a cocktail of disinfectants and bleach had been her only soap. As she now dried naturally, she laid out the makeup Canny had given her.

She slouched. "I have no fucking idea what to do."

The clothes the officer from the precinct had donated to her were steaming over the spent bathwater. A white shirt, and a black skirt and jacket were the only contents, but she'd found a pair of shoes that'd go with it at least. She'd need to figure out how to stick the wig on, but there were plenty of tools left about Jim's boat that'd surely solve that problem. So the makeup was the only hurdle left to jump.

Eyeing the late night hour, she decided she had a bit of time to practice and dived right in.

Her lowly kayak made few waves as she traversed the gentle river. The silence of the early morning was almost serene, and with the smoke gone from the Estates after the brutal Eviction, it almost seemed normal. Yet the Embankment had already been walled off and distant radio communications could be heard through PEA speakers.

She pulled up beside the rundown Charing Cross station where she hauled herself to dry land and slid from her hazmat suit. Her false hair fell like ringlets as she'd spent hours putting them in rollers, and a quick check of her mirror revealed her makeup had fared well. She touched up a few areas before applying more lipstick, and then she slid into her shoes.

'You look smashing, chick.'

"I look ridiculous is what I look."

She sighed heavily and set off, not bothering to hide her raft. "I'm a Casual," she muttered as she made for Whitehall where the sounds of the market were already rather lively, despite it being just after six a.m. "I'm a Casual, born in Quad: North and I just happen to sound like a Walker, is all. No big deal. I can do this. I can look civilised…"

She'd tried to make a beeline for the Houses of Parliament, but stopped short at the sight of Westminster Bridge. She'd not been back that way since the attack, but it seemed the gated outpost had been sealed shut. Amassing outside it were Agents and their vehicles, as well as a tank which she'd not seen before; big and black, with a small cannon and two automatic rifle arms either side.

Walkers were gathering in protest, shouting for the way to be opened up. Even with a bunch of Smaz Gazzars pointed right at them, the people wouldn't relent. They wanted access to the Religious District and they were getting uppity.

Even if she dressed like her usual self, she'd never have joined that mob. Groups were good for keeping discreet, but not when Agents had a tendency to open fire indiscriminately. So she hurried across the road that streamed with more Walkers coming from the market, and headed for the towering Big Ben's Obelisk in the grounds of the Westminster Palace. It shined like glass with a perfectly smooth surface and beams of light running up the corners. The gentle ray of purple that exuded from the point barely reached the clouds today, showing atmospheric pressure was high and the day may well lead to a bright one. If she got her way, it'd start with some good news, at least. But the digital numbers at the top of the obelisk showed it was nearly half six. She didn't have long.

The grounds around the palace had been fortified with concrete barricades and wire fencing, and there were Agents keeping watch. She'd barely begun her approach when sirens sounded. Agents from their outposts raised their guns but didn't fire as Walkers rushed in her direction, armed with makeshift shields and blunt weaponry. Within an instant it felt as if the riot had turned into a war and for the second time in a few days she was running towards Agents for safety.

"Hurry!" one shouted from the gates, pulling her through as they closed and soldiers stood the line, waiting for things to boil over. And yet there were no shots fired. It wasn't like them to be so restrained. She wondered if they knew that the anger the Walkers were feeling was justified.

"How'd you get caught in that?" the Agent asked as he walked her to the gaping entrance of the archaic building, fronted with scaffolding and floodlights.

She panted, "My driver, he saw the commotion and bolted, just leaving me-"

"Make sure you report him. Casuals caught in that get slaughtered. Head inside and don't leave until it's clear."

She pushed through the doors into a large foyer. The floor was marble and the stone and wooden walls went as high as the towering ceiling. She'd expected it to be filled with people, but there were only a few standing around in suits, stuck in their tiny groups talking quietly and looking tense.

She saw evidence of walls having been removed and supports added, and a collection of soft furnishings and tables were off to the right, but no one was waiting there. A desk ahead of her was manned by a single lady, smart looking, middle-aged, and talking quietly on the phone. Val made sure to come across confident as she approached, passing a trio of men.

"Gas the bleeding lot of them, I say!" one hissed.

"Like insects. Disturb their hive and they go into a frenzy," another added.

"Well, that's what they get for harbouring criminals."

The first scoffed. "Which of them aren't?"

As she went further, she spotted a glass wall off to the far right. The stone had been knocked away to make room for it, and it spilled light, looking rather modern in such an old-fashioned place. Atop the double doors read A.P.D in frosted writing, with the boarder underneath stating it was the Agency Parliamentary Division.

"Hello?" said the receptionist, making Val look with a start.

She didn't mean to come across flustered, but her words came out too fast. "Good morning. I've got an appointment with De… Commander Bernard Devron."

"Oh?" The receptionist checked her computer.

"Yes! I'm going to be a guest speaker on his station. It's all rather last minute," she droned, trying to sound how she imagined a Royal to speak. "I'd have been here sooner but those god-awful Walkers jumped me and my car."

The woman looked genuinely pained for her. "Awful business. Could you scan in, please?"

She used Pranav's blue and white striped key-card on a portable module. The light went from red to green and the woman didn't even bother checking her computer as she said, "Let's pray the recent eviction of Old South Quad holds better results than the last time it was tidied up, hey? Commander Devron's office is up those stairs, first floor. Have a good show."

I will, Val thought. *It'll blow his mind.*

The glass entrance to the A.P.D was brightly lit and carpeted in blue. The brick walls were exposed and half of the stairwell had been decorated using segments of the clock face from the old bell-tower.

She was nervous as she climbed for the first floor; she'd not been searched yet and she just hoped when they did look into her things that her little *trick* would work. Surely enough, when she was buzzed through into a corridor with wood panelling for walls and a bright red carpet, an officer called her to the desk.

"I'm here for an appointment regarding the broadcast and I-"

He held up a hand to calm her. "That's fine, ma'am. Card please."

She gave him it.

He checked his computer and shook his head. "Well, you have clearance but no appointment. Are you-"

"I've already been through this with the receptionist. The riots have thrown our schedules about and I spoke to Commander Devron personally who assured me-"

"Mrs Abad, is it? It's fine, you have clearance but I don't know when he'll be free to see you. You're permitted to wait for him at his office, but I need to search your bag first."

"Oh, I really wouldn't-" she began, backing off.

He rounded his desk and reached for her arm. "I need to. It's the rules."

"Sir, I would *not* recommend-"

"Miss, please!" he demanded and took the bag from her. She was stiff as he up-ended it, spilling pens, a notepad, a PDA, and what looked like an IV bag filled with brown sloshing liquid. The man was confused before realising a plastic tube went from it to her waistband.

She feigned embarrassment as she hurriedly packed the contents away. "I did try to warn you. The Sickness, you know, it does irreversible things to our bodies. Don't worry, it looks full but it really can hold much more than that."

As he realised what he was looking at, he allowed her to shoulder the bag as he collapsed into his chair. Just then, the radio behind his desk played the PEA intro, meaning the broadcast was starting.

"Ma'am, do you have any sharps or-" he paused to hold back the nausea before saying, "-any sharps or offensive weapons on your person?"

"No," she said, going for the buttons on her shirt. "Would you like me to undress and-"

"No! God no, no please just… I'll be here if you need anything," he said, pushing his knuckles to his mouth as he tried to keep control. "The Commander's office is at the end, just go in and wait."

She thanked him repeatedly and hurried off.

'*That was brilliant!*'

She slowed before reaching the last door where frosted glass read

Commander Bernard Devron
Agent Superior's Office

She could hear his voice as clear as day inside, but now she was shaking. Every cautionary voice in her head was screaming as she slipped the gun from inside her skirt. In all her years she'd handled less than five firearms, and she'd never used any to kill with. Now she'd change that and using Jim's old 9mm pistol seemed fitting.

'Whoa, chick, easy now...'

As she opened the door an inch, Devron's words spilled.

'Let me begin by addressing the rumours, the vicious claims that the PEA had conducted an execution-style raid on the people of the Embankment. These are senseless lies from Undesirables who want you to risk your safety in an uprising against us.'

His blasé tone gripped her with more hatred than she'd ever felt.

'In as little as a day, we've dug out hundreds of wanted men and women whose crimes against the Quads are extreme, from soliciting to drug dealing, murder to rape. There is no surprise at all that these foul people lived safely in the folds of the Estates, and if they had merely stayed in there then things might not have been so bad. But they turned Waterloo into a kingdom of vice, producing weapons and drugs to threaten our way of life and I, for one, couldn't stand by as that happened.'

She couldn't take any more and leapt into the room, gun drawn and finger on the trigger. The blow was instant, but it hadn't come from her weapon. She staggered into the wall, her eyes flashing with colours as a large hand landed around her throat and she was pinned.

'...I will be the first to express regret over the losses of life that day. Not just Walkers, but Agents, too. The biggest loss came when my men rushed several illicit weapons factories...'

Devron went on, barely missing a beat as the figure stood over her, his white boots, blue Agent uniform, and bullet-proof vest looking immaculate. Except this wasn't Devron.

It was Erga Roman.

"Who the fuck are you?" he growled.

Adrenaline caused her to see in hyper-vision, with the scene playing out at speeds she that couldn't comprehend as she looked over his fierce expression, and then to the corner of the room where a desk sat. The radio terminal was unmanned as a PDA had been plugged into it, playing Devron's recorded message to the masses.

He threw her into a padded chair and snatched up her bag. He cursed in surprise at the fake colostomy bag, but emptied the rest on the desk, pushing aside the rubbish until he finally turned on her. His large hands made light work of her blouse and jacket, infiltrating pockets and patting down her arms. He moved to her torso and she didn't have time to squirm as he felt about her chest, stopping as he sensed an irregularity. He showed no hesitation in tearing out the item from inside her bra, freeing the picture Pranav had given her.

His horror was instant. She could only imagine what he felt seeing a picture of himself from over fifteen years ago, and of a life that must've been very much different to now.

"Who the fuck gave you this?" he barked, grabbing the collar to her shirt as if he might beat the answer out of her. And then he stopped as if seeing her for the first time, and the realisation drove him back. "You…"

He rubbed his shaved head and sat against the desk. "Fool," he said. "Such a bloody fool. How did you even make it this far? Shit." He actually laughed, as if fatigue was draining him of control, but the anger soon returned as he spat, "You're a bloody idiot walking in here with a gun, and for what?"

"Jim's dead. My friends have been murdered. I want revenge."

"But you being here won't bring him back. I risked my

balls getting you released, do you know that? The amount of times I've stuck my neck out for you two is unreal."

"You got me out of the precinct?" She should've felt shock, but the adrenaline was still numbing her. "You knew who I was."

"I've always kept an eye out for you. And Jim. You have no idea and that's how it should've stayed. But I knew as soon as I'd seen the notification on my system that he'd died that you'd be on a downward spiral. He promised to Register you, but I bet he didn't."

"He adopted me."

"Not good enough. Look what this has led to. I expunged his record, I gave him some distance, and he still fucked it up." He looked almost weak. "I could've done without this."

"Agents just tore through the Estates killing thousands, and you think *you're* having a bad day. This is on your head!"

He didn't argue. She watched as his jaw clenched, almost as if fighting the words he wanted to say. Then he nodded. "I couldn't stop it," was all he uttered. She didn't care and he saw that, so he said, "You came here looking for Devron. You want him dead?"

"He needs to pay for what he's done."

"He's not the only one who signed off on the Eviction."

He was quiet but she didn't speak. He came closer in order to say, "You want to make an impact, one that'll hit as hard as the Eviction? I think I can help." He moved to the door and locked it. Turning to her, he said, "We haven't long."

PART THREE

41

She woke up groaning. She hadn't slept long, nor would she have been able to as her head was stinging from where the Agents had chipped her. The one that'd been implanted in her arm had been bad enough, but this time they'd cut her scalp by half an inch and shoved the chip into her skull, and apparently it was just as corrosive as the first.

A dozen other people shared a cell with her. Most looked unremarkable and she'd been stuck with this lot for over a day, first meeting them when she'd been thrown in the back of a PEA cattle truck. With no room to sit, they'd been made to stand for hours before they'd set off, with no windows to show where they were going. Even when the doors finally opened, it'd been inside a massive garage with other empty trucks. After that they'd been put in a cell for twenty-four hours quarantine. It'd felt longer, though.

Welcome to the Dwells, she remembered one Agent muttering before the door had slammed shut. Now it was opening to an Agent who growled, "Move it," though he sounded more tired than angry. Men and women dragged their bags and other personal effects that they'd been permitted to bring with them, though she didn't have anything like that. Still, she was happier for it since it meant she had nothing to protect.

The corridor was wide and there were no doors except for those at the end, made of thick metal with reinforced glass. A racket escape them and she soon saw why when they were heaved open. Beyond it was a caged area where lights flashed and alarms sounded, and Walkers amassed outside it, filling an atrium as large as a football field. The sirens stopped as the doors were closed, and the gates opened to allow them to join the others.

This wasn't what she'd been expecting. Sure, there were Agents, but they were standing patiently atop walkways watching the docile prisoners of which there had to be well over three thousand people. Along the walls, families had gathered who'd made camps, and she was shocked to see kids and babies mixed in it all. But then it started to make sense. She'd already known the real prisoners had been flushed out and replaced with Undesirables. That's all she was seeing now, the Agency's Registration Programme in full effect.

An automated voice broke out over the constant drone of Walkers. *'Cafeteria will open between nine and ten. Please form an orderly line.'*

She could just about see a sign over on the far left wall reading *cafeteria* and that's where people churned out. She went further along, spotting turnstiles for toilets and washrooms, and televisions played behind bars showing silent images of Registered Walkers and Casuals working together. It was followed with *Soon, this will be you* though it sounded much more like a threat to her.

As she approached it, she could finally hear a speaker spilling the happy voice of a woman. *'Do you lack skills vital for a hard-working, lawful life? Join our work programmes today.'*

Val suddenly bristled with adrenalin. This was what she'd been told to find. Erga had been vague on most things, but he'd been clear that she needed to stand out from the crowd, but not be obvious. To do this, she needed to get herself a job. She'd not been sure what this'd meant, but now the speaker listed off all the many jobs she could apply for within the Dwells.

'Learn to bake, garner a skill in engineering, or become a civil worker, all trained here for free. Just sign up today.'

Beneath it was a terminal that'd been left slightly battered and mucky. The screen offered information on work programmes and schooling, and she tapped about the tabs, checking boxes and swiping left and right to navigate the options. A list of skills filled the screen and the third one down offered beginning courses in engineering. She went to tap it but she was jostled from behind. Snapping around, she barked, "Hey!"

She felt dwarfed under the tall, pale man in goggles and a hard hat who growled, "Act natural!" before suddenly walking off.

'Thank you for signing up to our work programmes-' the voice rang out from the terminal, but she ignored it as she realised the man had bumped into her on purpose. It had to be Erga's contact. She'd not expected to meet him so soon, but she forced herself to be ready and followed.

He was a tall man, but it surprised her how easily he could lose himself in a crowd. She found him some way down by a set of turnstiles leading to a restricted area. A Black Eye atop it scanned him and a green light flashed, and through the winding bars he vanished. She paused before it and the light went red, denying her access.

She looked around as Agents noticed her. She didn't like that. It went red again and the lens of the Black Eye kept trying to focus on her features.

"Look up, Walker! Let it see your face," an Agent said from above, but she couldn't. It just went against her nature to do so. But just as the Agent grew impatient, the light flashed green and she threw herself through without delay, landing in the man's arms.

"Oh, I didn't think that'd work for a moment," he laughed, sounding so much brighter than before. She pulled away, insulted that he'd been so friendly with her, and looked about the large corridor she and several others had entered. Most of them were wearing hard hats and hazmat suits, and all about the walls were warning signs for radiation. Above their heads a speaker said, *'The NPP is running at optimal capacity. All departments are in Green. For more information, contact your line manager.'*

"What is this place?" she asked.

"*Mon cher*, you're going to love it here."

She froze. Suddenly she recognised the smiling face beneath those mucky goggles. Just to help her, he removed them so his blue eyes could dance freely and his blonde hair remained slick to his head.

"Pierre!" she snapped, sounding angrier than she was feeling. "How?"

He hurried over, taking her arm to guide her further down the corridor and away from watchful eyes.

She went on. "How? I saw the raid. I saw what they'd done-"

The corridor took on a change as tracks in the ground

allowed for automated mining trolleys to bring rubble to an unloading area. Guys driving buggies with flashing lights on the back sped off down adjacent passages, and warnings to workers were constant. Still, she noticed none of this as she kept her eyes glued to him. "I thought you'd been killed because I saw Vord's body being dragged out."

"It was bad. It was very bad," he said, his smile finally dropping.

"So Vord, he's…"

He was unable to find the right words, but he directed her down a passage leading into a room so large that several trucks could've easily fit inside. And to top it off were two mechanised doors sat partly open, exposing men in suits carrying detailed electronics, scanning what looked like a massive reactor. There was no doubt about it; she'd walked into a nuclear power plant.

One man turned and had his suit unzipped, making it easier to pull down so that he could shout, "Get that boy out of here, Pierre. We don't want his sort around here."

She coughed against the laughter as Vord came marching over, his angry smile one of the best things she'd seen in a long time.

"I never thought I'd be so happy to see you guys," she admitted.

Vord rolled his eyes but Pierre said, "Come, I think there's much to explain."

They'd called it a penitentiary, and they hadn't been wrong. At one point, cells containing the worst of the worst had busied the upper levels of the Dwells, and one such room may well have held Garboa. But in an extraordinary move, Devron had flushed them out and changed the cells to bunkhouses for imprisoned Undesirables. At first it hadn't made any sense, but now that Vord explained that the Dwells had always been a fully functioning nuclear power plant, and that inmates were used as cheap labour, it fit perfectly. After all, Bandits weren't the easiest to train up, and Devron needed the facility more than he needed the prison.

Many of the cell-blocks had been gutted of their bars and walls, leaving huge halls transformed into training areas and workshops. Some had been fitted with false partitions and bunks, housing over fifty men and women that'd live out their sentence there, being assigned jobs they likely weren't qualified to do, but doing them all the same.

Vord and Pierre had claimed a corner of one such room as their own and they'd decked it out with furnishings and supplies. She didn't know how they'd managed it, but Vord had mentioned that his contacts within the PEA were extensive.

"Devron questioned me for days," Vord said as he mended a PDA whilst sitting on his bed. She was sitting on Pierre's bunk eating rations. "I didn't break until the end, and even then I only told him that my base was the only one left and there weren't any other Palacers about. He didn't believe me, but honestly he didn't seem to care. He thinks he's won the war against CTG's and he couldn't be more wrong."

She looked to Pierre. "He beat you up?"

Vord laughed. "He broke in minutes. Told them everything."

"No I didn't! I just told him who I was. I knew they'd run my profile and that'd alert a few of my contacts. It was *my* friends in the Agency that got us transferred here and lost us in the system, remember." He turned to Val at this point, saying, "Devron hasn't even bothered trying to look for us, maybe thinking we're dead. This place is a shambles. When the time comes, escaping will be easy, but we just aren't sure when the best time will be."

She didn't say anything, but she knew his contact must've been Erga.

"Anyway," Pierre went on, "I was shocked when your ID showed up yesterday. I've been walking that atrium for hours looking for you."

She should've been grateful, but she couldn't pull it off. No matter what, she still held the resentment over the fact that he'd never told her about Jim or Erga. She changed the subject, asking, "Did they salvage much from the base?"

Pierre shook his head. "It was my fault they'd found us. I opened communications looking for any surviving Groups because I'd heard of raids taking place. The next thing I knew, Devron was shouting down my line because he'd infiltrated a base linked to ours, one of the last covert groups. I… well, I panicked. Vord was unconscious after I'd pulled some of his teeth, so he'd been no good to me. I just dragged his body to the panic room and blew ATOM up."

She hadn't meant to, but she'd laughed at that.

Vord scowled. "That's two centuries of history gone, you half-wank!"

She couldn't kill the smile, but she was apologetic as she said, "I'm sorry, it just seems so typical, but if I'm honest I'd have done the same."

Vord got to his feet. "Oh, well now I feel miles fucking better. And what the fuck did you get caught for? How could you've been so fucking stupid?"

That took the wind from her sails. "Agents killed Jim. I attacked them out of anger and Devron arrested me. A few things have happened since then, but I couldn't avoid getting caught."

Pierre went pale. "Jim…"

She couldn't risk him suddenly divulging the truth about their relationship, so she stood up as well, saying, "I have stuff I need to do."

Vord scoffed. "Like what?"

It was easy to ignore him, and by the time Pierre was up, she'd already navigated the many beds filling the hall. She needed to be above ground, that much she knew, and if it meant keeping away from Pierre and his secrets, then that'd suit her fine.

Erga had told her to get into the skills training sessions. She'd tried to do just that before Pierre had found her, and she'd been sure that she'd chosen electrical engineering. It didn't turn out to be the case.

After an awkward night of lining up for a bowl of lumpy stew, and finding an empty patch of ground to camp on within the atrium, she'd woken to yet another cafeteria rush. She'd joined in, not too impressed with the porridge hosed into her bowl that'd tasted far too much like the stew from before, but she'd sat beside a fellow wearing a hard hat. It'd gone against her better judgement, but she'd asked, "Where do people go to work?"

At first she'd assumed he'd ignored her, but he'd eventually finished his chore of a breakfast and tapped his hard hat. "Know where the works are?"

"Yeah."

"To there. Go up, not down."

He'd left with his bowl empty and she'd done the same soon after. Sure enough, the top right of the atrium which led to the NPP also had a security booth before a pair of reinforced doors where men and women were lining up to be scanned. She followed suit, trying not to look awkward as the line trickled down, before stopping at the booth where an Agent said, "Be still."

She avoided looking at the Black Eye, but it picked up her chip all the same.

"Walker 33GR/E163D. Assigned to kitchen. Move through and await your call."

She'd staggered backwards from the door when it'd sunken in. "No, I chose engineering."

"Well now you're in the kitchen. Move."

The door swung open and several officers with an armed Agent were collecting Walkers into groups. She was almost bustled through by other prisoners, and most instinctively found their groups waiting in the wide, almost sterile corridor that felt like a different building from that of the mucky atrium. The ceiling was almost fifty feet above and a corridor went beside the stairs to what looked like a school of some sort. This had to be a new-build; it just looked too clean.

"Kitchens," one officer called, urging people over.

"Technical labs, this way," another called, of which that group seemed much smaller. The temptation to join it had almost won, but with slumped shoulders and a heavy sigh, she took her place amongst thirty frightful looking Walkers by the stairs.

"This should be fun," she mumbled, garnering a few looks before they were directed for the stairs at gunpoint.

At least the kitchen workers were expected to shower before each session, and she'd ended up spending so long in the communal bathroom that an Agent had hurried her out.

She left the showers wearing a white overall over thin shorts and a vest that'd been pulled from a hamper. She and several other new-starters were taken down a corridor lined with tall windows overlooking the east side of the penitentiary's grounds. This was technically the first floor, but it was still a good eighty or so feet up.

The first thing she saw was a stand-alone structure next to the prison, though it was only separated by thirty-feet. Its roof was just below her level, but a smaller penthouse-like office had been built on top with square windows revealing a round table inside, computers, and a digital whiteboard, so she assumed it was an office.

Also sharing this roof space were air-conditioning units. Between that and the office was a cordoned part of roof where a metal and concrete base was being erected. She knew it'd eventually support a buffer tower, though a small one.

It didn't take much to make her look beyond where the concrete yard around the Dwells ended on a medley of metal fences. From there spanned miles of fields flush with dark grass, some shrubs, but the distance boasted a wealth of trees. Val had never spent much time in the north, but seeing this made her wonder why.

It was almost beautiful.

"Come on," an Agent said as they were brought to a pair of doors leading into a massive kitchen. It had stations for over forty people to prepare dough, cook food, and man ovens. Everything was tiled or covered in stainless steel, and the people already set to work were red from the heat and exertion.

A rotund man in a chefs' jacket and hat came waddling over, and didn't seem keen on the sixteen new prisoners brought in. He asked, "Ever baked before?"

They shook their heads.

"Ah! Why do you do this to me?" he whined, pressing sausage-like fingers to his head. "You will have to be teamed up. You, go stir soup. You can sift flour. Little boy, go knead dough."

Val followed where he'd pointed, making for a table with a large machine punching into and tearing apart what looked like thirty-kilograms of flour and water. The prisoner already assigned to it didn't pay her much attention as he raked the product from the turning arms. Then he dragged some of it out, slamming it onto a tray where he used cutters to separate smaller portions from the rest.

"Like this," the man said, rolling the balls before dropping them on a baking tray. She looked around, wondering if this really had been what Erga had expected her to do, and took some of the dough to roll. She was slow and her specimens came out looking lumpy.

"Gotta get faster if you want to become a baker," he said.

"Oh aye, that'd be a dream," she muttered and went about rolling more.

She'd been making bread for two days now. She'd thought the strenuous exercise might do her in, but it was the dermatitis she couldn't stand. Damp hands and irritating flour had left the skin on her knuckles cracked and sore, but she'd suffered worse. At least they were allowed to take their breaks at the back of the kitchen rather than down in the cramped cafeteria.

The fat baker had been down the front when he suddenly rattled a pan and lid. "Listen now," he called, his effeminate voice travelling well over the mixers. "Gather the trays for the main office, come along."

This had happened yesterday when food was taken to the staff room down the corridor. She'd not been able to attend that one, but this time the Agents chose her row and Val was handed a tray of rolls to carry.

Eight of them walked in single file, some carrying bread, others with pots of stew, and a few with pitchers of water. Two Agents kept close eye as they passed the stairs for the last door on the right, and they went inside where a large observation window was overlooking the heaving atrium. From this angle it looked astounding; camps ran along the walls, people moved in herds, and Agents walked the platforms above. She doubted the guards would've had enough bullets to settle a riot if one ever did break out.

Agents were manning terminals and security cameras, but most turned to watch them entering. "Dinner's up!" one Agent said and seemingly out of nowhere over a score of Agents came in from other doors, unclipping their helmets that released with sharp hisses, freeing up their fed-up faces. Still, a few officers approached, looking excited for the bread.

"Are those hot cross buns?" one officer asked. "Oh great, I missed yesterday's batch."

"They went down a treat," one of the prisoners said.

Val half-ignored it. She'd spotted something to the end of the room that'd taken her interest. There was a wall there where helmets and PDA's could be plugged in to charge, but also an Agent with gold chevrons running down his shoulder-armour was standing with another, as well as a smaller man wearing a long brown coat, riding goggles, and thick gloves. She knew that look as he was a Peace Ranger; bounty hunters for the PEA.

"Get in, these are massive," said one Agent when he'd made it to the trays, grabbing rolls in both hands.

"Fresh out the oven," the same prisoner said.

"I hope you lot ain't been spitting in these," another Agent grumbled, to the chagrin of others.

"We wouldn't dare," another prisoner insisted.

"I would," Val muttered. She hadn't. Not yet...

Her eyes wandered back to the Agents. Their conversation seemed tense and now that most of the Agents had taken their food to the tables, she could just about hear them.

The most senior Agent said, "To scan prisoners takes time. This ain't the same as AbysMA. People get lost in here. People die and we don't find out until their bodies are processed, and if you ain't noticed we got a backlog. If she ain't been showing up…"

The Peace Ranger looked listless. "Are you kidding me? How do you keep tabs on people?"

The senior Agent said, "We normally wait for them to turn up at the cafeteria..."

"Everyone's gotta eat," the other Agent added.

"I have a legal writ here," the Ranger said, trying not

to get annoyed as he took out his PDA. "It needs acting upon."

The Senior Agent said, "We'll see what we can do, but if you want-"

Val was nudged by another prisoner who nodded to her empty tray. "We're done here. Move."

She didn't argue as they continued out; anything to get her away from that lot. But she noticed the prisoner who'd urged her out was keeping awfully close. She'd been about to say something when he'd leaned over and dropped his tray atop of hers.

"Thanks mate, anything else?" she asked angrily, but he didn't seem to care as they were allowed into the kitchen by an Agent. Once in, he said, "Take them to the sinks and check them all before throwing them in the water. Check them first, got it?"

"Right, will do," she grumbled, too tired to argue as she trudged to the back where the basins sat in rows. She threw them on the side and tossed the top tray into the suds without checking it. However, this exposed a cloth bag on the tray beneath and for too many seconds she just stared at it. Then her heart skipped as she came to the realisation of what this was and did her best to subtly unzip her overalls to slip it inside.

She'd finished dunking the trays by the time the others had brought back their soiled kitchenware. From there she hurried back to her workstation looking for the bloke who'd slipped her the items. He wasn't about and she wasn't surprised. At least now she could plan on getting some real work done.

CHAPTER 44

44

As he peered into the bottom of the well, the wind kicked up dust as sharp as glass. His goggles and cumbersome coat protected him, but little rocks would hit the flesh between his breathing mask and goggles and it'd sting. Still, it didn't distract him from the skeletal remains that lent its name to Dead Man's Well. At eleven years old, he had quite a job climbing up in order to see down, but he was captivated as he dangled there.

"Rocky," shouted his father by a derelict building still standing when so many had turned to dust. Sand was all they could see for miles around as the earth had been levelled by storms, and what little remained was as skeletal as the well's lodger.

Rocky ran to him, adjusting his clothes that'd belonged to his older brother, altered by his mother, but not washed unfortunately. Still, at least he was able to get out of the base for a change. It was time they stopped treating him

235

like a kid and keeping him locked away with the women-folk back in the bunkers.

His father slapped Rocky's arm. "Hold that properly!" he barked over the mounting wind. Rocky almost dropped his rifle, but he repositioned it so that the barrel pointed up. "Getting lazy will get us killed."

Rocky wasn't lazy, he was tired, but he'd not tell his father that.

They climbed a ridge overlooking miles of open land, with dilapidated buildings in the distance and a huge road covered in dry earth, as well as rusted cars leading over the horizon. In the midst of these metal corpses were a handful of people and it made Rocky's knees instinctively bend; he wanted to get to cover, to hide, but when Father continued down, he realised these were the people they'd been sent to meet.

They waved as they approached and showed relief in their handshakes. One man took Rocky's father by the elbows and squeezed endearingly, saying something that was too muffled for Rocky to hear. But one of them barged to the front and pointed at Rocky. His words barely left his mask, but his father had understood and staggered at what he saw. Rocky even corrected his rifle, thinking he'd been holding it wrong again, but his father dropped to one knee before him and grabbed something from the ground. It was the handset to the radio Rocky had been carrying on his back; it'd slipped from its pack and he'd been unknowingly dragging it along the road, ruining it in the process.

"You dropped this!" he barked through his mask.

"Papa, I didn't know," he began, but he couldn't speak as he was grabbed by both arms and shaken violently.

"How are we to radio home now? What if something happens? You idiot, *idiot* child!" As his shakes turned to attacks, the men jumped on him, dragging him off his son.

One of the men said, "If you'd beaten the road as hard as you beat him, you'd have made it to us hours sooner, huh? Settle, I will fix this."

"We don't have time," another said. "Men were seen off to the East…"

Rocky's father cursed, still angry from his son's failings, but he asked, "The soldiers?"

"No, didn't look like soldiers."

"It's no problem," the other man said as he knelt before Rocky, taking up the handset of which the casing crumbled.

"I've ruined everything," Rocky whimpered.

"No, you haven't," the older man said. "But you have at least learnt a valuable lesson. Know what that is?"

Rocky sniffed through his tears and shook his head. The man held his chin and went to speak, but there was a sudden gush of red before the man threw himself into the small boy. The blast had made a dry sound that'd echoed in his ears more than the valley, and Rocky was caught under his him as the man's open head pumped blood.

The group dropped, finding cars to hide behind and shouting for someone to see who'd taken that shot.

"*Papa!*"

His words were lost over the raining gunfire. Rocky couldn't tell who was shooting and managed to push himself behind the same car as his father.

"Keep tight," one man shouted.

"I see two at my five."

"Two at my six! Not soldiers! They're not-" His words were cut off by gunfire.

"Hold this line!" his father barked. "*Just hold this line!*"

A man flew back in a similar fashion as the first. Rocky saw a huge part of his gasmask had been torn from his face. He twitched as if trying to sit up to take his gun, but he was blind and senseless. Eventually, he was left quivering on the ground.

"Boy, do you have your gun?" his father barked. Of course he could see it, but Rocky still took it up and said, "Yes Papa!"

"Shoot! Don't aim, just shoot!"

"They have us. They have us." shouted a man, shooting off towards an area of the landscape whilst another shot in a completely different direction. Rocky dared not look.

A man cried, "I don't see them. Where are they?"

"I see a-"

The third man lost most of his neck. His death was fast, but he'd been conscious enough to realise he'd been struck and his eyes were wide with fear as he lay motionless.

Ting ting ting as bullets hit the car. Some went straight through. A window shattered, a bare wheel spun as sparks flew…

His dad cried, "Rocky, Fire! Fire at them!" His eyes were pleading. It was as if he needed his son more in that moment than ever in his life, yet Rocky couldn't muster the strength to lift the gun. All he could remember thinking was *I hope I die so he doesn't take me home and tell everyone how scared I was*.

A bang, a flash of blinding light, and then silence save for the ringing in his ears. Rocky had the sense of being lost and held onto the car as if he'd float away if he didn't. His vision returned one patch at a time, but sound took longer.

His father was unloading every bullet. The last of their group went down, rolling about in agony. Just as his dad turned to shout, a bullet took out the top of his face, ripping through his temple in slow motion, and feeding Rocky vivid images that'd never be unseen.

In a moment that felt unending, he realised he was now surrounded with bodies.

As his hearing returned, the sound of his own sobs frightened him. He threw he face down into his arms and cried, waiting for the very last bullet to end him. Instead, hands landed on his shoulders and he screamed.

"*Non*! *Non*!" the boy cried. "*S'il vous plait non*! *Momi*!"

"What the fuck?" Jayms asked as he tore off his mask to see the boy better. "Just a kid?"

"Oh fuck, did we just kill a bunch of frogs trying to get home?" asked Gaber.

"Ssh!" Ashley said. "He can hear you."

Gaber barked, "He can't fucking understand us, though. Can he?"

"No," Jayms said. "What do we do?"

"We gotta take him with us," said the fifth member of the group as he approached, his radio still in hand. His bright eyes were barely visible behind his scowling expression, of which Erga had always been known for.

"No we fucking don't," Jayms scoffed.

Erga held up his radio. "Well I just called it in and Anderson said to bring him back. You want to argue with him?" He held out the device, but Jayms didn't respond.

Ashley stooped to the boy, trying to get him to look at her. His pleas were in another language, but they knew who his cries were for. In the end, he relented and she hoisted him up, his sobs wetting her shoulder.

"Great, another mouth to fucking feed," Jayms growled and led the group west for extraction.

Val had never seen Pierre looking so old before. He may've been ten years younger than Jim at around thirty or so, but he was starting to resemble him an awful lot.

"I'm sorry your dad died," she said, sitting on his bunk within the hall half-filled with weary workers. Vord wasn't about, which had been why she'd finally broken and told Pierre all she knew about his relationship with Jim. In return, he'd told her about how they'd first met. "Well, I'm not really sorry. He actually sounded like a prick. I think you were better off here in London than over there, but I'm sorry that…"

Pierre was smiling at her attempt at empathy. "It's fine." He sat up from Vord's bunk, rubbing his face and sighing. "It was another life, but I am the one who is sorry. I should've told you about how me and Jim had met, and how we'd come to be almost family."

"And then enemies?"

"He'd hated me for ditching Anderson, and for joining the PEA with Erga." He shrugged as he picked at his overalls. "What can I say? I just didn't buy into Anderson's schemes. He thought there was a civilisation out there in the Unknown World and was willing to risk everything to get there."

She was silent as she considered this.

Pierre said, "I honestly thought Jim would've told you."

"He probably would've eventually. Then he died and it took Devron to tell me the truth. Can't imagine a worse way to find out."

He looked exasperated. "It's not easy to start a conversation such as that. What was I to say? *By the way, Val, did you know your parents were radicalised extremists who believed the*

Unknown World held the secrets to the universe, and that they'd killed dozens of people to progress plans on finding the Promised Land?"

"Yeah, that would've done fine."

He sighed.

"Did Jayms believe the same?"

He looked troubled. "I don't know. He acted like he did but, frankly, I think he just saw Anderson as the dad he never had. It might've been why we'd feuded because Anderson had always treated me well. Even after I'd betrayed him and left with Erga, he'd always spoken to me like he loved me."

"Why didn't Jim go with them on the last mission?"

"Leg injury, I believe. Took a bullet to the knee and he might've caught the Sickness. I suppose he'd been tasked with looking after you due to it. I'm more than sure they'd expected to return. When they hadn't, he must've been overwhelmed and thought the orphanage was a better place for you."

"Yeah, it had been for a while."

She pushed closer to the edge of the bed to speak more openly. "You'd been an Agent when I'd first met you. I'd crawled into your car to steal your gun, but when you'd caught me did you have any idea who I was?"

"No, I promise you that. I'd thought you were just some poor girl from the Quad. I'd held onto you because I'd known a Mist was coming. Letting you go could've seen you killed."

"So when I finally led you to Jim, when you two were shouting-"

"It was the shock! Honestly, I'd thought he'd died, so to see him alive and with you was just… it was amazing. Neither of us had known how to handle it. I mean, it'd been ten years nearly."

"Had Jim ask you to keep an eye on me and give me a job?"

"Did he fuck. No," he laughed. "I think Jim was upset I'd made contact with you again. But I'd finally ditched the Agency once and for all and Vord had taken me on full time. I just wanted to give you a chance and, if I'm honest, I was worried Jim had turned you into a merc."

She chuckled, but she didn't explain why. Instead she asked, "So you'd had nothing to do with rescuing me from Garboa?"

"No."

"It was all Erga?"

"And Jim. I never got the full story. All I know is Jim found you in that camp and couldn't rescue you on his own. He must've told Erga and whether the Agency had always planned on wiping out the Bandits or not, it'd happened."

She sighed heavily as she stood up. "And then Devron ruined it all."

"Yeah, he's a twat. Where are you going?"

"I have a shift in the kitchens to go to."

"You really like it up there, don't you?"

"Got you free buns, didn't it? Listen, I probably won't be back down here in a while. If you get out of here before then, do me a favour."

"We're not leaving without you."

She gave him the hard stare.

"All right, fine, what you need?"

"Don't let Vord go mad."

He gave her a sideways look.

"He's going like his dad, all fucky in the head. Keep him sane and stop doing all those surgeries on him. You hear? Things are going to change and, well, I think

Walkers are going to need the Palacers more than ever now."

"What you know?" he asked, genuinely curious.

She shrugged it off as she headed away, but she wanted to say, *'jack shit,'* because frankly she had no clue what was coming. She just hoped when her end came, a new beginning for the Quads would finally start, as long as Erga kept his end of the bargain that is.

CHAPTER 46

46

It was a stupid idea. She'd known it as soon as she'd started. Who hides in flour? How many crime novels had ERD ever read where the criminal got away scot-free because they'd thought, *you know what makes for a good plan? Flour. Flour makes for a good plan.*

She'd started work as normal that morning and had waited for the shift to end. It'd dragged on until the late evening hours, and then she'd nicked off into the dry-stores where the flour was kept. She'd dived in just after the last of the Agents had walked out. It'd taken hours for the kitchens to finally shut down, and now that she'd not heard a sound for a while, she slid out coughing and itching.

She felt her way through the dark and cracked open the door just an inch. A few lights allowed for minimal visibility, but it was enough for her to find fresh overalls to change into. She made sure she still had the bag of tricks Erga's contact had provided, and fished from it the first weapon of choice; a mucky-looking key card. As hoped, the door clicked when she scanned it and a quick peek revealed the corridor was dark and empty. When she was confident enough, she darted across the corridor for the doors giving access to the adjacent building. A quick scan of the card and she was through where she paused for a moment after the doors closed, making sure she really had gone unnoticed.

'You're a sneaky one,' Jim's voice echoed. She always recalled how he'd catch her creeping around the ship, not necessarily looking for anything, just restless. And he'd always find her. Despite his big boots, heavy coat, and scarred lungs that'd make his breaths rattle, he'd always move about unnoticed.

The passage she was in now was dark and windowless. It was almost thirty feet long before the next set of doors opened freely, giving access to the conference room. Most of the walls were lined with windows; the tough, triple-glazed kind with sills integrated with buffer technology. The view wasn't much to go on since the only light came from the watchtowers every three hundred yards, though she could now better see the grounds before the penitentiary. It looked as if it was being kitted out as an exercise yard. On the other side, where the roof led to what she assumed were air-conditioning units, was the finished buffer tower. It was powered down, so approaching it shouldn't be a problem, or so she hoped.

She slid a screwdriver from her bag and mumbled, "A window will be loose. It'll give access to the roof. Well, not this one."

She was repeating the instructions on the note she'd found in the bag, except that first window hadn't budged. The next one popped free with a little persuasion from the screwdriver and she pushed it wider in order to slide out.

The cool air smelt like emissions, but at least it didn't make her itch.

She shuffled to the back of the tower to hide from anyone who might walk by the windows. She even remained motionless for a moment in case she'd alerted either of the watchtowers. As the silence stretched, she collected herself yet again. It was only now that she realised she'd practically escaped one of the most feared places in the Known World and yet freedom hadn't even crossed her mind. To think of it, the Dwells may well be awfully grim, but it wasn't the hellish place it had once been. If she allowed herself time to consider it, maybe the change was for the best and the Dwells was the key people needed for accessing a better life and future for their children. Maybe through this scheme, though harsh, the PEA were achieving what the Palacers and all those other CTG's had been striving for over the past century and a half?

She looked down at her mucky, cut up hands and wondered what life would've been like if she'd grown up in a complex like a Casual. Then her fists tightened as she realised that such a life would've surely been hers anyway if Bandits hadn't captured and tortured her for years; the very same creatures Devron had made a deal with and tossed right back down into the Wastes to torment more generations of vulnerable Undesirables like her.

"Fuck him right up the arse," she growled and got to work unscrewing the hatch on the side of the tower. "If we'd wanted educating, we'd have spent our Reds on books and not Bruch." She laughed darkly to herself as she set the panel aside, revealing the blackened tunnel leading up through the tower that'd give access to those wishing to maintain its inner workings. As she poked her head inside, the deep silence magnified a voice in her head.

"There's a good chance you'll get caught," Erga had said after he'd cuffed her to the chair back in Devron's office. *"I can't guarantee you won't get shot, either."* He'd slapped her hard enough to swell her eye, making her *capture* look authentic. *"You came here expecting to die. If you're still willing to give your life for a cause, then this is your chance to make a difference. Just survive long enough to see it through. If you live-"*

"*I won't*," she'd said pointedly.

"If you do, I'll make it worth your while."

"It'd have to be something fucking freaky to make me survive this," she muttered as she took several items from her bag.

"What do you know about sandstick compounds?" Erga had asked.

"Plastic explosive that blows like a pancake. A little goes a long way."

"Think you can make a sandstick device?"

"I can make anything if I have the parts."

The two sticks of explosive plastic came in fabric packets that she tore with her teeth and warmed in her hands, bending them until they formed a circle with each other. The detonator came already made, like a metal starfish that she pressed into the middle of the plastic sticks. With it came the remote, a small, round device with a trigger-switch that, once used, would detonate the bomb as well as breaking the trigger-switch into several smaller pieces for easy disposal.

To link the two devices, she pressed a tiny red button on both the trigger-switch and the detonator. It gave no indication that it'd linked, but she wasn't going to risk playing around with it anymore and climbed further inside the tower. It took far too long to do, but she'd made space behind a panel and fastened the explosive at a forty-five degree angle using wires, all whilst ensuring she didn't damage anything; the last thing she wanted was for an error to draw technicians back in to investigate.

"You'll need to be near it to detonate the device. That's something I can't avoid," Erga had whispered as he'd travelled with her in the back of the wagon to the precinct for further interrogations. *"If you cop out, our deal is over."*

"Over my dead body," she muttered as she clambered back through the window. Regardless of what deal she'd made with Erga, what she had with Devron was personal.

47

She'd spent the rest of the night in the dry-stores, losing all track of time. Still, she slipped out once the workers spilled in, but noticed there was an air of excitement about them. Even the fat baker had turned up early and was calling for cake mix.

She kept her head down, hoping she'd not missed something important. Then the doors opened and in came several Agents with their guns drawn. The Senior Agent took to the front as he ordered the mixers to be switched off, and for a time he only watched them. Val shrunk out of sight, peeking out from around another prisoner as the Agent finally addressed them.

"The opening of the new complexes in Quad: North is happening tomorrow. Commander Devron and Prime Minister Andrews will be here in a few hours for a meeting and a photo opportunity. Its purpose is to show the Known World that what's happening here is for the betterment of everyone. Due to this, twenty of you are going to be selected for early release and domestication into Quad: North. The rest of you will be required to finish your sentences here as first outlined."

Tension grew. No matter how tame the Dwells had become, they wanted out.

"Those I point at are to leave. The rest remain at your stations for further instructions."

He showed no emotion as he flicked his fingers at seemingly random faces, as if he was delivering a fatal shot. He went along the lines, picking off the majority of them before moving onto the next row. For whatever reason, his eyes hadn't even landed on Val whilst several around her wept due to being chosen. Once they were marched out, those that remained were patting each other on the back and smiling.

Val wasn't.

The Senior Agent returned to the front once more and said, "The rest of you will need to pose for pictures. You may even get to speak to Commander Devron and Prime Minister Andrews. Until then, you're to get cleaned up and be on your best behaviour. If any of you show me up…"

He didn't need to finish.

At that they left and the remaining Agents gathered them up for the showers.

Clean clothes, clean hats, and clean faces were all the Agents were looking for as the score of prisoners were led from the washrooms. Val had the trigger-switch in her bra; there was an odd comfort with it being so close to her heart.

'Devron and Andrews have to die,' Erga had whispered before she'd been thrown into the back of that cattle truck. *'I'd understand if you got cold feet-'*

"I won't," she muttered as she waited with the others standing behind an Agent who was watching the corridor. The stairs were in sight and atop them were ten or so Casuals and officers. Some were holding notepads and recorders, others had filming equipment, and the fat baker was standing before the kitchen doors looking pleased with himself.

From where she was standing, she could see the buffer tower. Its sides gleamed from where the generators had been fixed into place and were now powering it. It'd make a tidy explosion and no mistake.

The Agents stopped them a way back down the corridor. Those about the stairs were growing in excitement and cameras flashed as people approached. She partly hid as Devron emerged at the top step, smiling with a bright set of white teeth and his hair slicked back. He'd tarted himself up for the occasion.

Following was baby-faced Prime Minister Andrews, out of breath and looking awkward. He hung back as Devron spoke to Casuals, greeted Agents, and posed for pictures. He even flinched when Devron nudged his elbow, reminding him to smile. They made a fitting couple she thought with little amusement and watched as the Senior Agent guided them to the doors leading to the adjacent building.

Val rubbed at her collarbone, her fingers itching to get hold of the trigger-switch. She'd have grabbed it if it weren't for the Senior Agent returning, and he raised a hand as if to usher them over. He paused when a commotion sounded at the bottom of the stairs, and the man who climbed to their level made the Senior Agent look visibly irritated. She couldn't see why until the Agent backed off, snapping, "This really isn't the time!"

Her heart skipped as the Peace Ranger was exposed. The Senior Agent was urging him back down the stairs, but he pushed his PDA closer and said, "Just look!"

It took a few seconds of reading before the Agent finally asked, "You sure?"

"She was scanned this morning. I have it here."

Val tasted bile. She'd thought nothing of being scanned before their shower. *He's not here for me,* she thought, rubbing her chest. *It's not me he's after.*

The Senior Agent pushed the PDA back in the Ranger's hand and marched towards the prisoners. Val slinked further out of sight, but the Agent said angrily,

"One of you apparently has a writ out for your extraction. We'll need to scan you all again."

"No need," the Ranger said. "Her description states she's around fifteen, dark skinned, and female." He glanced at some of the darker prisoners. "Goes by the name Val?"

Silence.

"Don't fuck around!" the Agent began, glancing back at the conference room. "I don't need this on-"

Prisoners made startled cries as Val tore from the group.

"Catch her!" the Ranger barked as she ran for the windows. Guns were drawn but no one took the shot, so she slammed against the glass with her hand in her bra, squeezing the trigger-switch that cracked like a metal egg as she snapped the button in.

She was thrown back as Agents grabbed her shoulders, tossing her face down into the ground before being dog-piled. But there'd been no explosion.

Her hands were zip-tied before she was thrown on her back where the Ranger hurried over and nodded excitedly. "This looks like her!" Ten seconds later and her hat was knocked off so he could scan her. The bleeps had the Ranger cackling.

The Senior Agent snapped, "Just get her moved, now!"

She hadn't even been given the chance to stand as her entire body was lifted off the floor. With the Ranger in tow, Val was hurried off.

48

It was odd being in the back of a sedan. It felt every bump, stank of exhaust fumes, and each hard turn had her sliding about the back seat. She couldn't see the driver due to the partition, and even the windows had been blacked out. She had no idea where she was going as the Ranger hadn't said a thing.

It was also an odd experience to still be alive.

The bomb hadn't detonated and she couldn't think what she'd done wrong. She was no explosives expert, but even she could wire a bomb. But for whatever reason it'd failed, and now as the car came to a stop and her door was pulled open, the bright white light of the day made her squint.

He gave her no time to register the situation before hauling her out. There he stood at barely a few inches taller than her, but stronger and angrier. Behind him was a taller fellow, older by a score, in a neat black suit and tie.

He looked confused and she was of the same disposition. She guessed he was a butler and it made sense when she looked about the stunning street. There were no houses, just mansions! Each one on its own plot of land with manicured bushes, black fences, and crystal-like Solid-State buffer towers ever six hundred yards or so. This was a Royal district.

"One Walker, matching ID, as described," the Ranger said.

"Quite…" the butler mumbled. "Right this way, ma'am."

"Err, 'scuse me," the Ranger said, tapping his PDA. "My creds?"

"They've been paid in advance to the office. Once we verify her for ourselves, the funds will be released."

"Are you kidding me?" the Ranger cried as she was guided through the gates for a long yard centred with a stone fountain. "Do you know how long I searched for her?"

The butler didn't look back, but she did and he cussed a bit before getting back into his sedan. He tore off up the street as they climbed the steps to a black front door that opened on a young, wide-eyed looking woman.

"Where am I?" Val asked.

"Chelsea. West London," the butler said as she was guided inside. The foyer boasted a grand staircase with a magnificent oil painting on the largest wall. It depicted an old war fought on horseback and had a shiny golden frame. The wallpaper was dark and the furniture was plush, but there was a strong smell of disinfectant.

"Who lives here?" she asked.

"This is the Alsguard family home, with Master and Lady Alsguard as well as their two daughters. Now please follow Ilain. She'll help you get cleaned up."

She was taken beyond the staircase to a servant's passage. A boy in a storeroom gawked as she passed, and a door at the end opened to another maid. "Oh, is this her?" she asked, looking Val up and down.

"Hey," Val greeted and went inside to see a bath spilling bubbles and steam. It smelt amazing.

"Now, I don't want any funny business from you," Ilain said as she tested the water. "I want you in this tub and scrubbed up with no messing around. Don't make me call the Agents, all right?"

Val was still.

"Well?" Ilain asked. "What are you waiting for?"

She smiled as she unzipped her overalls. "A coffee wouldn't go a miss."

Ilain looked amazed, but the young maid chuckled as she left to do as requested. Val leapt into the tub where the bubbles spilt onto the floor. "Oh god, this is lush," she groaned, stretching out and sinking beneath the surface where the water stung the cut to the back of her head. She surfaced with a satisfied sigh and suddenly didn't feel all that bad about surviving anymore.

"Comfortable?" came a soft voice.

"It'd be better with that coffee," she said before glancing to the door where she'd expected to see a maid. Rather, it was a girl her age with long blonde hair, a smile, and teary eyes. She came over and knelt beside the bath, taking Val's hand in her own where Val realised several fingers were missing as well as some of her thumb.

Her heart skipped a beat as the girl said, "Welcome home, Val."

They'd tried to get her into a dress, but Val wasn't having it, so they'd provided her with a pair of jeans, a blue shirt, and a bandana for her bald head. They'd even taken her stitches out and left a few antibiotics with her coffee. Now she was sitting on a couch with a family of strangers except one, the girl she remembered as Drea.

They'd both been very young when they'd had shared a bunk back in the Sacred Hearts orphanage. Drea had been one of only a few faces she could recall, well, not so much her *face* but her hand. Back then she'd been cute, but now she was positively stunning. She'd grown into a gorgeous young woman with a full face, pert features, dark blonde hair and an overly-skinny figure that the Casuals seemed to love.

The woman sitting next to her was her older adoptive sister, and while her blonde hair was fake, she was no less pretty. In an armchair was adoptive mother, her hair now naturally brown and set in curls, and though she sported plenty of wrinkles, make-up worked well to cover them up. Between them was a tea table that the maid had filled with china and some finger cakes, of which Val had helped herself to plenty.

"This is nice," Val said, looking about the room. One wall held a huge window where the fake light from the many emitters about the street could shine through. The other wall was filled with books that looked brand new and free of distress, unlike the books she occasionally found in the Quads. It made her think of ERD and she asked, "Do you read much, Drea?"

"It's *Andrea*," Lady Alsguard said sternly, and for the

second time as well. "I was quite clear before, we don't do *nicknames* in this house."

"What's Val short for?" Ivanna asked.

"It's not short for anything," Andrea said knowingly.

"Valery?" Lady Alsguard suggested.

"Valentina?" Ivanna asked.

"Andrea's right, it's just Val. Always Val."

Andrea set her cup down as she said excitedly, "You'll love it here. I've prayed for this day for so long and now we can be together again, like proper sisters."

Lady Alsguard stiffened, but she kept her opinions to herself, for now.

Andrea went on, "I've been asking around for you for years. A family friend was the one who found you. He'd said you'd been naughty and that he'd had you *bang to rights*," she whispered, as if it would be their little secret. "I asked him to bring you and at first he wasn't going to and Mother had been nervous, but I convinced them and then… well, he said you'd been released accidentally and that he couldn't find you. I thought maybe he'd just been saying it, but he promised to find you again, just for me, and here you are."

Lady Alsguard said, "Your name was on Andrea's lips the moment she first walked through our door. We couldn't understand her fixation in the beginning, but then she explained how she'd saved your life and it'd made sense."

Val looked to Andrea but she refused to catch her eye. Still, her cheeks had reddened.

"As long as my daughter loves you then this is your home," she went on. "Do not abuse such a privilege as the safety of my family outweighs my want to please her. Trust me, *Val*, I have not brought you here lightly."

Andrea took her mother's hand. "I'll never ask for

another thing. I promise. I'm happier now than ever before."

She patted Andrea's leg before standing. She said, "I hope you find it comfortable here. In the meantime, seek the maids if you need anything and be sure to watch yourself and your conduct. Take a single step out of line and I will reprimand you, heavily. I'll see to dinner. Father will be home shortly. Ivanna, you can help me."

Ivanna had wanted to stay, but together they left the reading room and Andrea sat next to Val.

"So," Val said, "*you* saved *me*, did you?"

She looked guilty. "I never actually told her that. Well, not really. I barely remember it, to be fair. It was all a blur, but of course I remember how you'd pushed me into the cupboard. If you hadn't, I'd have been captured, too. But you obviously did all right if you're here now. Did the Agency rescue you? Where have you been living?"

"It's a long story."

She grabbed both of Val's hands. "I'm just so happy to see you! I've thought about you every night. I always hoped you'd end up adopted like me. How fortunate I was. You know, they only took me in as a temporary thing, to be charitable, but Mother couldn't have any more children and she just fell in love with me. I guess you didn't have a family out there if you'd ended up being a bit of a criminal. Don't worry, you'll not need to do any of that now. I can get you anything you want."

Val forced a smile.

The door opened and a young maid looked in. "Honey, we've just received a call. Ocky's been held up at the office. Lady Alsguard says dinner will be late."

"Oh," Andrea said, looking deflated as the door closed. "Dinner was supposed to be a celebration. I mean, it still will be now that you're here because I want them to meet you. But Ocky's just proposed to Ivanna and he's been too busy to celebrate.

"He's friends with so many powerful people. You'll meet them all soon. Never mind. I bet you can't wait to see your room."

Val was almost dragged from the chair and they hurried down carpeted corridors smelling of fresh flowers before reaching the staircase. Heading left, they passed beautiful photographs of the Old World and new pictures of family members. Val's room was fronted with a white door and Andrea burst through singing, *"Ta-daa!"*

An azure carpet was contrasted by gentle mint walls with cream curtains framing a huge window. An ice-blue four-poster bed sat centre stage and she even opened a door to show off her very own bathroom.

"Isn't it the best room ever?" Andrea asked, but Val didn't answer as she sat on the edge of the bed, noting just how gloriously soft it was.

Val asked, "How did you find me, Drea? You said you had a friend. Who is he?"

She was quite happy as she said, "It's Commander Devron. How amazing is that?"

She ran cold.

"He's an old family friend. He got Ocky into office and now they're two of the most powerful people in the K.W."

Val sighed as she said, "Ocky, that's Prime Minister Andrews, isn't it? Where are they now?"

"Well, I'm not really sure, but I know they had a big event planned in the Quads, something to help Walkers. They're going to be home soon and then we'll have a big dinner to celebrate, I promise." She landed on the bed next to Val. "I couldn't believe it when he'd come home and said he'd found you. He'd said he had you in a cell, of all places. But then a mistake happened and you'd been released. I thought I'd lost you."

"So he put a bounty out on me?"

"Yes, barely a week ago. It took that long to convince Father to sign off on it. I'd not known you'd been found until a few hours ago. To know you were on your way, or to even have you here now… Val, isn't this just a miracle?"

"It really is," she said in all seriousness, though she wasn't so sure who the miracle was for.

"Just you wait. You'll live so well here, you'll forget entirely of everything that came before. Now you have a family."

"But I don't belong here."

Andrea sighed. "I know. I'm not naïve. I knew you'd be different. In fact, I wasn't surprised to find out you'd ended up in prison. But with enough coaching you can change. Ocky says that Walkers are changing all the time, now. They're becoming more civilised. Last month they even voted." Andrea leaned over to take both of Val's hands once again. "Just promise me you'll do your best to fit in. Promise to try."

Val wasn't so sure, but Andrea looked as if she might put on a serious sulk, so she nodded. "I promise that, while I'm here, I'll try to fit in."

She beamed. "If anyone can help you do it, I can. Bernie says I'm like a poster child for change. I was born in the Wastes and no one wanted me. I should've ended up a drug-addled rad-walker, but I did my best to be a good girl and now look at me. He says anyone can be a civilised human being as long as they work hard and be - oh!"

Val had suddenly coughed and it'd cut Andrea off. It was forced and noisy and Andrea watched on as Val shook her hand as if to say 'don't worry'.

"Oh man, my throat's dry," Val finally said, sounding hoarse. "I could smash a drink right about now."

"Well, I'll grab you one. Just wait here. Don't go anywhere."

"I won't. I'll wait," she said and smiled pleasantly as Andrea closed the door. Once alone, she sighed heavily and fell backwards into the bed.

"I fucked up good, Jim." She allowed her eyes to close as her head continued to whirr. "Real good."

For a while, all Andrea had done was show off all the clothes in Val's new bedroom. It was surprising to see that she'd been preparing for this day for so long. What was more astounding to Val was that Erga must have had a much greater involvement in Val's release from the precinct since Devron had assured Andrea that he'd return Val to her. Erga had prevented that and it'd left Val wondering how things would've turned out if she'd ended up at the Alsguard's a few weeks sooner.

Canny still would've died, but would Val have been caught in such a vengeful mind-set? And if so, would it have made things easier in offing the murderous Commander? She didn't like dwelling on *what ifs*, but she knew one thing; if Devron really was such a close family friend, then she may well get a second chance to fulfil her end of the bargain with Erga.

Andrea eventually led her down to the dining room at around quarter to eight. Ivanna and her mother were already seated when they arrived, but the maids and butler had apparently been busy in the foyer with the arrival of Master Harriet Alsguard. She hadn't understood why it needed a team of people to prepare him for dinner until he'd squeezed through door. The man was huge!

"Darling," Mother said endearingly as she kissed his sagging cheek that rested atop his many chins. The girls stood quickly in excitement to see him, but they didn't leave their places and merely waved sweetly. Then he sat as a chair was forced beneath his rotund frame and the butler pushed a napkin into his collar.

"How has your day been, darling?" Lady Alsguard

asked. Now that they were near each other, Val could tell why they'd been unable to have another child after Ivanna.

"Blasted day. Wasters everywhere, blocking roads and being a pain. Dig a pit and throw them in," he mumbled, his chins wobbling.

Andrea laughed awkwardly. "Daddy, look who's here."

He had a job opening his eyes wide enough to see due to the fatness of his brow, but he seemed suddenly aware of Val. "This her? No one told me she was so dark."

"I just look that way because everything here is so clean," Val insisted.

His cheeks wobbled as he laughed, but Lady Alsguard looked appalled.

He pointed at her head. "And this? Some sign of tribal allegiance, I dare say. Are you in a clan?"

Mother jumped in before Val could be sassy and said, "No. It was shaved by doctors. It'll grow back. Maddie, tell the cook we're ready for starters."

The maid hurried off as if her life depended on it. Maybe Master Alsguard would eat them if they were too slow?

He began to ramble. "Shame about all this rain, bleeding stuff, getting in the way of everything. And we had to divert on the way home. They're implementing one of those darn fans. As big as Parliament it is, somewhere near Mayfair. They're calling it a test, though. We're expected to have more disruptions."

The small talk continued until the butler entered with a trolley of small dishes. The maids helped serve, but Val wasn't sure what she was looking at. Andrea was straight on it, saying, "This is avocado, wheat crackers, salsa, and cheese."

"Bet you don't get any of that where you come from," Ivanna said as she nibbled a cracker.

"Of course she does," Master Alsguard huffed. "What else is she going to eat? Dust?"

Val ignored them as she ate her *starters*. She was surprised by all the tastes available in such a small dish and felt at a loss when it was all gone. Even Master Alsguard was done in one breath, though the girls seemed keen to take the littlest bites imaginable.

"I sat in on the environmental awareness discussion as well," Master Alsguard said. "Damn long guff is what I say. They say if these fans go down well, they'll build more outside the Quads. For who? Feral dogs and rats?"

"Quite, dear." Lady Alsguard humoured him before the doors opened to several maids bringing more food. This was more like it as a heartily sized meal of meat, veg, and gravy was set before them. She was even stunned to find it was real beef.

"How much does a slice of this set you back?" Val asked, prodding it with her fork.

"Excuse me?" Lady Alsguard asked.

"She wants to know what a cut of beef costs now-a-days," Master Alsgaurd said before asking, "Alclay, what's our meat ration come to now?"

The butler said, "Eighty-four credits a week."

"That little?"

"It went down since we complained about the leanness of the meat, sir."

He nodded as if he suddenly remembered.

"It's a shame Ocky and Bernie couldn't be here," Ivanna sighed. "Ocky loves beef."

"You're honestly engaged to him?" Val asked, hoping they'd burst out laughing as if it'd been some inside joke.

"Great fellow," Father said suddenly, wiping his mouth on the back of his hand. In turn the butler wiped his hand with a cloth. "Really coming out of his shell. You know, a year ago, he wouldn't leave his office. Now look at him, off here and there, giving speeches, outlining development for our city, inspecting the prison and really showing he's got some fight in him.

"He has big plans for that place. I mean, we need a prison, but what an ingenious idea of his to turn it into a correctional facility and training centre. Why pay for workers when we can get them for free, is what I say. Walkers don't know any better unless we teach them."

Lady Alsguard coughed. "Let's not talk of that dreadful place at the dinner table, dear."

"Uh, very good," he mumbled and tapped his plate with his fork. At that, the butler worked hastily to refill it with meat and veg. As he did, he spotted Val as if once again realising she was there and half-smiled as he spoke. "Must be nice to be out of that filthy place?"

"The Dwells?" she asked.

"Huh? No, Central. I remember when it was a cleaner affair, back when Walkers weren't allowed in. Those were the days."

Val said, "Before my time. It's not all bad. Can learn a thing or two working there, I guess."

"Well, you'll go to school now, be taught how to be human, no more nonsense. Proper ladylike and all that."

"School?" she sulked. "I prefer working."

"She's an engineer," Andrea said. "She builds machines."

"Engineering?" Ivanna asked. "Like, a mechanic?"

"You could work with Oscar in our garage," Andrea said as if it'd been an amazing idea. "He's been looking for an apprentice."

Lady Alsguard set down her fork so that it made a clatter. "No girl in this house is becoming a mechanic. Really, just go to school and get an education." As if realising herself, she calmed and said as pleasantly as she could, "The school Andrea goes to is open six days a week and it provides you with your own uniform, a nice hat, a bag to carry your laptop in, and every year in which you succeed will earn you a new pin for your lapel, just like Andrea."

"I have two so far."

Val scoffed. "I'd rather be a prostitute."

The gasps came in union and she realised how bad it must've sounded, so she tried to explain. "Honestly, it sounds weird, but you learn quite a bit from the other girls and it'd allow me to be flexible."

Ivanna's jaw dropped.

"Hours! Flexible hours…"

"What did that dirty Walker just say?" Father asked, turning to Alclay as if wanting it repeated.

"Daddy!" Andrea cried.

"Oh god…" Lady Alsguard groaned, coming over all weak.

Master Alsguard threw his napkin down. "I won't have that sort of talk here at my table. I'll be damned!"

Andrea flooded with tears, but Lady Alsguard gestured for a maid to comfort her as she said, "This is what happens when we speak out of turn. Think before you say something because we can't have such dismal conversation when company arrives."

The maid kissed Andrea's head whilst telling her that everything will be all right. Val could only watch. For the first time in her life, she felt like holding her tongue really was the better option.

Dinner finished around half-eight, and Val had a feeling she was the reason for its sudden end. Still, she'd eaten well and when Lady Alsguard had instructed them to go to their rooms to prepare for bed, Val had been happy to do so. However, after the maid had gone, Val had snuck out to wander the quiet house.

She crept about the second floor to find all the rooms empty. It smelt dusty, too. Not dirty, just unlived in. None of the maids bothered with the back of the house, it seemed, and she wandered idly, peering out the windows where the street lamps had been dimmed and the darkness was but a gentle sheet; nothing like the invasive blackness she experienced in the Quads.

She'd heard nothing of a radio or television for as long as she'd been there, so the sound of a radio hissing its static caught her attention. She followed it to another set of stairs, though these were narrow and without carpet, and it was hidden behind a door at the end of the corridor.

After a moment of consideration, she began climbing, eventually entering what looked like the loft. The walls were bare and the floorboards creaked, and most of the doors were closed save for the ones nearest. It was from there the static sounded and she paused before it, listening.

"I can hear you sneaking about out there. I'm blind, not deaf!" barked a man. She actually jumped, but that was as far as she went. There she remained with her breath held and feet ready to run. It must've had an effect because when he spoke next he sounded fearful. "Well? Who is it? What are you playing at? Do you think you're funny playing with an old man's nerves like this?"

His genuine fear made her feel guilty, so she said, "Sorry," and stepped into sight. "Didn't mean anything by it. I was snooping and heard the static so I…"

She trailed off not in surprise but in wonder. The old man was aged indeed, but his room was bare save for a chest of drawers lined with books beside the door, a medical bed to the far wall, and a table holding a rather fancy looking radio. Other than the curtains on the window, there was no décor. Even the carpets and wallpaper was missing.

"Who are you?" he asked. He was sitting in a wicker wheelchair with a line coming from his nose to an oxygen tank at the back. His eyes were milky from cataracts, but he could make out her outline as his eyes followed her when she entered.

"Val."

"Val… Ah, you must be *Val* Val?"

"Most just call me Val."

He laughed somewhat awkwardly, but said, "You're the girl Andrea's been talking of all these years. Are you truly her?"

"Ask her. She knows me better than I know myself."

"I would but she doesn't come up this way much anymore."

"Are you imprisoned?"

The man allowed the question to register before barking his laughter. "Goodness! I suppose I am, but it's self-imprisonment, I do suppose. It's warmer up here and I can hear the birds better. And it's close to what I love." He indicated the radio.

She came nearer to see it. The fancy rig had wiring going up the wall and through the roof, but she noticed the station he'd been testing recently was the same one the

PEA broadcasted from. She said, "You've been tuning into Devron's channel."

He looked shocked. "I say, I certainly have not. Those blundering idiots are the reason I've got this white noise to listen to." He snapped the nob to the right and the signal began to click and stutter to show it'd been jammed. "I used to hold my own little radio show, you see. A few people I know liked to listen, or so they'd say. But now…"

"What show?"

"Mainly morning ones. I'm a light sleeper, you see. It helps me pass the time."

Out of curiosity, she turned back to the drawers and eyed his books. "One of those doesn't happen to be something like *A Guide to the Galaxy* does it?"

He seemed a little dumbfounded before asking, "Do you mean *A Hitchhiker's Guide to the Galaxy*?"

"Yeah. I used to listen to someone who'd read to us over the radio. He'd once told me about a story where the character had lost his entire world and he should've died with it, but he'd been saved and taken into space where he went on all these adventures."

He started to fidget and stutter his words. He finally coughed to clear his throat and held out his hand, saying, "Then I must say that it's a pleasure to meet a fan. Hello my dear, I'm ERD."

She was a little dumbstruck as she shook it.

He said, "I had no idea my show reached outside the Quad."

"It goes as far as the edges of the Known World, maybe even further. I've seen market places go quiet just to listen to you."

It was hard to read his expressions, mainly due to age, but also due to a certain solidification to one side of his face. It wasn't like a stroke. It was almost as if part of him had turned as rigid as stone.

"I'm staggered," he whispered.

"Did you honestly not know?"

"No one around here listens to the radio. It's somewhat taboo; a restriction of free speech. But a few of those who care for me, Casuals, they listen and they used to say people liked to hear it. I always thought they were being polite."

"And Devron just took it over?"

He grew bitter. "I didn't know for a while. Then one of the porters told me. I told my daughter, Lindsy, but she didn't do anything about it. A few of my carers tried to send my shows out, but they'd have landed themselves in trouble if caught. I couldn't risk it. It's probably for the best I just let it go."

"Your show had meant a lot to people like me. It still does. Do you know how many people there are out there who've never been raised?"

He tried to answer but he couldn't find the right words.

"Thousands of kids without mums or dads, not a single guiding word their entire lives, and then there you were. You didn't judge us or call us names. You didn't tell us where we're going wrong or how undesirable we are. You made every one of us feel like we had a life to live. When everyone else wanted something, money or servitude, you asked for nothing."

She rubbed at her eyes. "My life's kind'a been falling apart recently and it all seemed to start when I lost you."

"My dear, I…"

Her tone grew sombre. "I grew up in a Bandit camp around the worst type of people, and for a while I was just like them. But then I found your channel and even though I didn't make an effort to listen, your words made their way in and stuck, so when a good man finally adopted me, I felt like I could recognise his kind heart because he… well he was a lot like you."

He must've heard her tears as he rushed to produce a white handkerchief. He said, "It's clean," as he handed it over.

"Cheers," she said, though she didn't use it. "Anyway, it's actually really awesome to be able to meet you. But what happened? To your face, I mean. And your hands? I thought you were just really old, but you look scarred."

He seemed surprised at her forwardness, but not hostile. He held up his rigid digits and said, "Let's just say I've made many mistakes in my life, but none as profound as the one which left me wheelchair-bound many years ago."

"What was it?"

He was hesitant but he admitted, "I was a foolish young man who had dreams beyond his station. I thought I could lead people to a part of this country that wasn't as plagued by the Mists and fallout, but all I did was walk myself into death."

"I hear a lot of talk about Promise Lands now-a-days," she said, begrudgingly.

"Ah, but I actually found it."

"Looks it, n'all," she mocked.

"I honestly did. It's a place well known, though for all the wrong reasons. I wasn't the first to discover it, either. Long ago, when London was too volatile to live in, our ancestors made camps to the north of here. Not under the PEA, but as free people, and we prospered. Even my Grandfather had spoken of this place where there was power, water, and low exposure, so I knew it was real.

"No one believed me and I was denied travel to find it.

So I did what all young and foolish men do and went there in secret."

"And what did you find?"

He smiled. "I found the Promised Land."

"And it put you in a bloody wheelchair?"

He scoffed, though it died down to sadness. "That was my own foolishness. I found the old bunkers left over from nearly a century before and I'd thought them safe. When a Mist hit, rather than hurry back, I took shelter inside, not realising there were years of built-up radiation in there and for as long as the Mist lasted I'd grown exposed."

"Wow…"

"They found me with acute radiation poisoning, but I was saved and, most of all, they realised I'd been right. The Promised Land existed!" His humour died to sadness. "They were able to dig deeper and they found what had caused the radiation build up. It hadn't been the geological nature of the land that'd kept our ancestors alive, but the nuclear reactor they'd built in an underground plant."

Her smile dropped. "A nuclear reactor?"

He nodded as he said, "Within ten years, they had it powering Central. It really was quite a feat."

"Is this the same nuclear reactor that just so happens to sit beneath a rather savage prison?"

"I'd been too weak to oppose them. I'd damned them all for making that place." He pressed a hand to his brow, but then he slammed his fist down on his wheelchair. "I never said they could name it after me, either!"

"What is your name?" she asked flatly.

His chin quivered. "David B. Dwells."

"You!" she snapped. "Do you know what kind of hell that place has been for my people?"

He panicked as he said, "I had no say! I never wanted it. I…" His tears made his cheeks shiny. "Please. God in heaven, forgive me." He grabbed her hand, but she tried to pull free even though he was insistent to keep hold. "Please, if you knew how much I'd opposed it, if you only knew-"

"No fucking way!" she snapped and yanked her hand back. With it he came, flying from his chair and crashing to ground.

Spiders. They weren't uncommon, but the little one that'd made a web between the door frame and the ceiling looked nimbler than the hefty buggers that used to live in her greenhouse. Val watched it as she remained hidden behind the door, squeezed between it and the set of drawers whilst the maid secured David back into his chair.

"I told you I'm fine! I just slipped, that's all," he snapped, shooing the maid away.

"I'll be back in a few minutes with a warm drink. Keep that belt buckled."

He grumbled as she left. Alone again, Val stepped out. "Quite a legacy, then?" she asked, plodding over to lean against his table.

He shifted uncomfortably. She wasn't sure if he was hurting, but she wouldn't have been surprised if so; that'd been a hard fall.

Still, he sounded annoyed as he said, "I never made that prison. I never gave it my blessing *or* my name. The reactor was a boon, but to turn it into such a place…"

"It used to be full of Bandits, but I guess they weren't very good at working in a power plant. Now it's just poor Walkers whose only crime was surviving, and they're being brainwashed into thinking that it's for the best. They're losing their freedom, having their faces washed and skulls chipped whilst being told that surrender is the key to living."

He winced.

She should've let it drop, but still she muttered, "The men behind the Dwells are monsters."

"No," he said, sounding tired now. "Not monsters. A

monster's entire nature is to be horrible. They have no excuse. Men do. Men know better."

"They need destroying, the Royals, the PEA, the Casuals who turn a blind eye, and the Agents who walk over us. Then we'd be free."

"You would think so, wouldn't you? No. You may be free for a time. It's a bit like that spider." He gestured to the doorway. "I've never seen it, but I know it's there. The maid hates them and makes an effort to vacuum it up whenever she cleans, but she always remarks how it keeps coming back. She's convinced it's the same spider."

He leaned closer to speak, as if it was a secret. "Destroy one evil man and another will take his place. It's the way of the world. They may have different eyes and accents, darker hair or lighter skin, but they will take the place of those who came before and they will do exactly the same.

"It applies to good men, too. And women. And children. Good people die daily, but good people still exist. We need to focus less on hunting the evil ones and focus more on helping the good ones. We'll always have darkness. In that sense, things will never change."

"But if killing them doesn't make things change, what will?"

"Education."

"I have to go to school to make this world a better place? Is that what you're saying?"

"Of course!"

She was growing annoyed now. "So only stupid people kill?"

"Not even remotely. And I wouldn't even say that only stupid people make great dictators. No no, the most evil people I know of are also some of the smartest. But people with less knowledge are easier to lead. And a good education doesn't just mean knowing you're ABC's, my girl. Education is knowledge in general. We learn from each other, of each other, and we become tolerant, thoughtful. We become thinkers.

"Men who think don't act on impulse, and men who don't act on impulse are less likely to hurt one another."

"But men who don't act when other men do bad things are the most evil in my book."

He smiled because he knew she was echoing quotes he'd shared on his broadcast. He said, "I've killed a man." He paused as if expecting her to comment. When she didn't, he said, "It wasn't long before I left for that land. In fact, it was his death that prompted me to go."

"Did you murder him? I mean in cold blood?"

"Would it make a difference?"

"Well, if he deserved it-"

"Who on Earth has the capacity and wisdom to solely decree what person is truly deserving of death?"

"The Bible?"

"Then yes, he deserved it. And so did the man that ate shellfish, and so did the man that laid with another man as if he had lain with a woman, and so did the woman who laid with a man without being married, and so did the man who worked on the Sabbath Day-"

Val rolled her eyes.

"You think I'm patronising you? Religion is the biggest tool of oppression in my book. Sorry, my girl. I don't mean anything personal by it, but my faith vanished many years ago. But I do know how important the Houses are to the people."

"You know what means just as much?" she asked and tapped the mic to his radio. "People who care."

He sank in his chair. "They think I've abandoned them and, to be honest, it's about time I let go. Clinging to this device had made it so much more unbearable when I'd actually lost it. It's clinging that brings suffering-"

"Fuck your wisdom. I got out of bed every morning to hear you; now all we have is that fucking pompous Devron. Pity yourself for the Dwells all you want, but if you don't get broadcasting, you'll be letting down a lot of people. If you can live with that then fine."

He seemed at odds and asked, "Should I tell them about the prison?"

She leaned down and kissed his bumpy head. "ERD don't know nothing about no prison."

He may've been half-blind, but his eyes sparkled with tears as she headed for the door.

"But how will I be heard?" he asked.

The sound of the maid's return echoed somewhere down the stairs. It was time to leave, but she said, "Leave it to me. Get practicing, okay?" Then she was gone.

"I promise," he said as he listened to her footsteps growing quieter.

CHAPTER 53

53

She'd only just made it to the first floor when she'd heard the commotion. She followed it to the foyer where Lady Alsguard, Andrea, and Ivanna were standng in their night clothes, holding each other. An Agent and the butler were at the front door.

"What's going on?" Val asked from the top of the stairs.

Andrea turned, her face soaked with tears. "They're dead. They're both dead!"

Ivanna broke down, forcing her mother and several maids to catch her.

"I simply cannot believe it. I won't!" Lady Alsguard said.

"Who?" Val asked.

"They were caught at the prison because of Bandits, apparently," Andrea said, sniffling. "Then an explosion killed them both. Ocky and Bernie are gone!"

"What exactly exploded?"

The Agent said, "A newly installed tower. One of them Solid-State kinds. It'd been wired wrong apparently. It blew up and landed on the office they'd been in and-"

"No more!" Ivanna wept. "No more. Make him *stop*!"

Val finally reached the bottom step as Ivanna was being led away. She asked the Agent, "You were there?"

"No. It happened hours ago, but we weren't permitted to give the news until confirmation was gained."

"By who?"

"Second – I mean, newly appointed Commander Roman."

Val looked astonished.

"A tragedy indeed," the butler said. "The Known World will be in mourning for the heroes taken from us this day."

Val scoffed. It'd been such a subtle noise, but all eyes turned to her. Suddenly feeling pushed to explain herself, she said, "I didn't mean anything by it, it's just that most Walkers despise the PEA and the government."

Jaws dropped simultaneously.

"Is this honestly news to you guys? I'd not be surprised if the Quads are literally celebrating right now."

Andrea began to bawl like a baby.

"*Get her out of here!*" screamed Lady Alsguard as the butler rushed over, taking Val by the shoulders where he hurried her up the stairs. "Out! Out! I want her gone right now!"

Before she knew it, he'd guided her back to her room where the door closed quietly behind her. There was a light *clack* as the lock engaged and still she remained standing there looking dumbfounded.

Sighing, she kicked off her shoes and jumped on the

bed, sinking into the luxurious duvet. "Well, I tried," she mumbled and felt oddly freer as she rested back to sleep.

———————

She'd spent the night undisturbed, but she was woken by her door unlocking. It was barely light out, but a maid slipped in with some towels and a pair of boots. "Best you shower now, Miss."

Val took the hint and dressed. She wasn't left waiting long before someone knocked. It was the butler who entered with a black jacket in hand. "I was asked to give you this."

She slipped it on and nodded approvingly.

"Have you all your things?" he asked. She was surprised at how caring he sounded. He led her down to the foyer where she saw a welcomed face.

"I hope you managed to sleep," David said. Behind him was the maid who held a black rucksack. "It's a shame it's come to this, though you don't look very upset about it."

She eyed the door with a slight smile. "I can't wait." She was a little solemn as she asked, "Will Andrea be all right?"

"She'll be fine. The deaths of Devron and Andrews have set them back a bit, more financially than anything else, but they'll recover." He gestured to the maid. "I had Maddie here pack some necessities. Just a few things to help you get back on your feet."

She was handed the backpack that she shouldered and said, "Cheers, I appreciate it."

The door was opened onto a dim morning where a PEA cruiser sat waiting for her.

"Take care," David called.

"And you. I'll be listening."

The Agent stepped from the vehicle as she approached. She asked, "Can I drive?"

"Become an Agent and maybe."

"Ooh, tempting," she lied.

Within seconds, the engine growled and they were off. She wondered if Andrea had been at one of those many windows, watching her leave. She couldn't help except feel that she'd looked at Val through rose-tinted glasses, convincing herself that the few years they'd spent together in the orphanage had cemented a bond between them that nothing could shake.

Val hadn't helped in that situation, but then the life of a Royal just wasn't her thing.

She'd convinced the Agent to drop her off at Central. Whitehall had been the usual level of busy as it seemed the riots were all but over. Life had to go on for those who'd been unfortunate enough to survive, but there was a definite sense of depression. Far more Agents lingered now and the public screens were replaying the *tragic* deaths of Devron and Andrews. She wondered if Erga's coming to power would change anything. Frankly, she doubted it.

She ditched the market for the rubble-strewn streets. She knew it was risky to walk this area since it hadn't been two weeks since the Palacer base had been ransacked, and yet she found herself clambering amidst the rubble, searching for the burnt-out corridor. That's when a familiar sound caught her attention.

Yip! Yip-yip-yip-

Val almost stumbled. "You're fucking kidding me."

Poopsie was at the end of the passage where the old security door had been, and his little tail was going like a good'n. He rushed off into the darkness, barking and whimpering whilst his little paws tapped the floor, though it was almost too dark to see. She made it to the Control Room to find nothing had been spared and even many of the walls had come down, and yet there were lights on and it was warm. Something wasn't right.

Poopsie had run down the residential wing so she followed, spotting a gentle green glow from the end room. Here she found the ground had been picked away at, and there sat a hatch. She approached it just as it flew open and a ghostly white face came at her.

"*Boo!*"

She almost shit herself!

"Pierre, you fucking-"

He held his arms up to protect himself as she'd kicked out. "Haha, *Je suis désolé*! Please, it is I!"

"What are you doing here? What the hell is this? How is that thing still alive?"

He plucked up Poopsie and ushered her to the steps. "Come, in here before you alert the world to us."

He trotted down the narrow ladders into yet another corridor. When she was next to him, she said, "Your backup base is right underneath the original? Are you guys' stupid? They'll be watching here."

"Ah, they have no idea. Trust me, we have people on the inside who've reworked just what the Agency knows. They'll be lucky if they find records regarding our takedown."

They headed down the corridor where a wealth of lights buzzed at the end. It came from a room not unlike the Command Room upstairs, except the terminals looked older and not all the monitors were working.

Pierre said, "The original ATOM. It's back up and running, though she needs a serious update. There's nothing I can do about that at the moment."

She didn't care for that right then as she asked, "Pierre, how are you here?"

He set Poopsie down as he said, "We escaped during the commotion, the commotion Vord and I started, I may add." He looked rather proud of himself as he leaned in and said, "We found your bomb."

"How?"

"You used a disposable trigger-switch, didn't you? I happened to have a *friend* who acts as a Senior Agent and he found remnants of it and brought it to me. I showed Vord. It was him who figured out your plan. I don't know how you managed it, but you'd planted a bomb."

"The switch hadn't worked…"

"I contacted Erga, well, a friend of his. I wasn't told much, but I realised then what you'd come to the prison to do." He looked solemn. "I wish you'd have said something. We could've helped. But never mind that because Vord found your bomb and made a stronger trigger-switch. He even got into the building himself and blew it. The whole fucking thing came down! But it wasn't what killed Devron and Andrews."

She was dumbstruck.

He explained. "I know, the news says the explosion of a faulty tower had killed them, but I guarantee by the time we were rushed out of the prison, they were still alive. Whoever got to them did so after."

"How did you two get out? Erga helped?"

"Did he hell! Vord was caught in the explosion, so a few of our friends got us into an emergency vehicle and headed here for the People's Hospital. They stopped at the station and I had to practically drag Vord home."

"He's bad?"

Pierre gestured her to follow. He led her through a sliding door for a long corridor where observation windows overlooked a ward of hospital beds. Entering showed it was run down and under equipped, but one of the beds had the curtains drawn and there were trolleys and diagnostic machines scattered about.

He nodded her towards the curtain. She pulled them away half-expecting a flurry of abuse, but whilst Vord was in there, he was in no state to ridicule her; his body was filled with tubes and needles, and a hose had been fed down his throat to breathe for him. But the most harrowing of his injuries was the fact that his entire left arm had been completely detached save for a few artificial vanes connecting the two, and the limb was now floating in a tank beside the bed.

"I should be able to reattach it if the limb shows signs of repair," Pierre said. "Until then, he needs to remain in a coma."

She shut the curtains. She'd seen plenty of sick and dying people before, but this made her weak. Pierre understood as he led her out, saying, "I'm confident he'll pull through, but it's the arm I'm worried for."

She pushed past him to make her way down the corridor. "I gotta get home. I'll come back to check on you guys tomorrow, but I just need to see what's still standing." She made it to the Command Room where he finally stopped her.

"He'll be all right, try not to worry. But I was told the Peace Ranger took you to Quad: West, is it true?"

She calmed herself enough to explain, quickly anyway. Then Poopsie came over and started whimpering excitedly, so she picked him up and said, "He did well surviving on his own all that time."

"It's a she, actually. And she's a good girl."

Val scratched behind her ear. "I always get mistaken for a boy, too."

"Come back tomorrow and I'll have an RDAC ready for you," he said as they reached the hatch. He stopped her once she was up and said, "Listen, before you go there's something you should know. It's about Jim, or something Jim owns." He shooed it away as if to start again and began to explain himself. "A few years after you were taken by Bandits, Jim approached me. I didn't know at the time that you'd been taken. Heck, I was just some grunt with the Agency and I'd simply been happy to see he was alive. Well, barely. He'd turned to drink pretty badly. I suppose it was his way of handling losing you.

"Anyway, he brought me a PDA and on it was a recording. He'd been very specific that he'd wanted it copying onto cassette tapes."

"A what?"

"An analogue audio tape for stereos. I don't know why and it'd taken me ages to find the technology to do it. In fact, it'd been during my search for such tech that'd brought me to Vord, but that's another story. Either way, I managed it. I fixed the PDA, I made the recordings, and I listened to the tape.

"I guess he never played it to you, and I really don't know if copies of it still exist, but it's something you should try to find. If you can't, come back to me and I'll tell you what's on it. But if you can hear it for yourself…"

"Great, I'll go on a merry hunt for some old-ass tapes."

"Come back tomorrow, yes?" he called as she trudged off. She planned to, but she didn't respond as she headed off into Central.

Val had been nervous that the chip in her head would've alerted Agents once she'd climbed aboard the shuttle. After forty-minutes, however, the end of the line came at Toll-gate Road where she and several others disembarked. She'd been a second from losing herself in the ruined estates when someone called after her.

"Hey, young girl, wait."

She snapped around as if expecting trouble, but the middle-aged man looked nervous as he said, "You okay?"

"Yeah, what of it?"

"It's just, well, I noticed you ain't been looking too good recently, and I'd heard…"

"What?" she asked, her defensiveness dropping to curiosity.

"Well, it was just a damn shame to hear about Jim, and I know you'd done a fair bit of good round here with repairing the generators over at the water farm back when the PEA wouldn't."

She was shocked he even knew it'd been her.

"Well, anyway, I live over at the Oaks, me and my own, so if you need anything, until you get back on your feet…"

He nodded his respects before heading off for the over-grown estates and, even once he'd gone, she remained there, looking amazed. Eventually, she took herself off, heading for her old apartment even though she knew it'd be as burnt-out as it'd been before. And yet she felt better climbing the water-logged stairs for the front door hanging on by a single hinge, and trudging through the ceiling that'd come down around the place. On the longest wall someone had spray painted *Jim's Girl's Alright By Us* and it actually made her laugh. Then a fat tear rolled down her cheek as she turned to a window that'd been totally blown out.

As she climbed atop the sill to sit, she heard the distant rumbling of an engine. It was a rare sound around those parts, so when she saw a PEA cruiser mounting the curb to vanish in a long line of trees, she had the sense that she needed to run. And yet she didn't.

A moment passed before she saw a lone figure strolling across the grounds, flicking aside a cigarette before losing sight of him behind the library. Eventually, his heavy boots were heard climbing the stairs before they stopped at her door.

"Wow, big place," Erga said. She didn't turn, so he said, "I picked up your BioChip on a shuttle bus. I'd hoped you'd be here. Devron really ripped this place apart, hey? Watch who you talk to around here now, apparently some folks were eager to show the Agents where you lived."

He took a case from his pocket, producing a nicotine pipe that spilled vapour as he sucked on it. He then rolled it through his fingers as he said, "I'm leader now. I suppose we'll be in need of a few new suits for the government elections since Andrews left a really big seat to fill. Keep that chip in your head and you'll be able to vote. I'm obviously going to govern in their absence."

"Naturally."

He was thoughtful as he watched her. Then he said, "I'm glad you made it. Shame you weren't too punctual with that bomb, but I made some good of it." He replaced the pipe into his jacket and said, "Why don't you come with me?"

"Is that what you say to all the girls?"

"I mean it. Come with me. Join the Agency and be an example to others. I really believe you'll come into your own and the world needs people like you."

"And what am I?" she asked, finally looking at him.

"Smart and resourceful, like your dad. Pretty and nimble, like your mum."

She resented his emotional manipulation, even if that wasn't what he'd intended.

He added, "I don't know who you get your humour and resolution from. Maybe Jim?"

She looked away.

He stood beside her as he said, "I'm fulfilling my side of the bargain. I'll reinstate stamps as Walker currency, I'll give the Undesirables their Estates back, though I don't know what they'll build in the ruins of yet another broken Waterloo. I'll even continue to fund the repair of the southern wall to protect them from Bandit attacks, because we'll be seeing enough of them in time."

"And give the people their radios."

"Excuse me?"

"Open the radios back up. I want everyone to be able to broadcast free from persecution."

"I suppose I-"

"And open Essex. Half the people I was in jail with were there because they'd moved into the Exclusion Zone. It's not necessary. Let us expand."

He seemed a little exasperated. "Anything else?"

"No."

"Will you come with me now and let me take care of you?"

"No."

He could've lost his temper, but rather he laughed. "You definitely take after Jim."

"Jim was a cold blooded killer…"

He leaned down and whispered, "Was. People change." Then something touched her shoulder. She looked around to see him holding the picture Pranav had given her, the one Erga had confiscated during her arrest, though he'd been wise to remove himself from it. Still, he'd circled two faces. One was of a young woman with skin like hers, her expression plain and hair tied back. Standing a few spaces away was a man as tall as Jim, pale and grinning like a fool. She'd not have imagined her dad would've been so jovial considering how many lives he'd end up taking.

She wiped angrily at the tears and heaved herself to a stand. "I need to go."

He grabbed her arm. She remained but didn't look at him as he said, "I agreed that I'd move the legal age to sixteen. You have another year to decide what you want to make of your life, and I'll respect that you might not want to join the PEA, but I can't have you joining the Palacers, either. They're as good as dead, you understand? If I can do anything to keep you from returning to them…"

She pulled her arm free and left the room. He didn't rush to follow, this time taking a real cigarette from his pocket and sparking up. When he left the ruined building, an Agent by a cruiser pointed east of the road. "She went that way, Sir."

"That's fine," Erga said, dragging deep. "That's just fine." He threw the half-spent cigarette aside and jumped into the cruiser.

The ship was cold. She didn't mind as she undressed to her underwear and pumped water from the WTU for a wash. She'd only left Andrea's that morning and already she felt like a dirty Walker again. Still, it was a look she pulled off well.

She'd left the bag from David by the sofa and only now had she decided to look inside. The first thing she found was a nice pair of heavy duty, fingerless gloves with padded palms and a bar along the knuckle; perfect for a busy Lancer and she immediately adored them. Under that was an E-tag loaded with fifty creds as well as a thin clip-box of thirty Reds. A toothbrush and some abrasive fluoride powder for *clean and healthy teeth* (or so the tub read) sat in a wash bag with some rolled up socks and a bar of soap. Underneath that was a tightly rolled towel. A big one, too. She hadn't ever owned a towel, and it'd taken up a lot of space that could've been used for more essential products. It was only when she pulled it out that she found the book hidden inside.

The Hitchhiker's Guide to the Galaxy.

The front cover had been torn off and the pages were browned, but a hand written note on the inner page read, 'A good adventurer always needs a towel; they're probably the most massively useful things ever'.

She dropped the book on the table and sunk low. She should've been touched, but her nerves were raw. And something was making it worse.

Beep

Beep

Beep...

She glanced over to the small cubby-hole where the

TriStar radio was housed. She guessed she'd make a good few Reds off that Jettison Mark II signal booster. That's when she spotted the VHS tapes on the shelves and remembered Pierre's words.

She nipped inside to have a look, though she was aware that these weren't the compact cassettes he'd referred to. Each one she checked showed serious signs of damage, so she threw them aside until she'd amassed a small pile of useless Lecky.

"Really?" she said as even the VHS players were broken.

Beep

Beep

Beep…

"And you're not helping!" she snapped at the TriStar radio, marching over in order to pull the power cord free, but the floor shifted, causing the cabinet to bang against the wall. It'd sounded hollow behind there, so she hauled it aside to expose a large opening.

"Sneaky twat."

She poked her head inside the hole filled with a mattress and a few thin pillows. The walls had been covered in shelves and pictures. She clambered in and switched on lights that exposed countless personal nick-knacks like drawings, coasters, gloves, and more, all pinned about the plywood walls. They must've meant something to Jim, but those stories had died with him.

One photo caught her attention and her guts hardened as she freed it from its pin. Derek and Esha were standing close to each other, and in her mum's arms were a bundle of blankets and the slightest hint of a baby's face.

She pushed the picture back onto its pin and whispered, "*C'est la vie.*"

There was something hard under one of Jim's pillows.

She pulled the heavy cassette player onto her lap and felt as if every muscle had frozen. There were several buttons on offer: play, pause, forward, rewind, record, but she was amazed to find the play and rewind button had been used so often that they'd reduced to nothing more than metal pegs. She rewound the tape to the beginning and hit play. For the longest time there was static that muffled a gentle beeping noise similar to the TriStar radio. Then it ended and heavy breathing and roaring wind filled the tiny room.

Then she spoke.

57

Jim? Jim respond, over.

...

Jim? Over!

...

[Sobbing]

Jim, god dammit! I'm sorry. I'm so sorry. You were right. All this time-

[Interference]

... they never left. We crossed the verge like Anderson had said and the Agents backtracked, so we thought they were giving in. We thought we were safe! We just kept going, following the signal, but they weren't running from us, they were running from a Mist! Our scanners didn't pick it up. Derek thought we had time to look for cover but Anderson demanded we searched for the End Signal. He pulled a gun on him-

[Inaudible dialogue]

... forced us to head for Valley of Hope. He was adamant it was over the rise. I was, too. All indications were leading us to that point. I don't know what this place is, but it's not Hope. It's not-

...

... was run down and empty, but the unit's sensors were still going. We'd been tracking the wrong lab all this time and it's useless. I think it's Valour. No walls, no windows, just a shell. Some of us are in here now, but...

[Interference and sounds of screaming]

He's trying to get in!

Close it! Go on, fucking push the-

...

[Long bouts of interference]

Jim? Come in! Oh god, this place won't protect us. The Mist's coming and Derek's been shot. Anderson shot him when he tried getting his gun and I don't know where he is now. Anderson's outside shouting at the sky and there's no shelter for miles. I thought Hope existed. I thought we could find it-

[Sobbing]

I should've listened to you. Please pick up the radio. Oh god please, I'm so goddamn scared. I shouldn't have left. I thought we could do this. Now he's gone.

When you come back, when you hear this message-

[Inaudible]

... Valley will need you now. You're all she has. Promise me you'll tell her how wrong we were to leave and that I love her. Promise me! And remember, I always-"

[Inaudible]

... there for us. Now you have to be there for her-

[Minutes of roaring winds and high static]

[Pained panting]

Anderson's gone. I can't see-

...

... never follow us. Hope isn't here-

...

... must promise me no matter what, you'll-

...

....

.....

Click

Val watched the silence.

The TriStar radio continued playing its requiem sound, like a beating heart to a moment almost forgotten. And all she could think of was that in the instant she'd found her mother, Val had lost her all over again.

To be continued…

Dangel Angello is the pen name of Charlotte Teece.

As a young child, teachers were quick to point out how far behind on her writing she was, to the point that even her own name was hard to spell.

One teacher was familiar with her constant storytelling, so recommended that she start writing them down as a means of improving her writing. She did and instantly fell in love with the process, even if her spelling was atrocious and grammar was an alien concept to her!

It wasn't until her late teens, after completing her first novel that came in at well over a thousand pages, that she realised she had the determination needed to make something of herself.

Ten years and several manuscripts later, she was happy

with her work. But whilst all her other works were fantastical and whimsy, her darker side truly wished to be set free. This path led to Toxic City.

To her amazement, Britain's Next Bestseller wanted to make her gritty sci-fi a reality.

Dangel lives in the North East of England.